Speak Low

Melanie Harlow

THIS BOOK IS DEDICATED
TO THE READERS OF SPEAK EASY,
WHO CANNOT RESIST A COCKTAIL AND
A MAN IN A THREE-PIECE SUIT.

Chapter One

Saturday, July 21st, 1923

I stood at the door and watched the red Buick tear down the street, my lips buzzing and my head spinning.

Joey had kissed me. Again. But for real this time.

I brought my trembling fingers to my mouth and closed my eyes. I could still see the barely-suppressed fury on Joey's face as he put everything together—my uncharacteristic nervousness, the thousands of dollars in cash I'd just handed over, the diamonds at my throat.

He knows.

He hadn't said so, not in so many words, but Joey and I had known each other for years. And even though we'd spent most of them at each other's throats, for him to get worked up enough to kiss me like that could only mean one thing: he realized what I'd done with Enzo.

Which was everything.

Twice.

At the thought of Enzo's naked body pressing against mine, my breath caught and my insides went weightless. For a moment I was back in his bed, pulling him deeper. A wave of arousal swept through me, and I leaned against the doorjamb for support, my knees nearly buckling. When my body felt grounded again, I opened my eyes and frowned in the direction of the Buick. Anger pinched off the warmth inside me. *Go to hell, Joey Lupo!*

Not once in seven years had he done anything but tease me and pick fights, and the one time he *had* kissed me, he'd made it clear he was only pretending we were a couple to fool the Prohibition agents who'd spotted our boat full of bootleg whisky on the lake. Now just because someone else had gotten their hands on me—as well as some other body parts—he got proprietary. Well, tough!

And he hadn't even given me a reason. He just announced I was making a mistake and grabbed me, muttering some nonsense about how he knew me, how he's always known me.

Huffing an angry breath, I slammed the door. *Screw you, Joey. I don't care how long you've known me or how much you helped me when my family was in trouble or how tempting your mouth is. That doesn't give you the right to judge me for my choices or tell me I'm making a mistake or kiss me with those perfect fucking lips. Goddamn you! I*

2

stomped up the stairs to my bedroom and slammed that door too. The more I thought about it, the madder I got—mad at Joey for kissing me, of course, but the truth was, I was just as angry at myself for wanting that kiss.

For enjoying it.

Going straight to the dresser, I placed the diamond and pearl choker Enzo had given me into its blue Tiffany box and clapped it closed. Then I grabbed my hairbrush and yanked it furiously through my hair, eyeing my flushed face in the mirror. How dare he make me feel guilty about finally going after something I want for myself! Damn him for waiting so long to show me he felt something for me. *And damn him to hell for making me feel something for him that has me questioning everything right now!*

Hurling the hairbrush across the room, I took satisfaction in the loud thwack it made against the wall. In fact, it felt so good I scanned the dresser for something else to throw. My eyes fell on the blue box, and I nearly picked it up. Instead I braced both hands on the dresser top, stared hard at my reflection, and took a deep breath. And then another.

A memory surfaced.

A few nights ago, I'd stood here in my room wearing nothing but that necklace as I touched Enzo in ways Joey could only dream about. *Let him dream, then. So he's mad, so what?* Served him right. Maybe I'd enjoyed that phony embrace in the boat last week, and maybe the impulsive kiss downstairs had me worked up a bit, but I wasn't the same person he'd known all

3

those years—and if I wanted to make a mistake with my life, it was mine to make.

Because if that mistake was tall, dark, handsome as a movie star and supremely talented with his tongue, then I was willing to risk it.

"You don't know me, Joe Lupo," I whispered to my reflection. "You don't know anything."

I felt superior for exactly ten seconds, which is how long it took me to remember that Enzo was counting on me to stay friendly with Joey so I could get some information from him. Specifically, Enzo wanted a way to get back at the River Gang and its leader, Sam the Barber Scarfone, for hijacking a shipment of booze he'd been expecting from the east coast a few days ago. It hadn't just been any old shipment—hidden somewhere in the cargo was forty thousand dollars worth of opium, which even the hijackers hadn't known about. Briefly I wondered what had happened when they discovered it. Joey worked for the River Gang, and he had just returned from Chicago, where they'd sold the hijacked load, but he hadn't mentioned the drugs.

Then again, he'd only been at my house for about five minutes before he got angry, kissed me, and stormed out.

"Shit," I muttered. I'd have to make nice with him again if I had any hope of discovering where the gang's next load of booze would come from and when it would arrive. Fear shimmied up my spine, cold and unwelcome. Enzo had promised not to hurt Joey if I came through with the right information, and though he hadn't given me a deadline, I knew I'd better act quickly.

Trust was shaky between us, to say the least.

I had to think of a way to get Joey to reveal something to me before Enzo decided to take retribution into his own hands. Maybe the best way to do that would be to come clean with Joey and see if we could get back to normal. Our version of normal, anyway, which involved a lot of bickering and frustration, but it was a hell of a lot more comfortable than what had transpired by the front door. I touched my mouth again...had Joey's lips really rested there just minutes ago? How many times had I allowed myself a little fantasy about it?

Too many.

I need a cigarette.

After searching my usual hiding spots and coming up empty, I decided to walk to the small grocery store my older sister Bridget owned to grab a pack. She had taken her three boys and our two younger sisters on a trip to the beach on the other side of the state, so I wouldn't have to worry about a lecture from her, although it seemed ridiculous to me that I was still sneaking around like a child in order to smoke. I smoothed my white blouse over the plain black skirt I wore, found a decent-looking hat in my sisters' room, and locked the front door behind me.

My stomach growled as I headed down the block and smelled a neighbor's dinner cooking. I ignored it and wrapped my arms around my empty belly, frowning at my scuffed oxfords. Last night Enzo had

5

promised to pay me handsomely if I helped him recover his losses from the River Gang—enough to cover nursing school tuition in the fall, and then some.

Those damn schoolgirl shoes would go first thing.

I'll get some new clothes. No more stained blouses or skirts I've worn since high school. For God's sake, I'm twenty years old, I survived kidnapping at gunpoint, and I'm sleeping with a gangster. Stretching out my strides, I tried to walk a little taller, which wasn't easy for someone who measured under five feet.

The other luxury I wanted was my own apartment. Daddy would probably put up a big stink since it would mean leaving him to tend to the girls and the house on his own, but Mary Grace was ten and Molly was nearly sixteen—the same age I was when Bridget left home to get married. I'd been keeping house and mothering two girls long enough. Now it was my turn to have a little freedom, a little fun. Even if all I could afford was a little room in a boarding house where I could come and go as I pleased, it would be better than living at home.

I turned left into the alley that ran behind the store, and right away I saw the dark sedan parked behind Daddy's auto repair shop. Narrowing my eyes, I focused on the back door—it was open a crack. The back of my neck prickled. I knew it wasn't Daddy inside, and the nondescript car screamed *cops* to me. Halting my steps, I debated whether to turn around and hightail it back home or find out who was in there.

But I took too long to decide, and when three men exited through the back door, they saw me.

"There she is." Martin, the grocery store's assistant manager, followed two unfamiliar men in suits into the alley. "Tiny, these men are federal agents. They're looking for your father."

He and I exchanged a careful look. Martin knew about my father's neighborhood whisky business as well as the work he did rebuilding cars and hearses for other bootleggers, but his face gave nothing away. I was damn glad he didn't know anything about the events of last week.

"Oh?" I kept an even tone as I walked toward the suits, sizing them up as they flashed badges at me. The one in brown was younger, ginger-haired, and overweight, sweating profusely in the summer afternoon heat. The older one wore blue; he was dark-haired, beady-eyed, and smaller-framed, and he too was mopping his face with a handkerchief. "My father isn't here. Can I help you?"

"My name is Agent Thomas, and this is Agent Janssen," said the one in blue. "We're with the Prohibition Bureau. Your name?" He traded the handkerchief for a small pad of paper and a pencil from inside his coat.

"Frances O'Mara." I racked my brain, trying to remember what damning evidence could be in the garage. All the booze had been removed, and I was pretty sure all the rebuilt hearses were gone too. They'd been sold last week.

7

"But you go by another name?" The agent glanced at Martin, who'd just used the nickname I'd had since birth.

"Tiny," I clarified through gritted teeth. I really needed to ditch the childhood moniker along with the old clothes, but being called Frances didn't appeal much to me either.

He nodded and continued writing, while I imagined *Alias, Tiny* being scratched in lead on the little white pad.

"Excuse me, but what is this about?" I asked him. "May I ask why you were in the garage?"

"We're looking for your father in connection with a crime that took place Wednesday evening of last week: a liquor heist, during which a few men were killed. We have reason to believe Jack O'Mara may have been involved, or at least supplied the vehicles used by the perpetrators. We have a warrant to search the premises." He didn't offer to show it to me.

"Do you know where he was that night?" asked Agent Janssen.

"Yes. He was traveling in Ohio last week. For business." Actually he'd been a hostage of Angel DiFiore last week, and I knew he'd had nothing to do with the crime these agents were referring to—the River Gang's heist of Enzo's shipment. It was me who'd sold those hearses to the River Gang, because I'd needed the money for Daddy's ransom.

"Where in Ohio?" Thomas queried.

"I'm not sure exactly. Around Cleveland maybe?" I met his eyes and widened mine slightly as I lifted my shoulders. *You catch more flies with honey than vinegar.*

"And he's still in Ohio?" asked Janssen.

"As far as I know." A hidden drop of sweat rolled down my chest.

"Gentlemen, I think you've taken up enough of Miss O'Mara's time, and I should return to the store. You've searched the garage and found nothing of interest. Why don't you wait for Mr. O'Mara to return and talk to him yourselves?" Martin had an open, honest face, and with his neatly combed hair and polished spectacles, he looked like the dentist he was studying to be, not someone engaged in criminal activity.

Thomas ignored him. "Miss O'Mara, when do you expect your father back?"

"Oh, probably within a day or so. Shall I have him contact you when he returns?" I spoke sweetly, coating the lies with sugar. The sun was at my back, which meant it was shining directly in their eyes, and the brims of their hats weren't keeping their faces too cool. I could tell Janssen wanted to finish with me and get in the shade as quickly as possible.

But Thomas spoke up again. "One more thing. Does this guy look familiar to you?" He reached inside his coat pocket and pulled out a photograph—a mug shot. I leaned forward and pretended to scrutinize it.

"Have you ever seen him around here, maybe talking to your father? Could he be a customer at the garage?"

9

The young man in the photo was perfectly familiar.

"No," I lied. "I have no idea who that is. Never seen him before."

I had to find Joey. Immediately.

#

After reassuring Martin that everything was OK—which, in fact, it was not—I swiped a pack of cigarettes from behind the store counter, raced home, and called Joey's mother's apartment, where he was staying. His older sister Marie answered and said he wasn't home but she'd tell him to telephone me as soon as he returned. I replaced the receiver on the hook and chewed my nails, trying to think of where he might have gone. It was warm and stuffy in the house, and my head felt sweaty in the hat, so I tossed it aside and opened all the windows on the first floor. Just as I finished, the telephone rang.

Eagerly, I raced for it and scooped up the earpiece. "Hello?"

"Tiny, there you are!" The voice was my best friend Evelyn's.

"Evvy, I'm sorry we haven't spoken in—"

"Days!" she exclaimed. "It's been days, you naughty girl. You left the club Wednesday night before all the excitement and I haven't heard from you since!"

"I know, I'm sorry. I've been...busy." I actually hadn't left Club 23 before the raid alarms went

10

off—Enzo and I were upstairs in his father's office, where I'd left my virginity, my sanity, and my purse. "Did you make it out OK? I heard it wasn't really a raid, just a false alarm."

"Oh yeah, we were fine. It was all very exciting, actually. Ted and I can't stop talking about it." The lilt in her voice told me she was dying for me to ask.

"Ted? That's the guy you met that night?"

"Yes, and he's wonderful. I've seen him every evening since, and he's taking me dancing tonight," she bubbled. "He's so handsome and sweet and he loves the movies like I do, and he's come into the bakery twice to see me."

"I'm so happy for you, Evelyn. You deserve someone like that." I scratched at a nick in the wooden telephone table with my thumbnail.

"So…" Evelyn prompted. "Tell me what's new with Mr. Dangerous. You were right—he does look like a Hollywood film star. Have you seen much of him?"

Every inch. "Um, yes. It's really kind of a long story, and I promise to tell you all about it when I have time, but I have to do something for Daddy before tonight, and—"

"Is he back, then?" Evelyn was one of the few people who'd known about my father's kidnapping. With Joey's help in negotiating with the River Gang, I'd managed to bootleg enough whisky to deliver the ten grand in ransom, but not without a huge amount of trouble involving men with guns—sometimes pointed at me.

"Yes. He was released yesterday."

"Oh, thank God! Now things can get back to normal."

A rictus smile stretched my lips. "I wouldn't count on it."

"You know what? You need to get another job, Tiny. The bootlegging business is no place for a girl."

I sighed. How often had Bridget said the same thing? But even though our operation was small, the money was too good to pass up, and it wasn't like I didn't have a plan. I'd been trying to pay for nursing school on my own for over a year. Daddy's business ventures brought in decent dough, but he had a weakness for gambling and an aversion to anything that would hasten my departure from the house. "I'll think about it. Let me telephone you tomorrow, all right? Have fun on your date."

"All right." She hesitated before hanging up. "Ooh, Tiny. I just got the shivers! Maybe something big is about to happen."

My stomach plummeted, but I tried to sound hopeful. "Maybe Ted is going to propose."

She squealed with glee. "Silly, it's only been a few days. But if he does, you'll be the first to know."

#

While I waited for Joey to call me back, I sat on the back stoop with my cigarettes and watched the sun turn orange and sink behind the trees in the yard. As I smoked, I decided on a plan of action. When Joey got back to me, I'd do my best to smooth things over between us and explain the situation to him. He had no real allegiance to Sam the Barber or the River Gang, and after all, they never would have known when and where Enzo's shipment was arriving if I hadn't told them.

Joey had probably made pretty good money on the deal, if his new clothes were any indication. And he'd told me this afternoon he was planning on moving back to Chicago. Maybe I could talk him into going sooner rather than later. With the local cops and now feds looking into the heist—not to mention the DiFiores looking to exact retribution—Joey would be safer out of town, and I'd feel better knowing nothing I did could put him in harm's way.

I'd also feel better with some distance between us.

No matter how much I tried not to think about it, Joey's kiss wouldn't leave me alone. And the more I tried to block it from my mind, the more I obsessed over it, analyzing every detail. The shock of his hands on me, the sudden heat of his mouth slanting over mine. It wasn't overly aggressive or demanding, but it hinted at something powerful underneath—as if Joey had been restraining himself, and if we allowed the barriers to fall…

I shivered, imagining the intensity of it.

God…I didn't want Joey, did I?

No, that was ridiculous. We'd known each other too long, had too much history. No one got under my skin like Joey did. He was distantly related to Bridget's late husband, Vince, and from day one, we'd done nothing but scrap. As a boy, he'd cheated at cards, teased me mercilessly about my height, and never once let me win a footrace. For chrissakes, he'd stolen a pair of my underwear when we were fifteen and made money by offering neighborhood boys a penny a peek! Just because he grew up more handsome than he had any right to be didn't mean he was any different—underneath that fancy new suit, he was still the no-good, pain-in-the-ass delinquent I'd always known.

My stomach growled again, reminding me I still hadn't eaten, and I decided to go in and forage for some supper. As I stood, a low voice traveled through the dusk. "Hey."

Gasping, I searched the shadows and slapped a hand to my chest. "Joey? You scared me half to death! You should know better than to sneak up on me."

"Sorry. I called home, and my sister said you were looking for me."

I lowered my arm, although my pulse still raced. *It's because he startled you, that's all.* "Actually, it's the feds who are looking for you. They were at the garage today."

Joey shrugged. "They don't have anything on me."

"Yes they do, Joey. They asked about the hijacking. They flashed a picture of Sam the Barber at me. Asked me if I knew him or if he was a customer of Daddy's." I twisted my hands together.

14

"What did you say?"

"I lied! What the hell do you think I said?"

"Don't worry about it. Sam's a big boy. He can take care of himself."

"I'm not worried about Sam." Our eyes met briefly before his gaze dropped to my lips, and I lowered my chin. I noticed he'd removed his suit coat and rolled the cuffs of his light blue dress shirt. His exposed hands and wrists made my stomach flutter a little—I had a thing about Joey's hands. God, I *did* feel something for Joey, but I didn't know what it was or how to put it into words. Was it gratitude? Affection? Attraction?

My plan had been to pretend everything was the same between us. But things weren't the same, and we both knew it.

My eye caught Joey's gold silk tie, which had been pulled askew. Without thinking, I reached up and straightened it. He sucked in his breath, his muscular chest straining against the shirt and vest of his three-piece suit, so different from the workmen's clothes I was used to seeing on him.

"Don't." He pushed my hands away and took over the task.

"Christ, Joey." My voice wavered when I spoke. "Don't be mad at me. You don't know what I've been through. You hijacked that booze and hightailed it out of town, and I had to deal with the consequences."

"What consequences? I left you the remainder of the ransom money. You were supposed to spring your

15

pop from the DiFiores with it and stay the hell out of trouble. Instead you dive right into it, headfirst."

"That's not how it went, dammit! And after the choices you've made, you have no right to judge me. If I want to dive into trouble, that's my business, not yours." I poked a finger into his chest.

He lifted his chin. "You've made that perfectly fuckin' clear."

Bringing the heels of my hands to my head, I exhaled. This was not going well. I was supposed to be smoothing things over with Joey, not making them worse. "I'm sorry. I'm extremely grateful for everything you did for me while my father was…gone."

"He wasn't gone. He was kidnapped, remember? By Enzo's father?"

Stay calm. You'll gain nothing by letting your temper loose. "Yes, I remember. But a lot has happened since you left, and I want a chance to explain it to you without you getting angry with me. Please." I put my hands on his chest. Joey wasn't too much taller than me, but he had broad, thick muscles, and I could feel the warmth of his skin through his clothes.

He took a breath, and I thought he'd swat my hands away once more, but he didn't. When he spoke, his voice was softer, but still had an edge. "Where's your pop?"

Distracted, I answered without thinking. "He's at a meeting with Angel DiFiore, trying to work out the terms of a business arrangement."

16

"Are you fucking kidding me?" Joey took a step back. "First the guy tries extortion, then when that doesn't work he kidnaps your dad, beats him to a pulp, demands ten grand in ransom—and now your pop's gonna do business with him?" He looked me up and down. "No wonder!"

"No wonder what?"

"No wonder you're crazy enough to jump in bed with the guy's son!"

Rage burned in my face. "Fuck you, Joey! You got everything you wanted out of this, didn't you?" I gestured toward him. "Look at you in your new blue suit driving a fancy red Buick wearing your shiny new shoes! You wouldn't have any of it if I hadn't helped you! How dare you judge me for getting what I want!"

"That's what you want? Him?" Joey yelled.

"Yes! For once in my life, I have something that's mine, something I'm doing just for me, and if you don't like it, you know what you can do!"

"Fine." He closed his eyes, took a few deep breaths and rolled his shoulders. "So why did you call me today after I left?"

"I was worried about you." Just then my stomach growled again, loud and embarrassing.

Joey's brows went up when the groaning noise refused to stop. "Jesus, Tiny. If you expect to grow anytime soon, you're gonna have to eat a meal every now and then."

A joke. That was a good sign. "I was too scared to eat."

"Have you had a decent meal since I fed you?"

At the memory of the pasta dinner he'd cooked at my house last week, my mouth watered, and I may have moaned slightly. "I think so. I'm not sure. It's been a tough couple of days." I still hadn't told him the whole story.

Joey shook his head and grabbed my elbow, pulling me toward the driveway. "Come on."

"Where are we going?"

"To my house. I'll feed you supper. But this is the last time," he warned, turning back to shake a finger in my face. "From now on, you're his mouth to feed."

Nodding gratefully, I didn't even toss back a sharp response. The thought of eating Joey's cooking again had me salivating.

He opened the Buick's passenger door for me before walking around and sliding into the driver's seat. Then he pulled two cigarettes from his pocket. "Want one?"

I placed one between my lips and he leaned toward me to light it. When its tip glowed orange, I sucked in a lungful of smoke and exhaled. "Thanks."

He glanced sideways at me. "So what happened after I left town?"

I shuddered. "What didn't happen? Things went completely haywire. When Enzo heard the guys who hijacked the load and killed a couple of his men were driving hearses, he knew they had to be the ones he'd seen at the garage the night of Daddy's kidnapping. And since his father had Daddy hostage the whole time, he figured I knew more than I was telling him. Which I did, of course."

"What did you say?"

"I admitted that I'd sold the hearses to Sam the Barber and the River Gang because I needed the money for the ransom, but I didn't tell him I was the one who told you guys about his rum shipment."

"He still in the dark about that?"

I shook my head and took another drag on my cigarette. "I don't think so. When he asked me outright this morning if I knew Sam was planning the heist, I told him I did what I had to do to protect my family."

Joey was quiet a moment, and I thought he might be reflecting on my bravery, but I was wrong. "This morning?"

I shifted in my seat. "Yes."

"Did you spend the night with him?"

Damn it, Joey, don't make me feel guilty! I was glad it was dark, so he couldn't see me blush, but I didn't want to lie. "Look, I didn't plan on it. There's another part of the story you haven't heard."

"I'm not sure I want to."

I bit my lip. How the hell was I supposed to be up front with him and ask for what I needed with all this odd tension between us? Did he really have feelings for me? Or was he just angry about what I'd done? "Well, while you were living it up in Chicago, I was—"

"I wasn't 'living it up in Chicago,' you know. It was business."

"Maybe, but all that rum plus the opium must have brought a good load of dough."

Joey studied me but said nothing.

19

"Well, didn't it?"

"We didn't sell the opium in Chicago."

My jaw dropped. "What? Why not?"

"Sam doesn't even know about it. It was in hidden containers that ended up in the hearse I drove with Angelo. When we found it, we agreed to keep it to ourselves. We sold the rum as instructed, gave Sam his cut, and brought the opium back to Detroit."

My heart hammered in my chest. "Why?"

He shrugged. "Honestly, I'm not even sure what made me do it. It just seemed like the opportunity was there for me to make a move on my own. Like I told you, I'm planning on going back to Chicago, and I could use a little money to get started down there."

"Jesus, Joey. If Sam finds out, he'll kill you." I put a hand on his arm, but when he glanced down, I removed it.

"He won't find out. Unless *you* tell him."

He meant it as a joke, but I couldn't make light of this. "And what about Angelo? Can you trust him?"

"Why shouldn't I? He gains nothing by telling Sam about it."

"So where is it? The opium, I mean."

Joey rubbed his lower lip, as if he was wondering whether to confide in me. Then he looked me in the eye. "This information does not leave the car."

I nodded.

"It's hidden in the boathouse."

"Daddy's boathouse? How the hell did you get in there?" My father had purchased a dilapidated old boathouse on the water for bootlegging purposes a few years back, and although Joey had occasionally worked for him, I didn't think he had a key.

"I took the key off your ring while I was at your house earlier. You were upstairs getting the money to pay me back."

"You stole the boathouse key from me?" Somehow that seemed worse than anything I'd done. Neither of us had behaved terribly well in the last week, but at least we'd been honest with each other.

"I was planning on telling you. I just got…distracted."

Our eyes met, and I took a drag on my cigarette, fast. "Joey, I—"

"I want to meet with Enzo."

"What?" I coughed, choking on the smoke. "Why the hell do you want to do that?"

"I want to make a deal."

"What kind of deal?"

"I want to know where he was going to sell the drugs and for how much. I don't know anything about that stuff."

"And why would Enzo even talk to you? You just stole thousands of dollars worth of booze and drugs from him!"

"I'll cut him in."

"On his own opium?"

"It's not his anymore, is it?"

"He's not gonna see it that way."

Joey shrugged. "His choice. Thirty percent or nothing. I'm the one that has something he wants."

21

I brought my cigarette to my lips again, inhaling and exhaling more slowly. If they met in a dark alley, Enzo probably wouldn't hesitate to shoot Joey, but he did want to get his money back. This information could change everything.

"I might be able to set up a meeting," I ventured, watching a ribbon of smoke drift out the open window.

"You can't tell him about the opium beforehand, understand?" Joey pinned me with a hard stare.

"I do, but that makes it a lot harder to guarantee he'll agree to talk to you. He's furious, Joey."

"I have no doubt you'll persuade him, now that you two are so close."

"Stop. Just stop it. If we're going to work together on this, you have to quit harassing me about Enzo at every turn."

He switched his focus to starting the Buick, and the engine came to life. "No promises there."

My jaw jutted forward and I tossed my cigarette out the window. "None here either, then."

Joey looked over at me once more. "You know, I may have been wrong before."

"About what?"

"About you. Maybe I don't know you anymore."

As he backed out of the driveway and headed for Jefferson Avenue, I kept my eyes on the road. Why the hell was my throat closing up? I should have been glad he recognized that I was different now. Wasn't that exactly what I'd been saying to myself? And I'd gotten what I wanted—information to give Enzo. If he'd agree to meet Joey without killing him on sight, maybe they could work out a deal. Thirty percent was better than nothing.

The fist of discontent squeezing my throat eased up a little.

I could do this. No one would get hurt. Joey would go to Chicago and stop distracting me with his mouth and his hands and his cooking, and Enzo and I would learn to trust each other.

Of all the lies I told myself that night, the last one was the most foolish.

And the most dangerous.

Chapter Two

Joey's mom ran a restaurant and boarding house near Eastern Market, and the Lupo family lived above it. With Joey's sisters married and out of the house, it was just him and his mother there these days. I hadn't been to the restaurant in years, but it smelled the same when I walked in, like tomatoes and garlic and fresh bread. The dining room was bustling with a noisy supper crowd, and Joey nodded hello to a server setting down a huge plate of what looked like steak in some kind of red sauce. My stomach groaned again, and I cradled it as we took the stairs up to his family's apartment on the third floor.

"How's your mother doing?" I asked.

"Not too good."

"I'm sorry." Bridget had told me his mother was ill, and I felt bad that I hadn't inquired after her very much, but with everything going on last week it had slipped my mind.

The apartment door was ajar, and Joey pushed it all the way open. "Ma?"

"She's in the bedroom." Marie walked through the wide arch in the wall separating the front room from the dining room, wiping her hands on a dishtowel. "Tiny!" She rushed up to kiss both cheeks before hugging me. She looked like Joey, same dark wavy hair and generous mouth, but had little crinkles near her eyes when she smiled and a huge pregnant belly. "It's been so long. How are you? How's your family?"

"Um, good." I exchanged a quick glance with Joey. "We're all well. And you?"

"I'm well too, thanks." She dropped a hand to her stomach. "Just exhausted."

"Go home, Marie." Joey set his coat on the back of the sofa and took the dishtowel from her. "I can take it from here. I don't have any plans tonight, and I promised Tiny a decent meal. As you can see, she needs one."

"Shush, Joey Lupo. She looks just fine." She winked at me, and I wondered if she thought there was something between us.

He turned to me. "Let me just go see how she's doing and then I'll fix us something. I haven't eaten either."

"And I'll say good-bye to Ma and be on my way." Marie attempted to undo the apron strings at her back.

25

"Here, let me." I untied them for her and she slipped it over her head.

"Put it on, Tiny," said Joey, grinning as he backed through the arch. "I'll give you a cooking lesson. God knows you need one."

I glared at him as Marie dropped the loop around my neck. He was right, I did need a cooking lesson, but I certainly didn't feel like one tonight. I couldn't stop thinking about that opium sitting in the boathouse. Could I convince Enzo to meet with Joey without telling him about it? What would he do if he knew it was there, unguarded? The boathouse was locked and Joey had my key—the rotten thief—but locks were never a problem for Enzo. A smile crept onto my lips and I tried to wipe it off. *Quit thinking about him. Joey will wonder why you're blushing.*

Left alone, I looked around the apartment. I couldn't remember the last time I'd visited here. The wood floors were clean but creaky, and the furniture was Victorian style, with curvy backs and sides and faded burgundy upholstery. Floral-patterned paper covered the walls, on which hung family photos and religious paintings. A crucifix hung over a Brunswick phonograph in the corner, and a porcelain statue of the Blessed Virgin rested on a side table. Sidestepping away from it like a skittish pony, I perched on the edge of the sofa. A photo album rested on the coffee table, and it was open, as if someone had recently been looking at it.

Glancing back at the doorway to the hall, I sat back with the album on my lap and turned to the front of the book. Photographs of the Lupo family were fastened at the corners onto black pages, beginning with a wedding portrait of Mr. and Mrs. Lupo. I studied Joey's 'father. He looked a lot like Joey, actually, and I wondered how old he'd been when he married. Twenty? Twenty-one, like Joey was now? He and Vince had worked for the Scarfone family, and they were killed the same day, victims of an ambush on the boss, Big Leo Scarfone, right outside the police station. Neither Bridget nor Joey had fully recovered, although more than two years had passed.

I perused photos of the Lupo family as it grew, quirking a lip at babies in a frilly white baptismal dress and chuckling aloud at the photo of Joey in knee pants, looking miserable and yet adorable in his First Holy Communion portrait.

"Cute little devil, wasn't I?"

I jumped at his voice over my shoulder, and stiffened when he leaned down over the back of the sofa to look more closely. His jaw was so close to mine I could smell his aftershave. If I tilted my head just the right way, my cheek would rest against his. "Devil being the operative word." I scooted sideways and stood up. "But I like the outfit. You should wear knee pants more often."

"Thanks, but I don't think that suit fits me anymore." He grinned as he straightened. "It'd probably fit you, though. You're about the size of an eight-year-old boy."

"Very funny." I pulled the apron away from my white blouse. "Do I really have to wear this? You're

27

not actually going to make me cook anything, are you?"

"I thought you wanted a lesson. Here, I'll tie it." He motioned for me to come forward and turn around, and I felt his hands at the small of my back as he tied the strings. A funny ticklish feeling fluttered through my belly. "There. Now at least you *look* like you know what you're doing."

I faced him. "Appearances can be deceiving."

Joey looked skyward. "*Now* she figures it out."

#

"Is that spaghetti?" I peered over Joey's shoulder at the large copper pot full of boiling water, into which he'd thrown two handfuls of some kind of long noodle.

"No, it's fettuccine. Please tell me you at least recognize the vegetable." He gestured toward a second pot.

I peeked in. "Green beans."

"Thank God. Now go slice the bread and set the table."

While I did that, Joey warmed up some meatballs in the oven and poured some red wine. When supper was ready, we sat across from each other at one end of a table meant for eight, and I quickly devoured the meal in huge, blissful bites. The meatballs and noodles were lightly coated with a savory tomato sauce, and the green beans glistened with butter and lemon. "Oh my God, it's so good." I forked my last bite of meatball and shoved it in my mouth.

"I've heard that about my meatballs."

I narrowed my eyes at him and was about to make a sharp-tongued remark when a face appeared in the hallway leading off the dining room to the bedrooms.

"Ma, what do you need?" Joey jumped up from his chair, throwing his napkin on his empty plate. "Why didn't you call me?" He led her into the dining room by the arm as she took small, unsteady steps in battered house slippers. It was as if she'd aged twenty years since I'd last seen her, perhaps only a year ago.

"Mrs. Lupo, hello. It's nice to see you again."

"Hello, Tiny. Please forgive me for not welcoming you to my home myself. I'm no feeling so well these days." Her accent was still pronounced despite fifteen years in this country. She offered me a rueful smile and let Joey help lower her into a chair at the head of the table.

"Think nothing of it, really. Joey has been a very welcoming host."

Her face brightened a little as she looked at her son. "Like his father was."

Joey cleared his throat. "Are you hungry?"

"No, no. I came out to say hello and finish the dishes."

"I'll do the dishes. You can rest. Would you like to listen to the phonograph a little?"

"I'll help with the dishes, too," I offered, stacking our plates together.

While he moved his mother to the sofa in the front room, I rinsed the dishes and silverware in the large kitchen sink and retrieved the soap from a low cupboard. Soon I heard music coming from the phonograph, which got louder when Joey propped open the swinging door to the kitchen. Wordlessly he took his place next to me, toweling off the dishes I washed and then setting them in the rack to finish drying. I ignored the light hum under my skin at his proximity, but I did steal a few looks at his hands as he worked. When the last dish was in the rack, Joey sighed and shook his head. "I need a drink."

"Sounds good."

He looked at me. "Let's go up on the roof."

#

Ten minutes later we were sitting in the starlight on the building's roof, each with a tumbler of whisky in hand and the bottle between us. Joey tossed back his drink in one gulp and poured another.

I sipped mine, enjoying the way it burned down my throat and spread liquid warmth in my belly. "Thanks for supper. It was delicious. I really should take a cooking lesson from you sometime."

He shrugged. "If there's time before I leave."

"For Chicago, you mean?"

"Yeah. Once I settle things with the cake eater and get my ma moved into my sister's house, I'm

30

going." He glanced sideways at me. "You'll miss me, huh?"

I punched him on the shoulder. "Yeah, what will I do without someone around to call me Little Tomato, make fun of my cooking, and tease me mercilessly about my size?" But I was unsettled by the realization that I *would* miss seeing him. I'd miss hearing his voice, knowing he was around if I needed him. As we looked at one another, a light breeze ruffled my hair, and the strains of a waltz drifted up from an open window. To break the spell, I sipped my whisky and changed the subject. "It's nice up here."

"I used to come up here with my pop."

"Yeah?"

"Yeah. We'd escape my mother and sisters, and he'd let me smoke while he told me about the stars just like his father did when he was a kid." His voice cracked a little.

"You must miss him."

Joey nodded, took another drink. "Every day."

"I'm sorry."

He was quiet a moment. "I wish I knew for sure who did it. I hate that the bastard got away with it. I'd like to make him suffer, you know? Pay for what he did."

I nodded, although I didn't know what it must be like to have that burning need for revenge inside me. I knew about loss, though. "I miss my mom every day, too."

"It's been rough on you, huh? With those kids at home."

"Yeah. Some days all I want to do is escape it all." Another silence followed, during which I grew increasingly uncomfortable with the way he was running his eyes over each feature on my face—my eyes, my cheeks, my lips. Was he starting to lean toward me?

"So you know about stars?" I looked up at the sky.

"Don't sound so shocked, college girl. You're not the only one with brains around here." Joey drank again and leaned back on his hands.

"Nursing school isn't exactly college. And right now I don't have the money to go back in the fall."

"Ask your pop for the money. He owes you, I'd say."

"Easier said than done. I have no idea what his business will be like from now on. If Angel insists on a high cut, he won't be making as much, especially if he's got to cut the River Gang in too. Are they still intent on transporting all loads across the river for a fee?"

"Yeah. But I still don't get why your dad met with Angel today."

"That's because I haven't told you the final piece of the story." I took a deep breath. "Angel released Daddy and me in exchange for making a business deal that sort of makes him a partner in the bootlegging operation."

Joey sat straight up. "What do you mean, released *you*?"

"Well, after you left for Chicago with the stolen load, Enzo's younger brother Raymond and his buddy Harry lured me to the boathouse with the ransom money, stole it, and took me to a cabin in the woods, where they'd also taken Daddy."

"What!" Shock rippled through the word. "What the hell for?"

"In their greedy little minds it made sense—they thought they'd use the ransom money to start running dope or something, and Raymond wanted to prove to his father he was a big-time player, like his brother." I took another swallow, grateful for the numbing buzz of the whisky. "But it backfired because Harry kept calling Raymond stupid, so Raymond shot him and dragged his body into the woods. Then Daddy and I convinced him we'd go into business with him to show his father and brother how important he was."

"Jesus Christ, are you kidding me?" Joey's mouth hung open, and he ran a hand through his thick, unruly brown hair.

"Nope. But once he brought me back to town, I managed to escape and get to Enzo."

Joey's eyelids lowered. "Let me guess. He's the fucking hero."

"Not exactly." I ignored his sarcasm. "Angel was furious with Raymond for interfering, and he was already mad at Enzo about the hijacked booze."

"Good." Joey picked up his glass for a gulp.

"So I got Angel to release us both by assuring him Daddy would work for him, or at least pay him the percentage he'd wanted in the first place."

"Fucking brilliant."

I stiffened. "I did what I had to, Joey. I was scared."

He closed his eyes, leaned back on his elbows, and tipped his chin up, exhaling toward the sky. "I'm sorry. I shouldn't have left you alone here."

Right then I made the decision not to tell him that Raymond had wanted *me* as part of the deal, or how he'd attacked me at the club last night—not only would he feel more guilt, but I'd have to tell him that it was Enzo who broke into the room and fought off his brother before I clubbed him with a heavy lamp. And then later, in Enzo's room…

I shoved the memory of sex with Enzo from my mind. "It's not your fault, Joey. You did everything you could to help me get that ransom money. I'm so grateful to you, and Daddy is too. We have our freedom, at least; the rest is just a business deal."

Joey didn't open his eyes right away. I wrapped my arms around my knees, and we sat in silence for a few minutes, listening to a scratchy piano waltz coming from the phonograph downstairs, before he spoke. "You need to go back to school. Get out of this business. It's not for you."

Tipping sideways a little, I elbowed him. "Look who's talking. Haven't we had this conversation before? I believe it was you who said, *'The movies make you want things. I'm gonna get 'em.'*"

He shook his head. "We're different, Tiny. You've got the brains to make something of yourself without being in danger all the time."

"So do you! I was thinking about it earlier, during supper. You could take over here, or use the money you get from the opium to open up your own restaurant or something. You're talented, Joey. You don't need to spend your life breaking laws or skulls to make a buck."

He sat up and rubbed a hand on the back of his neck. "We're not talking about me. It's you who got the good marks in school. I screwed around too much, didn't care enough. If I could go back, I'd do a lot of things differently."

"You mean school?"

"I mean a lot of things."

What I would do differently if I could go back and change something in my life? For the most part, I'd done well in school and stayed out of trouble. Taking care of the house and watching over my sisters took up a lot of time, and I'd worked for Daddy a lot the last few years too. There may have been a boy or two I wish I hadn't kissed, but I had no major regrets so far—unless Enzo turned out to be a big mistake. *Which is entirely possible.*

Joey looked over at me. "So why don't you get a different job? Make the tuition money on your own?"

I groaned. "I think I'll have to."

"How much do you need?" His eyes were serious.

"You're not giving it to me."

"I didn't offer anything. I just asked how much."

Tipping back the last swallow of my whiskey, I set the glass down next to me and leaned back on my

35

hands again. "It's not just tuition. I feel like there are so many things weighing me down. I want more freedom. I want to move out of my father's house. Get my own place and start living, you know? I'm tired of feeling as if I'm waiting for my real life to start."

Joey nodded but said nothing. He finished his second drink and propped his arms on his wide-spaced knees, looking straight ahead. When he finally spoke, the words stunned me. "Come with me."

"What?" I couldn't possibly have heard that right.

He looked at me over his shoulder. "Come with me. To Chicago."

"Why would I go with you to Chicago?"

"You said yourself you wanted to get out of your pop's house. I'm offering you that chance. You could go to school in Chicago. It would be like going away to college or something."

"That's nuts, Joey! I can't afford that! Where would I live?"

"With me."

"With you!"

"We could find an apartment."

"Together?" I picked up my whiskey glass, found it empty, and tipped it to my lips anyway, hoping to suck up any miniscule drop left at the bottom.

"Why not?"

"Why not? I'll tell you why not. Because *we're* not—" Frantically I moved my hand back and forth between us. I didn't even know how to put it.

"We don't have to be. I just want you away from here, away from people who…put you in danger. I want you safe, that's all."

Suddenly something clicked. "No, you don't."

"What?" Now it was Joey's turn to be surprised.

"You don't care if I'm safe. You'd be doing the same things down there you're doing up here. I'd still be around the same kind of people breaking all the same laws. You just don't want me to be with *him*."

Joey shook his head. "That's not true! I'm offering to take you away from all the crummy things weighing you down. I'm offering you a chance to start living your life for you, like you said!"

"Bullshit!" I jumped up. "You're just jealous!"

Joey popped to his feet too, fists clenched at his sides. "He doesn't care about you!" he roared. "You'll never be anything more to him than a good time!"

"Which is more than *you* can say, isn't it? And that's really what we're talking about. You're mad because he got something you want." I poked him in the chest.

Joey breathed hard, his brown eyes flashing with angry fire. "Maybe he did."

Those three words stunned me silent. It was the closest he'd ever come to admitting he felt anything for me, and I had no idea how to react. Weren't you at least supposed to kiss the girl if you were asking her to run away with you?

Before I could speak, Joey went on. "This is the only time I'll make this offer, Tiny. I want you to come

37

with me, but I won't ask you again. You have to tell me tonight."

I narrowed my eyes at him and cocked my head. "An ultimatum. How romantic."

He pressed his lips together. "Forget I asked."

The fight left my body. "Come on, Joey, can't we at least—"

"No. You're right. I don't know what I was thinking. It would never work." He leaned over, picked up the whiskey bottle and his glass, and walked to the stairs before I could argue.

And why would you argue? You don't want to run away with him. What the hell kind of offer was that, anyway? It wasn't like he'd confessed his love and begged me to return it. He was just being a sore loser. Frowning, I followed him through the apartment, down the stairs and straight into the car.

Neither of us spoke on the ride home, and the tension between us grew thicker and more awkward with every wordless second. It made me realize how comfortable our silences had been before.

Those days were over.

I was dangerously close to tears by the time he pulled into my driveway, but the sight of the Ford Model T Daddy and I shared parked next to the house was a relief—he was home from his meeting with the DiFiores.

"Thanks again for supper," I said quietly, one hand on the door.

"Tell *nobody* about the opium. Got it?" Joey's tone was as cold as his stare.

"I got it."

"Forget I said a word about it. In fact, forget every single word I said tonight." He switched his focus straight ahead, out the windshield.

I stared at his stubbornly set jaw in disbelief. Was he really going to be such a child about this? He'd had plenty of opportunities to admit he felt something for me—not that he was admitting anything now, either. Why couldn't he just say something, *anything*, about his feelings? Give me some reason besides his jealousy to consider his offer?

But he remained silent.

Chapter Three

"Daddy?" I called the second I got inside the house.

"In here."

I followed his voice into the kitchen, where I found him sitting at the table with a notebook, pencil in hand, and a glass of whiskey. "What are you doing?"

"Just running some numbers."

"Feds are looking for you," I said breathlessly, sliding into the chair across from him and studying his face. We didn't look much alike. I had my mother's Irish farm girl coloring—red hair, fair skin, blue eyes. Daddy was dark-haired and brown-eyed, and even before Raymond DiFiore beat him bloody last week, his face had worn the faint scars and crooked nose of a youth spent boxing in underground fights.

"So I hear. I saw Martin earlier." He didn't sound particularly worried about it.

"Are they going to arrest you?"

"They got nothing on me. Most they can do is bring me in for questioning."

His lack of concern reminded me of Joey. God, men were so exasperatingly overconfident. None of them ever thought anything bad would happen to them. *Maybe that's how they live like this, day after day.* "So how did the meeting go?"

"Uh, good."

"And what's that mean?"

He swallowed some whiskey before answering. "They want me to move my auto repair operation to one of their buildings downtown."

"Why? So they can keep a closer eye on you?"

"It's bigger."

The way he refused to look up from his notebook made me twitchy. "And?"

"And it's got a second floor where I can run a poker game. And maybe a sports book. Might be organizing some fights too."

Aha. I sat back. Nothing was more irresistible to Daddy than an opportunity to place a bet. Didn't matter on what—cards, dice, horses, dogs, fights, ball games…he couldn't resist. When our mother was alive, her presence had kept the habit in check, but since her death he'd been increasingly susceptible to it. Fear oozed into my bloodstream and my heart thumped a bit quicker. "I'm not sure that's such a good idea."

"It'll mean more money coming in."

"It'll mean more going out too. And don't pretend you don't know what I mean."

41

His ruddy face flushed. "That's my concern, not yours."

"Bullshit!" I slammed my hand on the table.

"You watch your tongue, Missy. I'm still your father, and this is still my house. Weren't you the one who told me to agree to their terms this afternoon, no matter what?"

"Well, yes—but I meant in terms of the bootlegging business. I wanted you to agree to whatever percentage Angel asked for in order to buy the protection you need to keep operating. That's what he wanted in the first place. If you'd been so agreeable then, we wouldn't be in this mess."

"I'm getting out of the whisky business."

Now I was thoroughly confused. "What? I thought the whole reason—"

"Things are different now. Smalltime bootleggers are done. The mob will eventually control all booze coming in and going out, and I'd have to pay up to somebody anyway. Plus, if I stick to the auto repair business, there's less risk of being caught. And Angel only takes ten percent of the garage."

I narrowed my eyes. "What's he take from the House once you start the poker games?"

"Seventy-five percent."

"Seventy-five. And that's agreeable to you, getting only twenty-five percent?"

"Those places make a fortune, Tiny! Twenty-five percent could be a lot of dough."

Anger spiked my bloodstream. "I see. And what about the girls?"

"What about them? This is good for everybody."

"Not for me. I'm leaving."

"What?"

My voice rose, matching the flare of my temper. "You heard me, Daddy. I can't keep living here and putting off my life any longer. I worked for six months to make enough money to go back to school this fall, and it was gone in a heartbeat last week."

"I'm sorry about that, Tiny. I never should have ignored Angel's letters. That was my fault, and I'll pay you back. You can have money for school."

I shook my head and spoke through clenched teeth. "That's not enough. I want to leave home and be out on my own. Save your money, because you might need to hire some help."

Daddy got to his feet. "You're not moving away from home, Frances O'Mara, and that's final. Your family needs you here." He planted a crooked index finger on the table.

"They need a cook and a housekeeper and a seamstress!" I shouted, jumping to my feet as well. "They need a *mother*, and I'm not her!"

"No, you aren't!" he yelled back. "Your mother never would have let her family down this way. But when she died, everything changed, and we all have to make sacrifices."

I gaped at him. Was this the same man who told me earlier how proud my mother would have been of my bravery and selflessness this week? "Sacrifices? I sacrificed five years of my life for this family! Ever since Bridget married Vince, I've been running this house and mothering my sisters, and I'm tired of it. Molly is fifteen now—just as old as I was when Bridget left!"

His face went nearly purple. "Your sister left to get married because she'd gotten herself in trouble! I know you're smarter than that." In his eyes I saw all the fury he'd unleashed when Bridget had announced she was pregnant at nineteen. But I wouldn't be cowed.

"I'm going, and you can't stop me."

Daddy closed his eyes and took several deep breaths. If I hadn't just risked my life coming up with the ransom money to free him, he might have slapped me. He didn't often get violent, but since I had a loose tongue and a fiery temper like his, I'd probably been slapped more times than my three sisters combined.

Tonight he managed to keep control. But his knuckles turned white as he pressed his fists on the table. "We'll talk about this tomorrow."

"There's nothing to talk about."

"And how will you support yourself, missy?"

"I'll find a way."

But the truth was, I had no idea how I'd support myself. Bridget certainly couldn't pay me enough at the grocery store. It kept Bridget's family fed and clothed, but it was just a little neighborhood place. I'd have to apply for a job downtown, and even if I got one right away it would be a while before I'd have enough saved to move out. I was still stuck here for the time being.

Goddamn it. Maybe I shouldn't have said no to Joey so quickly.

#

"Come with me."

Joey's words floated toward me through the dark, whispered in a low voice, raw with need. Masculine scents of smoke and whiskey and aftershave filled my head, and I breathed deeply before a sigh escaped my lips. Then his mouth was on mine, hot and hard and heavy. Too heavy.

Joey, I won't fight you. Take me away.

I tried to murmur words against his lips, but the pressure on my mouth wouldn't let up. *I'm dreaming*, I thought in a haze of confused arousal.

But when I opened my eyes, the man in my room was real.

And it wasn't Joey.

"Shhhh," Enzo whispered, his hand over my mouth. "Come with me. Now."

My pulse, already racing, kicked up even higher at his invitation, at his touch on my lips, at the promise of sneaking somewhere alone with him in the dark. Clothed in only my light summer nightgown, I followed him past my father's closed bedroom door, carefully moving down the stairs in my bare feet. It didn't surprise me at all that Enzo had come right in the front door—he had a way with locks I'd learned not to question.

45

Outside, I hurried toward a gorgeous cream-colored Packard sedan parked at the curb. Enzo opened the passenger door for me and I slid in, tucking my hands underneath my legs. As I watched his lean, muscular frame move around the front of the car and open the driver's side door, my insides tightened with desire. He wore no coat, no vest, and no collar on his white shirt. The top few buttons were undone, and my fingers itched to pull the shirt from his trousers and undo the rest of them so I could work off some of the tension inside me. I dug my fingernails into my thighs.

As soon as the motor was running Enzo hit the accelerator, speeding down the street and turning onto Jefferson so quickly I had to brace myself against the door. My heart thrummed hard in my chest. Neither of us spoke, but when his right hand slid across the seat and under the hem of my short nightgown, I moved closer to him.

His expression remained impassive and his eyes on the road, although I saw the slightest twitch in his jaw. I held my breath when his hand settled on the inside of my thigh and slowly crept higher. When his fingers brushed against the soft folds between my legs and he realized I wasn't wearing underwear, he glanced sharply at me.

My eyes pleaded with him to continue. I wanted to lose control, lose my mind, lose myself. I wanted the heart-pounding abandon that overwhelmed us when we let ourselves forget who we were and why every moment between us was stolen. Ten days ago I hadn't even known his name, but he'd awakened something in me, something instinctual and insatiable that would not be ignored.

And I didn't want to ignore it. I wanted to indulge it—now.

With my eyes locked on the exquisite lines of his profile, I put my left hand between his legs. His cock was already hard, but as I rubbed him up and down, it swelled further and strained tighter against his trousers. He slipped a fingertip inside me, sliding it up the slick seam at my center, keeping it torturously shallow, before moving it gently back and forth over the tiny spot that electrified my entire body.

With one hand I slipped the buttons of his trousers through the holes and slid my palm down his hot, tight abdomen. When I wrapped my hand around his solid flesh, he grabbed the steering wheel with both hands.

I said nothing, just moved my hand up and down the hot, thick column, squeezing tight and keeping the rhythm steady, the way I knew he liked it. My lips curved into a smile. The thrill of touching Enzo this way filled me with a sense of power and freedom so intoxicating I often felt drunk when we were together, even when no alcohol had been consumed. The forward motion of the car, the rush of night flying past the windows, the hum of the tires on the road—all of it added to the maelstrom building inside me.

Suddenly the Packard swerved. At first I thought it was accidental, but then I saw that Enzo had turned down a silent residential street with large homes set back from the road. He turned off the engine, looked at me with glittering black eyes, and uttered just one word: "Now."

The keys barely hit the floor before he hauled me onto his lap.

I straddled him, one knee on either side of his hips, and he took my head in his hands, crushing his mouth to mine. We weren't in love, about that I had no illusions, but our desire for each other was volatile and fierce, and we kissed as if we were starved, as if our hunger could never be satisfied. Enzo slipped his arms from his braces and I shoved at the sides of his trousers. Without taking his mouth off me, he lifted his hips and managed to shimmy them down just enough. I grasped his swollen cock in my hand again, anxious to feel it inside me.

But we'd already been careless once the night before. "Wait," I breathed. Do you have...you know..."

Without answering, he tilted sideways and reached under the front seat. When he righted himself, he held a small condom tin, and with one hand, he opened it, slipped one from its paper wrapper, and slid it on.

I lowered myself onto him, intending to go slow since I was still tender from the night before. But Enzo had other ideas. He grabbed my hips and yanked me down hard, both of us gasping at the shock of it. Bracing my hands on the top of the seat behind him, I turned my face away from his and kept still, allowing my body to push past the sharp twinge of pain.

His mouth, hot and wet, traveled down the exposed side of my neck as the ache inside me eased. He swirled his tongue in an intricate pattern along my throat and down to my shoulder. Instinctively, the muscles surrounding him contracted, and I gasped when I felt his teeth sink into my skin. Then he brushed his lips over the spot, soft as a feather.

Aroused by the whisper of his lips on my neck after the sting of the bite, I began to move, slowly rocking my hips forward and back, and clenching him tight inside me. He picked up his head and our eyes met, our mouths open and breathing hotly against one another.

Then he took control of the rhythm between us, using his hands on my hips, pulling and pushing my body against his, increasingly harder and faster. He cursed and closed his eyes while I smiled and reached up, flattening my palms on the car's ceiling. I let him move me the way he wanted, but I arched my back a little to feel the base of his cock just where I wanted it. A sheen of sweat broke out on his forehead, glistening in the dark, and my back prickled with trapped heat under my nightgown.

Oh my God. Yes, yes, yes…

Pressure built inside me, the powerful need for release a gathering storm at my center, and I wanted to widen my knees even farther to take him deeper. My blood roared, my skin hummed, and every muscle in my body began to tighten.

"Yes," I said, my voice soft and pleading. "Don't stop. Oh God, Enzo—yes, like that. Don't stop…"

He cursed again, and I could feel him start to throb inside me. He dug his fingers into my skin and held me tight to him as he came, and the sight of his gorgeous face and the pulse of his powerful orgasm and even the knowledge that we could be seen through the windows sent me flying over the edge of my own pleasure. I closed my eyes, dropped my head back, and let the waves crash through me.

Breathing hard, I stared at the ceiling of the car as stars swam in front of my eyes. Enzo touched my throat, trailing five fingers down to my chest. "I want you," he growled.

I laughed lazily, picking my head up. "Again? Already?"

He didn't smile. "I want you for myself." His palm flattened over one breast and he squeezed it before sliding his hand to the small of my back. "I don't want anyone else to have what I have."

My body was still tingling, but his words abraded the lingering hum a little. I wasn't interested in being anyone's possession.

And Enzo had no room to talk.

"You're the one with the fiancée, not me."

"I told you last night—that's a business arrangement."

"I remember." Irritated at the thought of the squeaking little chippie he was engaged to marry, I tried to get off his lap, but he held me there. His flesh was still relatively hard inside me, but I was no longer in the mood.

"Jealous?"

"No." But my cheeks were burning. "I just don't like being reminded of your goddamn girlfriend while I'm sitting on your lap."

"That's more than just my lap you're on, isn't it?"

"Stop it. You know what I mean. Here you are talking about not wanting others to have me, but I don't even know when we can see each other, between my father and your fiancée, and—"

"Your father won't be a problem. He'll be so busy with his new business venture, he won't even notice you're gone."

"New business venture…you mean the new building?"

"And the gambling. I set that up, you know."

I blinked in surprise. "Your father let you do that?"

"I'm a grown man, Tiny. My father doesn't control me." Anger edged its way underneath his words.

"Sorry, but I thought it was Angel who'd made the deal with my father today. He never said anything about you."

"Well, I was there," he said, irritated. "It was my idea to move Jack to a new building, let him run a few games, and let Raymond take over the bootlegging from Canada on his own."

At the mention of his brother, I froze. "Raymond was there?"

Enzo smiled. "No, he's still recovering from the wrath of Tiny O'Mara."

In my mind I relived the adrenaline-and-terror-fueled blow to his head. I felt no guilt, but I did fear further violence. "Is he going to come after me again?"

"If he does, he'll have me to answer to."

"But he's your brother."

"I don't fucking care who he is—anyone touches you, anyone even looks at you in a way I don't like, I'll kill him."

Unease slithered up my body, wrapping itself around my chest like a boa constrictor. I tried to shake it off and speak lightly. "So it's OK for you to have a fiancée, but no one can even look my way?"

"You know, if your friends hadn't stolen that shipment, I wouldn't be in this position. I could probably even break it off with Gina."

I raised an eyebrow. This was something new. Yesterday when I'd confronted him about the engagement, he hadn't said anything about leaving Gina Meloni, whose father owned a whiskey distillery in Kentucky. "Oh?"

"But now I can't postpone anything until I pay for the fucking whiskey I ordered. It's in Meloni's warehouse, but he won't deliver it until I pay him. And his men won't let anyone else deliver booze to the club, which is a big fucking problem, as you might imagine."

I didn't much care about his whisky problem. "Postpone what? I thought you were already engaged." I tried to recall a ring on Gina's finger, but couldn't. The couple times I'd seen her at the club, I hadn't known about the engagement so I hadn't thought to look for one.

Enzo turned his head and stared out the window. "I asked her father for more time to get the cash for the whiskey, and he offered a deal."

"What kind of deal?"

"If Gina and I get married now, he'll forgive the debt."

The irony that it was now Enzo forced to come up with thousands of dollars on a deadline wasn't lost on me, but I couldn't help obsessing over the word *married,* especially in light of our intimate seating arrangement. "Wait a minute...you're actually going to marry her?"

"I'm trying to get out of it."

My mouth fell open "Jesus Christ, Enzo!" This time when I wrestled my way off his lap, he didn't stop me.

"What's the problem, Tiny? It's not as if you didn't know about her. We discussed the fact that you and I are a secret, remember? That's half the fun."

We *had* discussed it, sort of—actually it was less a discussion and more his telling me how things had to be. If I wanted him, those were the terms. And while the secrecy did add a certain clandestine thrill to our meetings, I wasn't sure I wanted to be a married man's mistress. Frowning, I looked away as he removed the spent condom.

"Listen to me," he said. "Gina's not important. What matters is that I can't let Meloni see I can be bested by a bunch of fucking upstart delinquents from

53

the Scarfone gang. He'll make my life hell. He'll think he can push me around. That's why I have to go after them myself. Forget what I told you about talking to Lupo."

At the mention of Joey, I froze. "What?"

"I need to handle this now. I can't wait around and hope that he tells you something."

"Can't you just ask your father for the money?"

"I'm not a fucking child, Tiny. I can handle this myself."

"So now what?" Pressing my knees together, I pushed my nightgown down and tucked it around my legs. My thighs were sticky.

"So now I get my money back from those assholes. I can't let it be known that you can steal from Enzo DiFiore. I have to send a message."

Chills swept down my arms. "How?"

He set his jaw and didn't answer, but I knew what he was thinking. My stomach heaved, imagining it could be Joey on the receiving end of that message. "Don't, Enzo. You don't have to hurt anyone—let me help you."

"You can't help me."

"Yes, I can." *What are you doing?* a voice inside me screamed.

But I ignored it.

"The River Gang didn't sell the opium. Joey brought it back to Detroit." I whispered the words, as if the volume at which I betrayed Joey might lessen its reprehensibility.

Enzo fixed his eyes on me. "What? Who told you that?"

"Joey wants to talk to you. Maybe make a deal with you." The words tumbled out quickly.

"Where is it?"

Finally I bit my tongue. "I don't know."

"Oh, I think you do." He leaned closer, slipping his arms around me and dragging me across his lap on my back. My legs extended along the seat, and I pressed my knees together as his right hand slid under my nightgown again. "And you're going to tell me."

"Enzo, please."

He kneaded my thigh, but his touch was gentle, too gentle for how I knew he must be feeling inside. And he was smiling. "Tell me, darling."

I chewed my bottom lip as his eyes searched my face. Despite his warm hands on me, the curve of his lips was as chilling as the calm in his voice. It was the Enzo I'd first met, the one who could mask his emotions so masterfully that I couldn't tell what he was thinking. He'd let some of that façade slip in the last few days. *But now there's something he wants more than you.* "I can't."

His smile widened as his fingers slid higher and worked between my inner thighs. "You can do anything you want," he said softly, bringing his lips close to mine as he began to stroke me. "You're still wet. I love that I make you this wet." Lowering his mouth, he slid his tongue between my lips and eased one finger, then another, inside me, his languid kiss mirroring the gentle rhythm of his hand.

55

Somewhere inside my brain was a voice warning me that this was wrong, that I'd made a promise to Joey, that Enzo wasn't kissing me this way because he cared for me. But I silenced it by telling myself I'd done the right thing by revealing Joey's secret—I'd prevented Enzo from hurting anyone. And even if Enzo didn't love me, he certainly loved pleasing me, and maybe that was enough. As his tongue swept mine, my arms snaked around his neck and I widened my knees a little.

"Good girl," he whispered, removing his fingers to caress my tender, swollen flesh before plunging them deep inside me again. "You're going to come again for me."

"Oh God…" I clutched at his neck and turned my face into his chest, but even the smell of him, smoky and masculine, drove me mad with desire.

He rubbed his wet fingers over the most sensitive skin on my body. "I know everything you want. And I can give it all to you, you know I can." His voice was dulcet, the words dripping from his lips like honey. "Your own apartment, money to do as you please, new clothes…the life you deserve. I've been thinking about it all day."

When I moaned, he rubbed faster and harder, and I could only think *yes, yes, yes.* I murmured the words, and he brought his lips closer to my ear.

"Wouldn't you like your own place? Where we can be together whenever we want? I'll make you come all…night…long."

His breath tickled my skin, his words echoing through the roar of blood and the buzz of nerve endings and—*oh my God* the way he touched me made me feel like nothing else mattered but the moment and the need and the heat and the spiraling climb toward release…

"Yes!" I cried out, lifting my hips against his hand as the second orgasm exploded inside me, no less powerful than the first. When the tightness finally eased, my bones were floating in my skin.

"Mmmmm." He kissed me again. "You'll need an apartment that has thick walls."

I managed a tiny smile.

"So what do you say?"

"I…can't afford an apartment."

"I'll pay for it."

"No." Orgasms aside, I didn't want to him to own me.

"Then I'll get you a job. Would you like to work at the club?"

"Work at the club? What would I do?"

"Whatever you want. Hostess? Hat check? Waitress?" He cocked his head. "You don't sing, do you? Or dance? You'd look fantastic on stage in a short little costume."

"Uh, no." Because one of my legs was slightly shorter than the other, the result of a difficult birth during which my hip was broken, I'd never felt terribly natural while dancing—sometimes even walking comfortably was a chore. And my singing made my cooking skills look good.

"Well, you can think about it then. But I'll see to it that you're paid *very* well, if you want."

I exhaled, closing my eyes. Of course I wanted it. I wanted everything he just mentioned—the apartment, the nights with him, the money to do as I pleased, the freedom to make my choices and own my mistakes as well as my successes. What young woman didn't want to live a flapper's life with all its wicked delights?

But at what price?

If I told Enzo where the opium was and he took it back, Joey would know I'd betrayed him. But if I didn't, Enzo would take matters into his own hands and people would get hurt, maybe even killed.

I opened my eyes. "If I tell you where the opium is, you have to promise me you'll give me a chance to talk to Joey before you take it."

"I can't promise that, Tiny. But I can promise that if you *don't* tell me, I'll have no choice but to settle this score my own way."

My heart stuttered. "Well...you can't hurt Joey. Promise that."

Enzo stiffened. "What is he to you?"

"A friend."

Silence. "I won't have to hurt him if he cooperates. And I won't have to marry Gina if I get the cash for the drugs."

It was so dark, I couldn't read his eyes. I wanted everything he was offering. And I didn't want him to marry Gina. What had he said to me this morning? *You and I are going to have to trust each other a little bit.*

I took a breath. "It's in the boathouse."

A smile crept onto his lips, slow and sinister. "Shall we take a ride?"

I struggled to sit up. "No!"

He shifted me onto the seat beside him and started the car.

Panicked, I put my hands on his arm and tugged. "Please, Enzo. Just wait, all right?" It occurred to me that I wasn't entirely positive the drugs were still in the boathouse. Even if they had been there earlier today, Joey might have moved them after dropping me off. I hung on as he swung the car around and headed back onto Jefferson. "Listen, I wasn't supposed to tell you anything yet, and now I'll be in trouble."

Enzo laughed. "Trouble is your middle name, darling."

Frowning, I scooted away from him and stared out the window. Enzo rarely used any terms of endearment with me, and somehow this one lacked a certain affection I was hoping to develop between us. Why the hell couldn't I meet a normal fellow like Evelyn had? One who took me to the movies or a dance on a Saturday night?

Enzo turned off Jefferson onto the boathouse drive, and I had to reach out and steady myself again as the Packard bumped and shimmied over the tree-rutted and potholed dirt. Low hanging branches scraped against the windows, and Enzo swore softly. "Fucking trees better not ruin this paint job. I just got this car."

I felt like spitting on the new upholstery, and I might have if I weren't so scared.

When we emerged into the clearing where the abandoned boathouse stood, a shiver ran through me. This is where I'd been abducted just a few nights ago by Raymond and Harry, and I didn't much feel like reliving that memory. Beyond the dilapidated old structure, Lake St. Clair loomed, black and silent. I wrapped my bare arms around myself, feeling exposed and vulnerable in my nightgown. "I'll wait here."

Enzo looked over at me but didn't reply. After pulling his braces back onto his shoulders, he got out of the car and opened the door to the back. I thought he might be looking for his coat but instead he reached down and retrieved a pistol from beneath the seat. My mouth hung open as he checked it for bullets.

"What the hell is that for?" I whispered. "There's nobody here!"

"Then there won't be any trouble." His tone was cool and confident—of course it was— but he glanced over both shoulders as he walked past the giant weeping willow to the boathouse door. The waning moon offered little light, so I didn't see how he managed to pick the lock, but within seconds his white shirt disappeared into the shadows of the building.

I swallowed hard, murmuring a quick prayer that the drugs were there, that Enzo wouldn't want to take them tonight, and that Joey would forgive me for this.

Before I even got the chance to say *Amen*, the gun went off.

Chapter Four

I opened the car door and took off running for the boathouse before I thought it through. "Enzo!" I yelled as I crossed the threshold into the cool, dark space. Stopping just inside the door, I was relieved to see him standing there, unharmed. His back was to me, and both his hands were in the air near his shoulders. Neither hand held the pistol.

"Tiny, go back outside please."

I barely heard the words over the galloping of my heart, which felt like someone's fist trying to punch through my ribs. I looked around, confused. The voice was deep and familiar, but it wasn't Enzo's. Inching forward, I scanned the shadows and saw Joey standing next to a large trunk, pointing a gun at Enzo. "Joey?"

"I said, go back outside." He kept his eyes and his weapon on Enzo.

"No! What are you doing?" I tried walking toward him, but immediately someone threw a thick arm around me from behind and pinned my back to

61

his chest—not hard enough to hurt me, but enough to prevent me from moving forward. I tugged at the wrist, to no avail. "Hey!"

"Take her out, Angelo." Joey's voice was colder than I'd ever heard it, which must have been why I hadn't recognized it right away.

"Hold on, just wait a second." I struggled to free myself from Angelo's hairy left arm. Like Enzo and Joey, he wore no coat and his cuffs were rolled. His right arm extended toward Enzo, gun aimed. "What is this?"

"It's a meeting," said Angelo. "Thanks for setting it up."

"What do you mean, setting it up? I didn't do this!" I panicked, imagining Enzo would think I'd sent him into a trap.

"I figured you'd tell him." Joey's voice was devoid of any emotion, but I felt the sting of his words as if he'd slapped me. "And I had a feeling it might be tonight."

"Joey, please," I began.

"Get her out of here," he said.

"Why?" Enzo asked. "If all you want to do is make a deal, why not let her stay? She's hardly going to run away in her nightgown."

Oh God—I'd forgotten I was in my nightgown, and barefoot. *Jesus, what Joey must think!* And Angelo—my face burned with shame that a strange man held me so close in my pajamas. Frantically, I wondered why Enzo wanted me to stay. Did he think they'd be less likely to shoot him if I was in the boathouse?

Or did he want me where he could see me?

This was a huge problem with us—we were rarely sure whose side the other was on. My hands shook, and I tightened them into fists to keep them still. "Let me stay." I forced myself to sound defiant. "I won't be any trouble. I was trying to do as you asked and set up a meeting, Joey, but he insisted on seeing for himself if the drugs were here."

"Of course he did." Joey never took his eyes from Enzo. "He probably wouldn't have met with me otherwise."

"You're right. I wouldn't have." Enzo sounded way too self-righteous for someone with two guns pointed at him. Silently I pleaded with him to show some humility. "You fucked up a huge deal for me."

"Tough luck, I guess," Joey said.

Angelo spit on the boathouse floor, and my stomach turned over at the splat. "You ready to talk business or you want to cry about the past?"

I braced myself for an angry reaction from Enzo, but he stayed calm as he regarded Angelo. "Who the fuck are you?"

"Shut your mouth," Joey ordered. "We came to make a deal. You interested?"

"Can I put my arms down?"

"Be my guest. But stay the fuck where you are."

Enzo lowered his arms. "What's the deal you're offering?"

"You have a buyer lined up for this?" Joey jerked his head toward the trunk next to him. It was large and rectangular, the kind used on steamer ships to make a long voyage.

"I might."

"We make the sale together," Joey said. "I'll deliver the product."

"And what do I get out of this deal?"

"A cut of the profit."

"What kind of cut?"

"I think thirty percent's fair."

"I think you're fucking crazy."

"I could just kill you, you know."

A high-pitched sound escaped my throat. Neither Enzo nor Joey looked at me.

"Killing me won't get you what you want."

Joey shrugged. "But it might be fun."

"Please, stop," I begged. Angelo tightened his grip on me, and I whimpered in protest.

"Let her go," Joey said.

"Hunh?" Angelo was as surprised as I was.

"You heard me. Let her go."

The arm around my chest didn't loosen. "What the fuck, Lupo?"

"Just do it."

After a moment's hesitation, Angelo released me and moved closer to Enzo, bringing his other hand to the gun.

"Tiny, bring me the pistol on the ground." Joey's voice was cool and steady, and he still didn't look at me.

64

I hurried forward, scooping up Enzo's gun from the cement floor and bringing it to Joey. As he took the gun from my hands, the moonlight shining through the high windows revealed the fury in his eyes.

I remembered a night not long ago when Joey and I had been alone in the boathouse, the night he'd kissed me on the lake…the night a storm raged outside and lightning had illuminated his features as he'd moved toward me in the dark, his voice teasing…I heard none of that levity now.

"So DiFiore, you can either agree to what we're offering here, which is an even three-way split—more than anyone else would offer, by the fucking way—or you can kiss thousands of dollars goodbye like a goddamn fool."

Enzo squared his shoulders. "I'm no fool."

"Then make the deal."

Unbearable silence followed. Finally he spoke. "How do I know you've really got the drugs? Could be anything in that trunk."

Joey nodded at Angelo, who grabbed Enzo by the upper arm and put the gun under his chin. They were about the same height, but Angelo was meatier, with a thick neck and a beefy chest that bulged inside his shirt. By contrast, Enzo's frame appeared slender. Angelo led him over to the trunk, which Joey opened. Tentatively, I tiptoed forward and peered inside too.

It was full of tin containers shaped like small bricks with rounded edges, and they were labeled, but I couldn't read the words in the dark. Joey shut the lid. "Well?"

Enzo studied Joey. "What's Sam paying you?"

"This is between us. Sam doesn't know about it, and he's not gonna find out about it, neither, understand?" Joey raised the gun a little higher.

Enzo's lips twitched. "Lupo, you have no fucking idea what you're doing."

My heart skipped a beat—that was exactly what I was afraid of.

But Joey stood his ground. "Deal or no deal, asshole."

Enzo stared at Joey for another few seconds, and then he glanced at Angelo. I might as well have been invisible. "Deal."

To my astonishment, the two shook on it before Angelo marched us out to the Packard at gunpoint. I couldn't even bring myself to glance back at Joey as we left.

#

Enzo was silent on the way back to my house, but he wore an eerily calm expression. He switched off the headlamps once he'd turned onto my street, and slowed the Packard to a crawl before pulling into the drive next to my house.

When the motor was silent, he looked at me. "Are you all right?"

"No."

He smiled, the bastard. "I'd say I was sorry for taking you out tonight, but I'd be lying."

"You enjoyed this?"

"Well...parts of it. Maybe even most of it." He brushed a finger over my shoulder, but I leaned away from him.

"You could have been killed, Enzo!"

"Those guys were never going to kill me. They need me."

"Well, it frightens me, all the guns and threats and posturing. Not to mention the stealing and the lying and the underhanded deals."

"That's how it works, Tiny."

I crossed my arms in a huff.

Enzo smiled again. "Are you angry with me or with yourself?"

"I'm angry with everyone and everything right now. No matter what I do, I can't get anything right."

"Come on, now." Enzo slipped his fingers up the back of my neck through my hair. When I tried to lean away, he closed his fist, keeping my head where it was and forcing me to look at him. "Everything is going to be perfect, Tiny. You'll see."

"How do you figure? Will your thirty percent cut of the opium be enough to pay off Gina's father?"

His lips tipped up, the smile of an adult tolerating an ignorant child. "Of course not."

"Well, then—how will everything be perfect? I don't understand." He couldn't mean he was going to steal the drugs—Joey would take them from the boathouse tonight, I was certain, and this time he wouldn't be foolish enough to trust me with their location.

67

Instead of explaining, Enzo leaned forward and kissed me lightly on each cheek. "Good night, Tiny."

"Enzo, I—"

"Shhh." He put a finger to my lips. "I'm going to take care of you. I'm going to take care of everything."

"But—"

"Leave it all to me."

I pulled his hand away from my mouth. "You can't hurt Joey. You promised."

"I won't have to." He released me and sat back. "If he's smart."

"And you can't go to Sam the Barber with this information. He'll kill Joey himself."

Enzo's voice took on a new edge. "You're awfully concerned about Lupo. I'm not sure I like it."

Be careful. "I'm just trying to prevent people from getting hurt, Enzo." That was the truth, wasn't it? I thought it was, but for me the *truth* was becoming more nebulous every day. It was nothing I could cling to for safety.

"I see the way he looks at you," Enzo said icily.

"You're imagining things. Right now he wants to shoot me. I'm surprised he didn't."

"He's not going to shoot either one of us. In fact, I think he's going to negotiate further with me."

"Why would he do that?"

"Because I've done a little research on your friend. And I have something he wants. I'm going to offer it to him." With that he put both hands on the steering wheel. "Now you better go in. I'll see you soon."

After shutting the car door as quietly as possible, I snuck back into the house and crept up the stairs, attempting to avoid the ones that creaked.

Wait a minute, what am I doing? Why am I sneaking around like this? It was probably three o'clock in the morning, but what the hell did I care? What's the worst Daddy would do—throw me out? *To hell with it.* I walked up the stairs as if it were noontime, actually disappointed that my feet didn't make more noise on the carpeted steps. How I would have liked to show Daddy he couldn't police me anymore! I wasn't his to control—I wasn't anybody's.

In the bathroom, I cleaned up a little before climbing back into bed. My body was tired, but my mind wouldn't rest. I lay on my side, hands tucked under my cheek and knees drawn to my chest. What could Enzo possibly have that Joey wanted? It couldn't be money.

The whiskey? No, he didn't really have that yet either.

But I couldn't think of any other asset Enzo had to offer Joey at this point, so I approached it from the other side.

What does Joey want?

Immediately, my stomach flipped. I curled my toes and squeezed my thighs together, bringing my legs tighter into my chest. *Knock that off. Even if Joey had felt something stronger than friendship for you before, which he'd never actually said, your behavior tonight was enough to splinter it.*

The hideous weight of what I'd done dropped onto my chest like an anvil and stayed there, pressing the air from my lungs. Tears burned beneath my eyelids. Without Joey's help last week, I never would have gotten the ten thousand dollars to free Daddy. And he'd never asked for anything in return. Yet I'd repaid him tonight with duplicity, giving up his secret to Enzo in exchange for my own pleasure, for promises whispered in the dark. The shame of it rained down on me—I gasped for air as if I were suffocating.

Hold on, just hold on, said a voice inside me. *You did what you had to do to keep Joey safe, right?* Inhaling deeply, I held my breath for a moment and counted to ten before letting it out, slowly. *Yes, I did.*

Somehow, it didn't make me feel any better.

Weeping into my pillow, I wondered how I'd ever make things right again between us.

#

By the time I left my room the following morning, Daddy was up and out of the house. I'd missed nine o'clock mass, which I felt some guilt about, but instead of dwelling on it, I dressed and took a streetcar down to Mt. Elliott Cemetery, where our mother was buried. Usually the girls and I did this together on Sundays, and when I entered the scrolling gates and saw other families at gravesites, pulling weeds and sprucing up flowers, or even just holding

70

hands as they strolled or sat on a bench in quiet contemplation, a lump formed in my throat.

Swallowing hard, I walked toward the section where our mother rested, keeping my head down. It was sunny but breezy, and I had to hold one hand on my hat, which was wide with an oversized brim. It wasn't until I was nearly upon her simple Celtic cross that I saw someone already there. I froze, my Sunday dress flapping about my knees in the wind.

Daddy stood, hat in folded hands, feet apart. From the side, I could see his head was bowed, and I had the feeling that his eyes were closed. When I took a step closer, I saw I was right. His lips moved in silent prayer, or perhaps confession or apology—he certainly had any number of things he might have told her in order to unburden himself. I couldn't even imagine what she'd have said back. Would she forgive him his sins and shortcomings as a father, as a man?

And what about your own?

An ache took hold of my heart, and the lump returned to my throat. What would she say to me if she could speak from beyond the grave? Would she tell me I was selfish to leave home? Would she ask me to think of my sisters first? Or would she agree with me that I'd done enough and it was time to move on with my life? She'd married young, like Bridget, and had a family almost as quickly. In fact, it was my mother who'd always talked of being a nurse if she'd had the opportunity or the education. She was always so proud of my high marks in school and my determination to go to college. After she died in

71

childbirth with Mary Grace ten years ago, I made up my mind that I'd do as she'd wished she could have.

At the time, I'd had no idea what an uphill climb it would be.

I said a quick prayer for my mother's soul from where I stood and turned to leave, having no desire whatsoever to converse with my father here. My mother deserved peace in her final resting place, and I wouldn't disturb it with another argument. Because I hadn't changed my mind—I still wanted to leave home.

And it wasn't only that I wanted to be with Enzo, although I'd be lying if I said my newfound sexual freedom wasn't influencing my decision. But the longer I stayed at home, the more I feared life was passing me by. I couldn't shake the sense that something was out there for me, and if I didn't try to find it now, I might lose my chance at it forever. Sure, I was only twenty, but I'd seen plenty of unfinished lives snuffed out too soon.

To stay out of sight, I tugged the hat down further over my eyes and made a beeline for the exit. But when I turned to glance one last time at my mother's stone, I saw another familiar figure standing over a grave about ten yards off to my left.

His back was to me, but I knew those wide shoulders that tapered to a trim waist. I'd seen that muscular back naked in my kitchen last week, the night I'd treated Joey's injuries after a fight. Biting my lip, I recalled the way I'd run my hands over his bruised ribs.

He was dressed more in the style I was accustomed to seeing him in—the plain black pants, a cream-colored shirt that even from here I could tell had seen better days, and brown braces cutting into his solid shoulders and making a Y down his back. His head was bare, his dark mop of wayward curls blowing in the breeze, and I figured he was holding his floppy old cap in his hands.

Were his eyes closed? Were his lips moving in silent prayer for his slain father? Was he asking forgiveness of the man who'd taught him about stars and had no doubt hoped for more for his son than the life—and death—he'd had himself? Or was Joey asking for guidance at his father's feet, the way I sometimes did at my mother's? In that moment I felt a kinship with Joey that I rarely felt with anyone other than my sisters, and before I knew it, my feet were stepping through the grass in his direction.

I came up beside him, and although I knew he recognized me from the way his back straightened, he said nothing. Perhaps he, too, didn't want to sully his father's final resting place with heated words.

But I needed to apologize.

"Hello." I braved a sideways glance at him.

Silence. I might as well have greeted the statue on my right.

"Joey, I'm sorry."

"I don't believe you."

I wasn't sure if he meant he didn't believe my apology was sincere, or he didn't believe I had the gall to approach him here. Neither interpretation boded well. "Please let me apologize. I never meant to tell Enzo anything last night."

"Pretty obvious your self-control ain't what it ought to be."

Deep breath. "I thought I was doing the right thing. He was threatening to hurt people in order to get his money back, and I was scared for you. He knows who stole that load."

Joey shrugged. "So *you're* a hero now too—he saved you, you saved me. Well done. You two deserve each other."

I stepped in front of him so he'd be forced to look at me. "Joey, please. I'm…I'm sorry too about last night on the roof. I wish I—"

"I told you to forget about that," he snapped.

"Have you forgotten about it?"

"It was a mistake. One of many I've made where you're concerned." His glare was more blistering than the sun.

"OK, fine. But I'm worried. I don't know exactly what Enzo is thinking, but I do know that things aren't going to go according to your plan."

"Switching sides already, doll?"

Jesus—I hadn't thought of it like that. Was I? Had I ever really been on Enzo's side? Before I could think it through, Joey went on.

"And what the hell do you mean by that, anyway? He shook on that deal."

A gust of wind threatened to carry off my hat, and I reached up to hold it to my head. "I don't know anything for certain, but I do know that you shouldn't underestimate him. When he wants something, he..." I swallowed hard. "He knows how to get it."

"I bet he does." He slapped his cap on his head. "You tell him I'll be in touch. I want this deal done fast so I can get out of this town. Nothing here but bad memories." With one last look at his father's stone he stomped away, and I noticed he'd traded his new shoes for his old work boots too.

He exited the gates and got into an old Model T parked on the street. Even the fancy red Buick was gone. A pang of regret squeezed my heart. It was the old, familiar Joey in every way except one—he despised me. And he had every right to. Until that moment I had no idea how much that would matter.

I broke into a run.

Chapter Five

Joey was just starting the engine when I reached the windowless passenger door. "Wait," I said breathlessly. "I want to talk about this."

"About what?" Joey spoke loudly over the noisy motor. "There's nothing left to talk about, Tiny. Just go home."

Without being invited—in fact, I'd been dismissed—I opened the door and hopped in. "No." I shut myself in the car, put my hands in my lap and looked at him. "I can't. I won't."

Joey turned off the engine and squinted at me. "Have I told you how annoying you are?"

"Not today."

"And also how weak and impulsive? And for such a smart girl, how stupid you act sometimes?"

I squirmed, but it was no less than I deserved. "Go ahead. I can take it."

"You deliberately betrayed me, Tiny. After everything we went through last week. I told you something in confidence and you went right to him with it."

"I didn't! I swear to you, I didn't. He surprised me by showing up in my room late last night"—and here Joey flinched—"and we went for a drive. We got to…" I flapped a hand in the air, unsure how to proceed. "…Talking, and he started in about taking revenge for the heist into his own hands because he owes money to a whiskey distributor. I got scared for you, Joey, I had to tell him!"

"I told you, I can take care of myself." Joey's knuckles were white on the steering wheel.

"I'm sorry. I know I did the wrong thing, but I never meant to betray you. It just came out. Please forgive me." I put a hand on his forearm, and he shrugged it off.

"You should have left it to me like I asked you to."

"You asked me to set up a meeting!"

"No, I didn't! You offered, and if you recall, at the end of the night, I told you to drop it. And I meant what I said."

"I know, but…"

"But nothing." He stuck a finger in my face. "You fucked up. If we hadn't been at the boathouse last night, he would have taken those drugs and left me with nothing."

No point in reminding Joey he'd *stolen* the drugs to begin with—these guys all played by their own rules. "I wouldn't have let him."

"Ha! You've got no sway over him."

"You're wrong. He listens to me." What *possessed* me to say such a thing, I have no idea.

Joey smirked. "If you think that, then you're a bigger fool than I thought." He cocked his head, looking more like the old Joey. "What did he do, tell you he loves you?"

"Shut up." My chest and neck flushed with heat.

"Ooh, she's blushing." Joey poked his finger in my side repeatedly. "Did he proclaim his devotion for you, is that it? Is he going to build you a house on Boston Boulevard and buy you a fancy electric car and name his yacht after you? The Tiny." Joey framed the words in the air with his hands. "Hmm, not quite grand enough, is it." He widened his gesture. "The Frances Kathleen. Eh, a little better."

Irritation bubbled up in me, but I was relieved he was back to teasing. "You remembered my full name. Impressive. Don't worry, I won't ask you to spell it."

He turned to me with murderous eyes and poked my side once more. "Get out of my car, ya no-good, backstabbing floozy. Or do I have to drive his girl around as well as feed her?"

"I'll take a ride home, thanks. Sweet of you to offer."

Joey looked at me a moment and exhaled. "I should put you out at the curb right now."

"But you won't."

A pause. "I guess not. "

I grinned. I couldn't help it.

"Why can't I stay mad at you, anyway?"

Linking my fingers, I tucked them under my chin and batted my lashes. "Because I'm so adorable?"

He scrutinized my face. "Nope. That ain't it."

I dropped the pose. "Just drive me home already."

Rolling his eyes, he started the engine again. "Sure thing, Little Tomato. I only live to serve you."

Crossing my arms, I turned my face to the window so he wouldn't see me smile at his nickname for me, which only a week ago would have made me scowl.

When Joey pulled into the drive at my house, I was reluctant to get out of the car, for some reason. "Have you had lunch?"

Joey looked amused. "And if I said no, what are you gonna do about it?"

"Um…invite you in? Scramble you an egg? I do know how to do that."

He smirked. "Sounds tempting but no, I can't. I have to work the dinner shift at the restaurant today."

"Oh. OK. Maybe I'll see you later this week?" What the hell was I doing? *Just get out of the car.*

"Maybe." His tone changed, as if he was irritated I'd asked about seeing him again. "But this week's busy with moving my ma to my sister's and all. Plus I'm looking to get out of town. You tell your boyfriend to get in touch with me, and fast."

"He's not really my boyfriend." Then I was embarrassed—Joey knew I was sleeping with Enzo. If he wasn't my boyfriend, what was he? "I mean…I don't really know what we are."

79

Joey switched his focus out the windshield. "It's none of my business. Just tell him."

I nodded as I got out, a funny, prickly feeling in the pit of my stomach, as if a cactus had lodged there or something. Lifting my hand in a stupid little wave, which Joey didn't return, I watched him back out and drive down the street. I was glad he wasn't angry anymore, but I still didn't feel right about things between us. Maybe I was just worried about the deal with Enzo.

That had to be it.

#

Five days later I hadn't heard from either Enzo or Joey, and I was nearly out of my mind with worry. I started checking the newspapers every afternoon to make sure I didn't read about any new gang warfare or heists that took the lives of young mobsters.

Perhaps I should have just left it alone. After all, I was lucky in some regards—the feds I'd seen at the garage had questioned Daddy on Monday but hadn't discovered anything incriminating enough to arrest him. The garage was "sold" to Raymond DiFiore the following day, and I nearly laughed at the thought of the feds constantly breathing down his neck. I hoped they caught him and threw him in the slammer. Sometimes I fantasized about Sam the Barber accosting him in a dark alley, demanding payment for hauling a load of booze across the river, and roughing him up when he refused.

And perhaps best of all, my monthly arrived Sunday afternoon. When I noticed it, I was so delighted I dropped my head in prayerful thanks, offering up a hasty promise that I'd be more careful from now on. Aside from a little fooling around, Enzo had taken precautions, but still—no girl wants to face the hell of discovering she's in a family way before she's married. It had worked out in the end for Bridget, but she and Vince were so in love, I'm certain they'd have married eventually anyway.

Bridget had returned from the beach with the girls and her three sons as well, and we'd all had supper together Monday night at her apartment over the store. Daddy and I ignored each other throughout the entire meal, each going out of our way to avoid even making eye contact. If Bridget or Molly noticed, they didn't mention it. Both of them knew about the ordeal last week, which was why they'd grabbed the younger ones and left town. I assumed they were each so glad to see us all sitting around the table again like nothing had happened, they didn't want to risk any more unpleasantness. It was easy to avoid talking about it, since Mary Grace chattered incessantly about their trip to the beach, showing off shells she had collected, a post card she'd purchased for her scrapbook, and her freckled skin.

Every day that week I worked a bit for Bridget at the store, and had to tell anyone who came in looking for "maple syrup," our password for whisky, that we were out of business. I mourned the income I'd lose since I wouldn't be making tips on deliveries anymore—finding a new job was a must, but I couldn't motivate myself to look for one.

After work, I'd go home and see to the girls and the house as if nothing had changed, but I just felt like something was off, as if my bones were jumbled up inside my skin. My appetite was nonexistent, I had trouble sleeping at night, and my fingernails were bitten to the quick. For a few days I thought maybe it was related to my monthly—doctors used to say women suffered from hysteria, a particular emotional frenzy caused by disturbances in a woman's body. It was quack stuff, but for a day or so I began to wonder if there wasn't a grain of truth behind it. My bleeding stopped after the usual four days, but the unease lingered.

This is ridiculous, I told myself Thursday evening as I scanned the headlines of Daddy's paper. *I've got to find out what's happening or I'll go nuts.* Had Enzo and Joey come to an agreement? Was Joey still in town? And what about the whisky—had Enzo come up with the money to pay Meloni or was there a goddamn wedding next Saturday?

Friday afternoon I went to the telephone and stared at it. Should I call Joey? What would I say? I felt even less comfortable calling Enzo, not that I knew how to reach him. But he would probably be at the club tonight...maybe I could manage to run into him and find out what was going on.

I called Evelyn, whom I still hadn't seen this week. Between her job at the bakery and her nights out with Ted, she'd been much busier than usual, and I'd been keeping to myself. She was thrilled to hear from me, and even more excited when I asked her if she'd like to go down to Club 23 tonight.

"Ted and I were planning on going dancing, so why don't you come with us? That's our favorite spot, since it's where we met. I can't believe it was only ten days ago, I'm so crazy about him." Her voice was thick and sweet.

"I'm happy things are going so well for you," I said, tamping down the jealousy in my gut, "but I don't want to be a nuisance on your date."

"Nonsense! You're never a nuisance, and I haven't seen you in forever. Besides, a whole slew of people are going down there tonight, I was going to phone you about it anyway. Ted says they've got a swell jazz band there from down south somewhere. Real Dixieland music, great for dancing."

"Sounds like fun." And it did, for the most part. Not that I was much of a dancer, but the prospect of being out with a group of young people all having a good time excited me. When was the last time I'd done that? "I just have to make sure the girls are set for the night. Daddy's been working late at the new location."

"New location?"

I sighed. "I'll tell you about it later. What matters is that we get together and have some fun tonight, just like old times."

She squealed with delight. "Perfect! We'll pick you up at nine, OK?"

"I'll be ready." I hung up the phone and took a deep breath.

"Ready for what?"

I jumped at Molly's voice behind me. "Oh! Uh, I'm seeing Evelyn later."

She raised a brow at me. Molly used to swallow my half-truths quite easily, but lately she'd become more perceptive. "Uh huh. And what are you wearing to see Evelyn? That?" She nodded toward my navy skirt and white admiral middy with the faint yellow stain on the front.

"Um…" I looked down as if to examine my clothing, but she caught the pink in my cheeks.

"Aha!" She crossed her arms. "No use lying to me, Tiny. I saw him, remember?"

I bit my lip. How could I forget? Enzo had come to the house to collect me one afternoon last week, and Molly had answered the door. It was the day he'd discovered the connection between the hearses from Daddy's garage and the heist. I shuddered recalling how angry he'd been that day

"Are you screwy in the head or what?" she asked. "I know he looks like a movie star and all, but don't be stupid, Tiny. He's dangerous!"

"He isn't," I insisted, although my tone rang false. "He's the one who gave me the money to send you and Bridget and the kids out of town—he's the one who told me it could be too dangerous for you to stay." That was true, at least.

Molly narrowed her eyes. "Men will say anything they have to in order to get what they want, and they usually just want one thing. S-E-X."

"Jesus, Molly. Where do you hear this stuff?"

She rolled her eyes—now *that* I was used to. "I'm nearly sixteen, I don't have to hear it from anyone. It's obvious."

"Well, good. Then that's one lesson I don't need to teach you. But as for me, I'm old enough and smart enough to handle myself, thank you very much." I drew myself up to my full height, but I was still shorter than she was by two inches. "Now. I've got a proposition for you. If you help me find something to wear and agree to watch Mary Grace tonight, I'll give you two extra dollars this week and let you go to the movies tomorrow night without her."

She considered it. "And an hour later for my curfew."

"Half hour. I already extended it to ten thirty, remember?"

"You also already agreed to give me two more dollars for helping with laundry and cooking, which I've been doing this week."

That was true. I hadn't eaten much this week, but Molly had made four suppers that looked and tasted much better than my usual underdone scrambled eggs and overdone bacon. "Three dollars, then."

"Deal." She grinned. "Now let's go upstairs and look at our closets, I might even have something you could borrow for tonight—I saved some money this spring and bought a dress I never told you about."

"Why?" I followed her up the stairs.

"Because it's short. And satin. And Rosie told me not to show it to you because you'd never let me wear it."

I stopped halfway up the staircase. Rosie was Evelyn's twin sister, although they looked nothing alike and had opposite personalities. When angel-faced Rosie wasn't breaking hearts or gossiping, she worked at J.L. Hudson's department store. "You went shopping downtown by yourself?"

Molly looked at me over her shoulder. "For heaven's sake, Tiny. A girl's gotta live a little, you know? And I'm not a kid anymore."

I blinked in surprise, and then nodded. "I'm counting on that."

#

At nine on the dot, Ted opened the door to the back seat of his car, and I climbed in next to a young man I'd never seen before. I was about to introduce myself when Evelyn let out a wolf whistle from the front.

"Jezebel!" she cried. "Look at you in that dress, Tiny!"

Settling in, I tried to arrange the ivory satin skirt so that it covered more of my legs. "It's Molly's. I borrowed it."

"Molly's? Your father lets her wear that? It almost looks like a nightgown!" Evelyn couldn't keep the shock from her voice.

"I doubt he's seen her in it. He's not around much." Her comments in front of the men annoyed me a bit, but I could see why she was stunned. The dress did look a bit like lingerie, with thin straps over my shoulders and a low square neck. It probably didn't show as much of Molly's chest as it did mine since she was taller and bigger than I was, but Evelyn's eyes were glued to the lace-trimmed bodice of the dress.

"And where did you get that?" she squeaked, pointing at the choker I wore around my neck. She looked at my hair, which I'd curled and styled, the black and silver headband Molly had lent me—also purchased on the sly—and my red lips. "Gee whiz, Tiny, you look like another person! I'd hardly recognize you as the girl I once knew." She laughed, but I couldn't help thinking she was right.

"It's 1923, Evvy." I took a cigarette from my little mesh evening bag. "And I've discovered I like living dangerously."

The young man next to me quickly offered to light my smoke.

On the way downtown Evelyn introduced me to Ted's friend Walter Lewis, my companion in the back seat. He was friendly and attractive in an Ivy League sort of way, with his natty bow tie and severely parted hair. But I hoped there was no expectation that I would be his date for the evening.

I had other plans.

87

My stomach flipped uncontrollably as we went down the cement steps into the hidden vestibule that served as the entrance for Club 23. Enzo and I had once shared a kiss in the dark, tight space between the outer and inner doors of the underground speakeasy. My toes curled inside my satin t-straps as I recalled the way I'd been backed up against the brick wall, one hand pinned over my head, one knee hitched up to his hip.

We were granted permission to enter, and walked down the long cement-walled hallway toward the music, our heels click-clacking on the tiles. A Dixieland beat thumped louder and louder as we approached the velvet drapes that opened onto the dark, ritzy club. As usual, the dance floor down in front, as well as all the cocktail tables and large crescent-shaped booths lining the two-tiered room, were packed with revelers. The bar along the back was mobbed as well. The room was hazy with cigarette smoke, and the entire place smelled of perfume, tobacco, and whisky, but underneath it all, I detected the faintest whiff of sex and sweat.

The men checked their hats at the door, and as I looked at the attractive, smiling girl who took them, I wondered again about Enzo's offer to work at the club. Would I be happy here, night after night, working while I watched my friends come to have fun? Watching Enzo as he played host, buying drinks and kissing hands and making deals under the table? I looked around but didn't see him anywhere.

"Hey, there's Rosie. Come on." Evelyn grabbed my hand and the group moved across the room, skirting tables dressed with white tablecloths and low candles. Along the way, Ted stopped a waitress to let her know we'd like cocktails at the end booth on the far wall, and I scanned the club over my shoulder again for Enzo. I was still looking back when we reached the velvet-curtained booth, but I heard Rosie's mocking voice above the music.

"Well, would you look what the cat dragged in. Heya, kiddo, nice dress. You knock over your sister's closet or what?"

Annoyed, I turned toward her. Despite the fact that she was only a few months older than me, she was always calling me kiddo because of my size, and she didn't mean it affectionately. We got along all right, and she was always up for a good time, but I much preferred Evelyn's sweet to Rosie's tart. Nothing Rosie liked more than stirring up trouble, which was why her eyes glittered with pure mischief as she poked at me from where she sat, right on some poor sot's lap.

I was about to bite back when I bit my tongue instead.

Because the sot was Joey.

Chapter Six

"What are you doing here?" I blurted. I couldn't help it. He hadn't contacted me in days and I'd been so worried, assuming the worst, and here he was at Enzo's club with Rosie's round little ass on his lap. What the hell was going on?

"I was invited." He raised his dark eyebrows. "It's nice to see you too."

"Invited by whom? Rosie?" I looked at her, and she smiled at me like a cat looming over the fishbowl, then blew smoke in my direction.

"No, not that it's any of your business," he answered.

My ears were burning hot, and furious energy vibrated throughout my body. But before I could think of what to say, a waitress came over to take drink orders. I requested Canadian Club, straight, and wondered if I'd survive the five minutes it would take to arrive.

"Have a seat, gang," said Rosie, sweet as pie now that she saw my jealous reaction. "Joey and I were just about to dance. You can save our table."

Blustering on the inside, I watched them slide out from the booth and felt like tripping her as she glided by me with a smug look on her face. "Don't look so put out, kiddo," she said over her shoulder. "Your man's around here somewhere, and he looks mighty fine tonight."

I glanced at Joey to gauge his reaction to that, but he kept his eyes on the dance floor and his expression blank. If it bothered him to hear her call Enzo my man, he didn't show it.

Evelyn and Ted decided to dance too, which left Walter and I alone in the dark booth to wait for our cocktails. He tried to make conversation with me, but I couldn't tear my eyes off Rosie and Joey. The band had eased from a hot-tempoed jazz number into a lazy, suggestive blues, and Rosie was draped on Joey like a jungle monkey. My whisky arrived, and I took two huge swallows.

By the time they were done dancing, my whisky was gone, my head buzzed, and my tongue itched to let loose on Joey Lupo. Exactly why I was so angry I couldn't articulate, but somehow it seemed my right to be mad. Rosie led him back to the table by the hand, and they slid in across from Walter and me.

"Joey, can I speak to you in private for a moment?" I attempted to look calm and sweet.

"Oh, don't be a spoilsport, Tiny," Rosie piped up. "We just sat down. Let the boy have his fun, why don't you?" She rubbed his arm and smiled at me with the devil in her eyes.

I wanted to kick her under the table, but I kept my eyes on him. "It's important. Please?"

"All right." When Rosie's face fell, he patted her hand. "I'll be right back."

She pouted. "You better. I won't wait around too long, you know."

Detaching himself from her grasp, he stood. "Need another drink?" He gestured toward my empty glass.

"Good idea." I slid out and made for the bar, and Joey followed. When I reached the crowd, lined three deep waiting for the bartenders' attention, I turned on him.

"What the hell, Joey? I hear nothing from you or Enzo all week and then you show up at his club? And with that....that"—I waved a hand in Rosie's direction—"tarantula on your arm?"

"She's more like a peacock, actually."

"Whatever. The point is, what are you doing here and *why* are you with *her*?"

Joey looked amused. "You know, your jealousy might actually be kind of endearing if it didn't make your face turn all red like that."

My mouth dropped open but I snapped it shut immediately. "*I* am not jealous of that two-bit man-eater."

"Oh. My mistake, I guess. Now what do you want to drink?"

"Whisky." I probably shouldn't have ordered a second glass so quickly, but rational thought had been supplanted by confusion and irritation and—yes, fist-clenching jealousy. I could admit it to myself, although I'd be damned before I'd let Joey see it. While he paid for the drinks, I took a few deep breaths, rubbed my lips together to make sure my lipstick was still on, and adjusted my posture to read cool instead of hot.

"Here you go, Little Tomato." Joey handed me a glass of amber liquid and clinked it with his own. *"Salute."*

I took a small sip. "So if it wasn't Rosie who invited you here tonight, who was it? And why didn't you call me?"

"What is this, the Inquisition? For your information, I was invited here by the cake eater himself, and he told me to come alone."

"What? Why?" I nearly choked on my whisky. In my mind there was only one reason why Enzo would invite Joey here alone. How could Joey be so dumb as to actually show up by himself? Wouldn't he see the trap?

"He said he had some information for me."

"About what?"

"He didn't say exactly, only that it was something I've been looking for." He drank again. "I assume he's ready to finish up the opium deal."

"And Rosie? How'd you end up with her?" I couldn't resist asking.

"I walked in here looking for Enzo, and Rosie accosted me."

I squinted at him. "Accosted you?"

He gave me a crooked smile. "I can't help it if I'm irresistible. It's the hair, you know?" He ran a hand along the side of his brown curls, which had been tamed into submission with hairdressing. "Or maybe the body in my sharp new suit." He puffed out his chest.

It's the mouth, I wanted to say, looking at his full lips, *and maybe the hands.* But I rolled my eyes and took a drink instead. "Well, it's certainly not your modesty, we know that. So Enzo invited you tonight. Well, he didn't say anything to me about it."

Joey shrugged before lifting his glass again. "What he says to you ain't my business."

In an instant his demeanor had shifted from playful to tense. "But—"

"Good evening," said a smooth, deep voice behind me.

I spun around and came face to face with Enzo, whose sleek appearance in a black suit and tie were enough to momentarily steal my breath. *Rosie was right. He does look mighty fine.* "Hi," I said. And then hiccupped, loudly.

Enzo's lips tipped up. "Welcome, darling. I'd buy you a drink but I see you've already gotten started." His eyes moved beyond me to Joey. "Mr. Lupo. You made it. You're alone?"

"As requested."

"Excellent. If you'll just give me a moment with Miss O'Mara here, I'll be with you shortly."

"I'm at a booth down front," Joey said, already backing away from us.

"I know where you are. Enjoy yourself."

It was all perfectly friendly, but something was off about the exchange between them. It wasn't just that they were being eerily nice to one another in a phony way, because even after Joey had gone, I still felt a sense of alarm. "So...you invited Joey here tonight?" *Hiccup.*

"I did. I have something to discuss with him, and I promised him it would be worth his while. In fact, I invited him a couple nights ago, but this was the first night he said he could get away."

"Oh." Briefly I wondered what had kept Joey so busy. His family? Was his mother OK? *Hiccup.*

"Shall I get you some water?"

"Yes, please."

Enzo snapped his fingers for the bartender's attention while I racked my brain trying to think up a way to get Enzo to let me come to the meeting he was planning with Joey. A moment later, he took my whisky and handed me the water, watching as I took a few sips. "Better?"

I nodded. "Thank you."

He leaned closer to speak low in my ear. "You look ravishing in that white dress, darling. I can barely keep my hands off you. Is it new?"

Heat bloomed in my cheeks. "I borrowed it."

"Ah. Well, soon you'll have a whole closet full of new dresses, each one just waiting for you to put it on so I can tear it off you. With my teeth."

"What?" *Hiccup.*

Enzo laughed as I brought the water to my lips again. "You heard me." Lifting his wolf eyes from my breasts, he glanced over my shoulder and straightened up.

"So what happened with the whisky shipment?" I asked. "Did you get it?"

"You're drinking it tonight, aren't you?"

"Well, yes, but…how did you manage it if you haven't gotten the money for the opium yet?"

"Just leave the business to me." He leaned forward and kissed me lightly on the cheek but seemed suddenly distracted by something. "Now, why don't you join your friends, and I'll try to send for you later."

"But what about Joey?"

His eyes darkened a little. "Leave it, darling. I'll see you later tonight."

He tucked the whisky back into my hand and strode toward the entrance. With dread in my stomach, I turned to see whom he'd rushed off to greet. The dread turned to fury when I saw Gina Meloni making her way toward him, wearing a gorgeous gold and scarlet dress and a feather in her dark hair. She threw her arms around his neck and he kissed her cheek, taking her arm to lead her to their usual table. Spikes of wrath needled my arms and legs, and I finished both the water and the whisky, slamming the glasses on the bar.

If I'd thought I could handle the back and forth between her and me, I was wrong. *Either he wants me or not.* No closet full of clothes was worth feeling so angry and inferior every time he left my side and went to her. So her father owned a distillery and supplied his club, so what? He shouldn't have to marry the guy's daughter if he didn't want to. And he didn't...did he?

As I watched him seat his fiancée and light her cigarette, it struck me what was so unnerving about his behavior tonight. He was acting just like his father—the amused detachment while calling me darling, the cool kisses on the cheek, the shrewd agenda I knew lurked beneath the polite treatment of his enemies. The comparison turned my stomach.

I walked back to the booth, where Evelyn and Ted sat holding hands. On the dance floor, Walter was doing his best shimmy with a black-haired flapper dressed in red, and Rosie had her arms around Joey again. He held her close, spun her out, and they laughed together. When he pulled her in even tighter to his chest and whispered something in her ear, I felt it like a punch in the stomach. No one wanted to dance with me that way.

My hiccups were gone. I ordered another drink.

#

At some point, Joey and Rosie returned to the table, and I did my best to appear unaffected by their flirting as well as by the whisky I'd consumed. It wasn't easy. My head was cloudy, the room wasn't holding still like I wished it would, and my skin itched with irritation. There was plenty of room in the goddamn booth—why the hell did she need to sit on his lap? And why the hell did I care, anyway? I held my tongue, not easy for me, and tried not to stare at them. I even attempted to flirt with Walter, and though my heart wasn't in it, Joey sat up straighter when I put my hand on Walter's arm and laughed at a silly joke he told. It made me feel a little better.

Around midnight, one of the DiFiore goons came to our table and asked for Joey to follow him. Joey excused himself, and I practically elbowed Walter in the face to scramble out of the booth after him. "Joey, wait!"

He turned and grimaced at me. "Go back and sit down."

"No. I'm coming with you."

"You can't. And you're drunk. Now quit acting screwy and go back to the table. I'm sure Arthur misses you already."

"Walter."

"Exactly." He took me by the shoulders, turned me around, and gave me a little shove toward the table.

But I wouldn't go. "I'm coming with you," I insisted, trailing his heels.

Joey shrugged and spoke over his shoulder. "Fine, I'll let the cake eater deal with you."

I hurried behind him, taking two steps for every one of his, stumbling a little in my high heels. When the goon reached the curtained doorway that accessed

98

a staircase to the building's upper floors, I tried to slip through after Joey.

"He didn't ask for you." The goon grabbed my elbow and held me back.

"I promise I won't be any trouble." I smiled sweetly at him, a younger guy with thick eyebrows and a five o'clock shadow. "I stayed here Friday night, and I think I left something in one of the rooms. I'll just retrieve it while I'm here."

"Oh, you work here, eh?" One of his bushy brows arced suggestively.

"What? No! I was sort of—a guest." And sort of a prisoner too, but I left that part out.

"That's a shame," said the goon. Joey bunched his fists at his sides.

"Listen, if Enzo sends me back down, I'll come without any trouble at all." I tried a flirty wink. "What harm could a little thing like me cause?"

Joey coughed, and I glared at him.

"No chance, doll. He didn't ask for you."

So much for my feminine charm. Helplessly I watched them disappear behind the curtain, then spun around and stomped back toward the booth. How dare Enzo shut me out! I was the one who told him Joey had the opium in the first place. Was he keeping me away for a reason? I was torn between being angry and being scared. If he was on the level about his promise not to hurt Joey, why wouldn't he tell me what he was doing? And how dare Joey fail to stick up for me and insist I be allowed to accompany him! I'd put this whole thing in motion.

Bastards, all of them.

I was almost to the table when I recalled another way to access stairs to the upper floors—the tunnels.

Subterranean passageways led from the club to hidden stairwells as well as to buildings across the street. They were used for escaping during raids or for booze deliveries, but if I could find my way into them, they'd sure be useful to me tonight.

Biting my lip, I scanned the club. There was a door to the tunnels in a room behind the bar, but I'd have to convince the bartender to let me back there, which seemed unlikely. One leg twitched impatiently. It would've been much easier to think through this plan if I wasn't so goddamn tipsy—the room was positively spinning.

With a loud blaring solo by the trumpet player, the band swung into a hot jazz number, and the crowd rushed the dance floor. I went along, the murky edges of an idea taking shape in the back of my head. I pushed through the dancers as they jumped and flailed to the two-beat rhythm, feeling the thump of the bass drum in my chest. Awkwardly I tried to dance along with them a little, lifting a knee here and an elbow there, hoping it looked like the Charleston, a smile plastered on my face. Thankfully everyone was either too drunk or too exhilarated by the music to notice me. When I'd made my way to the front, I skirted the stage over to the side. An unguarded door led to the backstage area, and I hurried through it without stopping.

I saw no one. Moving quickly, I walked past doors labeled Dressing Room and kept my eyes peeled for one that might access the tunnels. There had to be an entrance to them on this side of the club—if the cops came in the main doors from the street, the room behind the bar wouldn't provide a safe getaway. The logical exit would be in the opposite direction. I congratulated myself on this brilliant deduction, and when I came to an unmarked door, I squealed inwardly and threw it open.

Unfortunately it led to a prop closet where two women and a man were engaged in an activity that was definitely not the Charleston, although it looked just as rhythmic and entertaining, with limbs extended every which way. "Oops, sorry!" I whispered, backing out and slamming the door.

Damn.

I hurried further along the backstage corridor until I came to another door. Crossing my fingers, I twisted the knob and pushed it open, and found myself inside a closet full of cleaning supplies. But at the back of the closet I saw something else—the outline of another door. Stepping around buckets and rags, I prayed the door would open without a key. *Who has time to fumble with keys during a raid, right?* I pushed the cleaning implements aside.

No lock. Just a baseball-sized hole in the wood, through which I stuck my fingers and yanked.

It opened.

I took a second to pull the outer door shut behind me and ducked into the tunnel, my heart pounding at the sudden darkness. Enzo and I had snuck up to Angel's office twice last week using the tunnels, but he'd had a lighter in his pocket that we'd used to illuminate the way. I fumbled in my purse, where I'd stuck a few cigarettes in a small case along with a matchbook. How many did I have left? My fingers shook as I felt for the number of matches—four. Saying a quick prayer they would last, I lit the first one and started walking.

With one hand brushing along the cement wall for balance, I moved as quickly as my legs would carry me down the dirt-floored tunnel. The music receded until I couldn't hear it anymore, and my breathing got louder. I stopped twice to light new matches and once when the passageway forked and I had to make a choice about which way to go. I stayed to the right, reasoning I was traveling clockwise around the perimeter of the club and wanted to stay close to it. When my third match was nearly burnt out, I came to another wooden door. Crossing myself with my free hand, I pushed it open. Just as the match burned dangerously close to my fingers, I saw stairs.

With a sigh of relief, I blew out the match in my hand and lit the last one.

Then I climbed two flights of stairs and pushed open the heavy door at the top.

Bingo.

Angel's office was just down the hall. Based on previous experience, I knew that office made Enzo feel powerful and confident, whether it was business or pleasure. Pushing the stairwell door closed behind me, I leaned back against it and blew out the match.

"Hey!" bellowed a deep voice. "How'd you get up here?"

I jumped. The goon in the dark suit who'd come for Joey was striding down the hallway toward me. He wasn't that tall, but he was wide and thick-knuckled, and I didn't like the way he was looking at me.

"I want to see Enzo." I planted my feet and stood tall.

When he reached me, his eyes traveled down my body and up again. "What's it worth?"

"Go to hell." I scooted around him and bolted for the office, but he chased me, catching my upper arm with iron fingers.

"Let go of me, you ape." I tried to wrench my arm from his grip. "Enzo! Help!"

The goon squeezed tighter. "Shut the fuck up."

The door to the office swung open and Joey burst through it. The next thing I knew Joey had thrown a punch so hard it knocked the goon off balance. As he stumbled backward, he let go of my arm and Joey landed a few jabs to his gut before taking a hit in the face. "Joey!" I cried.

With the back of one hand he touched his nose, which was bleeding. He looked at it and then delivered a series of blows to the goon's face and stomach that had him reeling. I flinched at each sickening crack and thump. Finally, the goon went down hard.

"What the fuck, Lupo?" Enzo elbowed his way past Joey into the hallway.

"He had his hands on her." Joey's chest heaved with heavy breaths, and he gingerly touched his nose once more.

Enzo looked at me. "Is that true?"

"Yes!" I snapped.

"Well, she doesn't need *you* to defend her here." Enzo took my face in his hands, brushing my hair back with his thumbs. "Are you all right?"

My stomach was roiling a little, but I nodded. "I'm fine."

He pressed a kiss to my forehead, which somehow seemed more for Joey's benefit than my own. "I'm sorry. Go into the office and sit down while I deal with this asshole."

Which asshole? I wondered. But I slipped through the office door and took a seat on the brown leather sofa.

Adrenaline had kept me alert, but once I sat still, I felt the effects of the whisky again. The pattern on the rug in front of my feet swirled like a whirlpool, making me even more sick to my stomach. Snapping my eyes closed, I put a hand over my belly and breathed deeply. The office smelled nice, like leather and tobacco. A moment later, I opened my eyes.

There. That's better.

Now to find out what the hell was going on between Enzo and Joey.

Chapter Seven

Enzo didn't return immediately, so I had a few minutes to myself. The office looked the same as I remembered—oak paneling, gold drapes at the windows, a sideboard along one wall topped with crystal decanters, and two red leather chairs in front of a large mahogany desk.

Oh, the things we'd done on that desk.

I pressed my knees together.

Stop it. This is no time to get distracted by sex.

But my body had never listened to my brain where Enzo was concerned, especially once I'd been drinking, and I felt the pull low in my abdomen as I recalled the way he'd set me on the desk, knelt in front of me, and run his tongue along—

"So here we are again." Enzo's voice interrupted my thoughts.

I turned and saw him pouring a glass of something at the sideboard. He'd entered so stealthily I hadn't even heard him.

"Darling, your ability to create chaos among men will never cease to amaze me."

I wasn't sure whether to be flattered or insulted. Glancing at the door, I asked, "Where's Joey?"

"He asked for a moment to clean up."

"Oh."

"He'll be back soon, otherwise I can think of a few things I'd rather do with you in this office than talk." He moved to the desk and sat behind it, looking more like Angel than ever. "Especially at this desk."

"Then you should have told me what you were planning tonight."

"Tiny, this really has nothing to do with you. Why don't you—"

"Bullshit!" I exploded, fueled by whisky and frustration. I wouldn't be brushed off. "You made me a promise and I intend to hold you to it."

He looked amused. "I make a lot of promises. Which one are you referring to?"

I nearly launched myself over the desk to slap his handsome face, an urge I had frequently. Instead I clenched my fists and counted to three. "Tell me why you asked Joey here tonight, alone."

"Leave it, Tiny." I stood as Joey entered the room, tucking a bloody handkerchief into his coat pocket. "It ain't your concern."

I looked from one to the other, seething. "So that's how it is."

"That's how it is." Joey's face looked pale, and I didn't think it was because of the fight, which was nothing new for him. *Something* had happened before

I'd gotten up here, but neither of them would tell me what it was. The idea that it was now the two of them against me drove me insane.

"Do you know what I went through to get up here?" I stamped my foot like a child. Enzo actually laughed, which only made me angrier.

"How *did* you get up here, anyway?" He sipped his drink.

"Never mind about that," I snapped.

"I need to go," Joey said. "I'll be in touch."

"Soon," said Enzo.

Joey nodded. "Soon."

"I'll call someone to escort you down." Enzo picked up the telephone on the desk and Joey and I stood in silence. It felt a little like we were two kids in the principal's office, waiting for our punishment. I thought of the time five years ago when Joey'd had the brilliant idea to steal and bootleg the sacramental wine from church. Michigan had just gone dry and he was positive it was a brilliant scheme, sure to make some quick dough. I'd had the brains to turn him down, thank God, but he'd gotten caught. That's when he'd entered the Bishop School, a sort of reform school for kids needing a last chance, and met the future members of the River Gang. He'd been tossed out of *there* for running crap games in the yard.

But he'd once beaten the tar out of this neighborhood bully named Timmy Toos for repeatedly eating out of my lunch box and stealing my milk money. And he'd threatened to cut off Mary McCarty's long hair in her sleep if she didn't stop calling me a dwarf. And when he found out I'd won a prize for mathematics in twelfth grade, he embarrassed me by announcing it at a family dinner at Bridget's that Sunday. At the time I thought he'd just done it to annoy me.

Now I saw it differently.

"*Grazi*," Enzo said before hanging up. "Someone will be here in a moment to take you both down."

"Me too?" I said, surprised.

"Yes. I have some more business to do tonight. And I can't leave the club just yet—my father is at his new establishment. With your father, actually," he finished, smiling. "I wonder who's having more luck at the tables." His dark eyes sparkled with mischief.

"The house always wins." Joey spoke quietly but firmly.

"That's true," agreed Enzo. "Now, darling, why don't you go back to your friends and I'll find you later."

"I might not be here later. It's already midnight, and I have to get up early." It was a lie, Molly was ready to handle things at home in the morning, but I didn't want Enzo to think I would just wait around for him.

"Oh? What a shame. Well, I guess I'll be lonely tonight." His tone implied he'd be anything but lonely.

A moment later, a couple moon-faced guys in dark suits showed up and took us back to the club. The music was still jumping, the dance floor was still packed, and the crowd at the bar was even thicker. All of it annoyed me. I marched ahead of Joey on stiff legs and flopped into our booth, across from Rosie, who, despite her threat, was still waiting for Joey.

"There you are!" shouted Evelyn over the music. She rushed from the edge of the dance floor over to the table and fanned her face, which was pink and sweaty. But her blue eyes were lit from within, and the glow in her skin was becoming.

"Here I am."

Her brow wrinkled at my glum face. "Everything OK?"

"I'm fine," I promised her. She deserved a good time tonight. Out of the corner of my eye, I saw Rosie tug on Joey's arm until he sat next to her. "Really," I went on. "Go enjoy yourself. I just have a bit of a headache, so I'm going to rest here a bit."

"All right." She glanced at the table and giggled. "Ted bought a couple bottles of champagne—it's the bee's knees! Maybe that'll cure your headache."

I plastered a smile on my lips. "It might. Go on, dance."

"All right." She tilted her head. "Sure you're OK?"

No. I looked across the table. Joey's face was stony; Rosie's was triumphant. She stroked his arm and whispered something in his ear. "I'm sure."

She patted my arm and hurried back to Ted, who scooped her up close. I didn't see Walter anywhere and figured he'd given up on me altogether. *Smart guy.*

"So where's that handsome man of yours? He dump you already?" Rosie's shrill voice grated my last nerve. My nostrils flared as I took in her bobbed blond curls, perfectly coiffed around her flawless face, set off by a headband that sat low on her forehead. Her porcelain skin appeared even whiter than usual behind splashes of scarlet on her lips and cheeks, like blood in the snow.

"He's busy." Turning my attention to Joey, I gasped. "You're still bleeding."

Rosie squealed and shrank away from him. "Ew, what happened?"

"Nothing." Joey pulled out his handkerchief and dabbed at his face. "Just a bloody nose." He met my eyes and the secret passed between us. My heart beat a little faster.

"Oh. I've never had one of those." Rosie sounded as if we were talking about a giant wart or a festering wound.

"It's nothing, but I should leave." He braced himself on the table to stand.

"Wait—don't go." I put my hand over his, which was already bruised from the fight.

"Yeah, don't go yet," Rosie put in. "I want to dance with you again."

But I wasn't about to let her take him away. Not when another slow, sexy blues had just started. "Dance with me?" The words slipped out before I realized what I was saying.

Surprise flashed in his brown eyes. "You want to dance with me? To this?" He didn't even bother to mask his shock.

"Yeah." I set my little mesh bag on the table and slid out from the booth. "I do." My heart was pounding now. Would he turn me down? Or worse, dance with Rosie instead?

"All right."

I had to look carefully to be sure he wasn't joking, but his expression was serious.

"Don't be too long, now" Rosie called, a false cheery note in her voice.

We walked onto the dance floor, my knees jittering uncontrollably. What was I thinking, asking him to dance with me to this song? We might have done a tame fox trot or an awkward waltz at Bridget's wedding, but that was in a room full of relatives, and we'd probably kept enough space between us to park a car. This was something altogether different. Where would he rest his hands? Was I supposed to put my arms around him like Rosie had? What if Enzo saw us?

Actually, that thought spurred my confidence a little. *Let him see us. Serves him right.*

In the back of my mind was the dim realization I'd had the same exact thought in reverse just a week ago—I'd wanted Joey to see me with Enzo and be jealous. Tonight...I didn't understand it completely, but I didn't want Joey to leave, and it wasn't only because I wanted to know what Enzo had said.

We found a sliver of open space and Joey reached for me, slipping his right arm across my lower back, and taking my right hand in his left. I rested my other hand on the top of his shoulder. Despite the crowded floor, he left so much space between us that I was disappointed. *We might as well do the foxtrot*, I thought grumpily.

111

But when he started to move, he pulled me into his torso, tight. As tightly as he'd held Rosie, maybe even tighter.

My breath hitched and my heart hammered my ribs so hard I was certain he could feel it. He swayed me in time to the lazy, throbbing rhythm, leading me so surely that my feet never fell out of step with his. God, the way he moved his body, and mine along with it...it was slow and sexy and sinuous. Warmth pooled at my center. My breaths started to come faster, and my dress felt heavy on my skin. Had it been this warm in here all night? I could smell the perfume I'd dotted behind my ears and between my breasts and at the backs of my knees, and hoped he could too. My left hand inched along the rough fabric of his coat until my fingers curved around his neck.

His movement slowed.

Rising on tiptoe, I pressed my face into the space between his ear and his collar.

He stopped dancing.

I inhaled deeply, letting the scent of his skin invade me. Soap and starch and aftershave, and the barest trace of something else—something delicious but not sweet, something herbal that brought the memory of cooking with him into sharp relief. My mouth watered.

His turned his head and I felt his lips against my temple. "Move your feet, Tiny." His voice was strained.

Oh—right. Was it me who'd stopped dancing? Recovering my senses, I let him lead me again, but I didn't let him pull away. Against my chest I could feel him breathing, and I adjusted my breaths to his so that every part of our bodies moved in tandem, even our lungs. My body hummed with pleasure, warm and decadent. And though I knew it was wrong and misleading and maybe even dangerous if Enzo was watching, I closed my eyes and pressed my lips to the side of his neck.

Immediately I felt him spring to life against my hip. Arousal fluttered between my legs and hollowed out my insides.

He pushed me away. "What are you doing?" His eyes swept the room, as if he was trying to make sure Enzo hadn't seen us. "Are you crazy?"

I found that extraordinarily funny and started to giggle. "Yes. I think I am."

Joey rolled his eyes and grabbed me by the wrist, yanking me back toward the table. "You're drunk," he said through clenched teeth over his shoulder, "and I can't handle this tonight. I don't know why I even bothered to try." We reached the booth and he shoved me in across from Rosie, who was fuming and trying to hide it.

"Well," she said, bringing her cigarette to her lips for a puff. "That looked cozy."

Joey looked around as he adjusted his pants. "Where's your ride home, Tiny?"

I shrugged. "Dancing?"

"I've had it with this joint." Rosie stubbed her cigarette out and looked up at Joey, batting her lashes. "You wanna go someplace quiet, sugar?"

"Yeah. I do."

"See you around, kid." Rosie offered me a smug look as Joey took her hand to help her from the booth.

It was my turn to fume. They walked off without looking back while I pursed my lips and tried not to stare at Joey's ass. *Fine, go!* Beside the fact that dancing with Joey had me so riled up I could hardly sit still, I hadn't asked him what he and Enzo had discussed, although he probably wouldn't have told me anyway. As usual, the men called all the shots.

The bottles of champagne were still on the table, so I poured the remains of one into a glass and drank it down. Fast. Then I poured from another and did it again. Nothing about this night had gone as planned. I was wound up, I was jealous, and I was alone.

I was also drunk.

Propping my chin in my hand, I scowled at the tilting, swirling room full of happy people dancing to happy music. I hated all of them but Evelyn. I hated Rosie for taking Joey away and I hated Joey for leaving. I hated Enzo for his games and his goddamn good looks, and I especially hated myself.

At that moment, a flash of gold caught my eye, and I forced myself to focus on it. Gina was headed toward the ladies room with a friend. *Good idea. I need to reapply my lipstick too.* And if I happened to engage her in a little conversation...

Picking up my purse from the table, I stumbled after her.

#

A lot of speakeasies had been men's clubs or saloons in the past, which, of course, were not equipped with bathrooms for women. I had no idea what the history of this building was, but the door labeled Ladies Room was near the hat-check, and when I entered, I almost ran headlong into the sloping ceiling. The room appeared to be tucked beneath a stairway or something. Ducking the sharply pitched angle, I headed through a little lounge area cloudy with smoke, nodded at the attendant, and entered the only unoccupied stall. On either side of me, girls chattered away.

"I still can't believe you're getting married next weekend," said the girl on my right.

"I can," squeaked someone on my left.

Fucking Gina. Her voice was like chalk on a slate.

"He's been putting me off all year," she went on. "I would have liked a ring by now, though, or at least some kind of diamonds. Last week he hinted around that he had a gift for me, but I got nothin' to show for it."

The necklace. I brought a hand to my throat, nearly gagging.

I was wearing Gina's engagement present?

"You know he'll get you something. That's how these guys work. They're all down and worried one day and riding high, flush with cash the next."

"He better." The toilet on the left flushed noisily. "I told him I want a rock for each month he made me wait around."

115

Her friend laughed. "That'll be one a hell of a gift, then."

"No kiddin.'" Gina exited the stall and I heard the water come on at a sink. "I just wish he'd pay more attention to me when I'm here. He's always so busy."

The toilet flushed on the right, and her friend joined her at the sinks. "Well, I guess that's the price you pay for marrying somebody like Enzo DiFiore. I still can't believe he's gonna go through with it."

"For cryin' out loud, Valerie, can you stop saying that?" Gina screeched. "What's so goddamn hard about believing he's gonna marry me like he promised?"

"Don't have a kitten, Gina. All I meant was that he seemed so reluctant to actually say 'I do' before this week. Now all of a sudden it's a rush job."

"Rush job! I been waiting six months for this. I don't know any other girl who had to wait so long. Daddy was getting as anxious as I was."

"Well, I guess he came to his senses," soothed Valerie.

"Yeah. Either that or someone showed him what would happen to his senses if he didn't do the deed." Gina giggled. "I think Daddy might have had a little man to man chat with him."

Her friend gasped. "Really?"

"Yeah. Hey, gimme that lipstick."

I waited in agony as they touched up their lips.

"Why does your father want you to get married so badly? Ouch!"

For a second I was confused and then I realized Gina must have slapped her or something.

"It's not about what he wants, dimwit, it's about what *I* want! It pays to be Daddy's little girl, you know."

"I know."

"I'm just trading in for a younger, handsomer model." Gina giggled. "One with all the right equipment. And boy does he know how to use it!"

My stomach heaved as Valerie squealed. "You're telling me! He's about the best-looking man I've ever seen. You're so lucky."

"Honey, it ain't luck. I know how to use my equipment too."

"You're so naughty," chided Valerie. I heard the clink of coins and figured they were tipping the attendant.

"At least I'm not boring," said Gina. "You've gotta be naughty to keep a man like that. Otherwise, they'll start running around."

"Honey, they all run around eventually," Valerie said confidently.

"Well, if Enzo does, my Daddy will cut off his balls before he even sees the knife coming. Or I'll do it myself." They laughed again as they exited into the lounge. "Val, you got a ciggie?"

The music got louder when they opened the ladies room door, and then it was muted again. They were gone.

My heart was beating so fast and loud it sounded like a locomotive in my head. Was there such a thing as a heart attack brought on by anger? If so, I was about to suffer one. I shoved the heel of my hand into the side of the stall, hard.

"Miss? Are you all right?" the attendant asked.

I sighed. "Yes, I'm fine. I just...bumped into the wall." Rolling my eyes at the lame explanation, I decided to actually use the facilities since I was in there. When I came out, I washed my hands, and tipped her with some loose change from my purse.

What I didn't do was look in the mirror. I dreaded the sight of my stupid, gullible face.

Ducking the slanted ceiling, I left the bathroom and started for the booth. I had to pass by Gina's table, and at first I hoped no one would notice me, but then I happened to look up and notice Enzo lighting her cigarette again.

"Fuck it." I swore softly and turned on my heel, heading straight for them.

Chapter Eight

"Good evening." I greeted the table with a friendly smile. Gina looked at me as if I were a bug to be shooed away but Enzo's face drained of color. *Good.*

"Miss O'Mara," he said. "How nice to see you again. You remember my *fiancée*, Gina Meloni?"

I wasn't sure if the emphasis was because he thought I didn't recognize her, or if it was supposed to serve as a warning to behave myself. Either way, I didn't much care. "Of course. And what a lovely dress you're wearing. I just adore it."

Gina smiled, smoke seeping from her lips. "It's from New York. It was a gift from Enzo. He's always buying me something."

"Mr. Generosity." I met Enzo's eyes. "Got a cigarette to spare?"

"Certainly." He removed a gold case from his coat and opened it. While I chose one, he glanced at Gina, who was staring at the diamonds at my throat.

"Allow me to light it for you and escort you back to your table, Miss O'Mara."

I lifted my shoulders. "If you insist."

"Say, that's some serious ice around your neck." Gina pointed at the choker. "Enzo, you see that?"

"I do." He brandished a lighter and flicked the switch, pinning me with a look that said *stay quiet*.

"That's the kind of gift I want next." Gina pouted as I leaned closer to Enzo and allowed the small flame to light the cigarette between my lips.

I took in a lungful of smoke and exhaled. "You should get her one, Enzo. When is the wedding anyway?"

"Next Saturday," answered Gina. "We just can't wait any longer, can we, darling?"

I feigned a swoon, putting a hand over my heart. "How romantic!"

"What about you? You got a fella?"

"Me? No."

If we were on the playground, the look she gave me might have been accompanied by a bratty little *nyah-nyah*. "So who bought you those goods?"

I looked at Enzo again, who was gripping the back of Gina's chair so hard, I thought he might break it in half. Oh, how I loved to see him squirm. "Just an admirer," I said airily.

Gina was intrigued. "Is he handsome?"

"Indeed he is."

"And rich?"

"Well…" I pretended to think this over. "He does have a nice new motorcar."

"So does Enzo," she said, smug-faced. "A Packard. Daddy bought it for us as an early wedding gift. Isn't that right, honey?" She glanced back at her fiancé.

I nearly vomited.

"Sure." He cleared his throat. "Tiny, are you ready to go?"

"Absolutely." I stubbed out my cigarette in the ashtray in front of Gina. "Enjoy your evening, Miss Meloni. And congratulations. I'm sure you'll be very happy together."

Enzo grabbed my arm and yanked me sideways before she even had a chance to reply. "What the hell was that?" he hissed in my ear. "Are you out of your mind? Her father will kill me!"

"Good," I snapped. "Saves me the trouble!" I shrugged out of his grasp and tried to run through the crowd, but it was too thick. He got me by one elbow and dragged me over to the booth, which was empty. "Stop acting like a child," he demanded, shoving me onto the bench. "Give me a chance to explain."

I looked up at him angrily. "Why should I?"

"Because… I have something for you."

I lifted my chin higher. "Not. Interested."

A knowing smile snuck onto his lips. "You will be when you see it. Meet me out front in ten minutes."

"You don't really expect me to go somewhere alone with you, do you?"

"I'll make it worth your while."

"You want to take me somewhere, you have to tell me what you said to Joey tonight."

Anger darkened his complexion. "I don't *have* to do anything."

"Then I'm leaving. Alone." I stood and tried to get past him, but he blocked my way, gripping me by the upper arms.

"No. You're going to stay here and wait for me."

Something in his tone made me clam up instead of making a sharp-tongued retort or kneeing him in the balls, which was another compulsion I occasionally had around him. I froze, my gaze sliding to one of his hands squeezing my skin.

He must have realized he'd gone too far, because he let go and glanced around to make sure no one was watching us. "I'm sorry," he said, softer now. "I know this sounds crazy, but I'll make it up to you."

"You hurt me." I rubbed my upper arms.

"I *said*, I'm sorry."

"Fine. You're sorry. I'd still be crazy to go anywhere alone with you."

"Tiny, please." He brought his fingertips to his forehead. "I'm sorry I grabbed you that way, but you just *do* something to me, something I can hardly control, and it drives me crazy when I see you and can't touch you. That's all."

"That doesn't excuse your behavior tonight. And there is no way I'm going to sit in this club any longer and watch you fawn all over the future fucking missus."

He sighed and closed his eyes. "What do you want from me?"

"I told you. I want to know why you asked Joey here."

He opened his eyes and stared hard at me. "Fine. Meet me outside in ten minutes."

#

When Enzo went to make his excuses to Gina, I tugged Evelyn off the dance floor just long enough to whisper my plans to her and tell her not to worry. "Now if only you can ditch Walter somewhere, you could have the back seat of Ted's car all to yourself." I tried to keep my tone bright.

She shoved me playfully but gave me a conspiratorial wink. "The front seat's just as comfortable, you know."

Yes, indeed I do. I made my way to the exit. But I wasn't going to let him touch me that way tonight. Not a chance. *I just have to be strong, that's all. I have to let him know that he can't expect me to sit idly by while he chauffeurs Gina around in his shiny Packard during the day, and then expects to fool around with me in it after dark. The nerve of him!*

Last Saturday night it had seemed glamorous and exciting, but now the experience had lost its allure, and I wasn't even *thinking* about the way the evening had ended in the boathouse. How dare he come for me in the car her father bought for them? As a *wedding gift!*

By the time he pulled up, I was fuming again.

I got into the Packard, and the familiar interior gave my surging temper a boost. After slamming the door, I slapped his face. Hard.

"How could you? This car was a wedding present from her father? You fucked me in the front seat!"

Enzo held a hand to his cheek and grimaced. "You didn't have any complaints at the time."

"Because I didn't know, Enzo! And this necklace—ugh, take it back!" I unclasped it and threw it at him, then I crossed my arms and thumped back against the seat. "I don't even know what I'm doing in here right now. I must be crazy."

He set the necklace aside and reached for my hand. I snatched it back, but he took it again. "Listen to me. You're not crazy. You're here for the same reason I am—I can't stay away from you, no matter how much I want to."

Something occurred to me. "You *knew*. You knew that night that you were going to marry her next weekend, and you lied to me."

"I said I was trying to get out of it, and I am. But I had to agree to marry her, Tiny. The club was low on booze and I have a business to run. But listen—it's all gonna be OK, I know it. I won't have to marry her."

I looked at him incredulously. "And why not?"

"Because I'll be able to pay off Meloni with the cash I'm getting from all the opium. That plus what the club brings in this week, now that I've got good booze to sell."

I shifted in my seat to face him. "And what makes you think you're getting all the opium again? I'm still confused about that part."

"I'll tell you. But first...your surprise." He dropped my hand and pulled away from the curb. I sat ramrod straight, wanting as little of my body as possible to touch any part of this car.

"Where are we going?" I asked as Enzo drove north on Woodward toward Grand Circus Park.

"You'll see."

In a few minutes Enzo pulled up at the ritzy Statler Hotel, and my temper flared again. If he thought we were going to enjoy a quick romp here, he was mistaken. "A hotel? That's what you wanted to show me?" I set my jaw. "Well, you can forget it. I'm not going to a hotel room with you."

"It's not a hotel room. Just trust me, OK?"

"No."

Enzo sighed as attendants rushed to open the passenger door. I was tempted to refuse to get out of the car, but figured that would embarrass me more than Enzo, so I allowed the uniformed man to help me out. He led me underneath an awning, where I waited with tapping toes and a scowl for Enzo to give instructions for parking the Packard. In a moment he took me by the elbow, and we entered the lobby.

My bottom lip dropped open. I couldn't help but be awed by the sheer size and splendor of the hotel. One of my secret dreams was to travel to big cities and stay in romantic, luxurious places like this. My childhood scrapbook was filled with advertisements and post cards from lavish hotels whose lobbies looked just like the one before me. Now that I was actually inside one, I felt like a child again, small and wide-eyed and dazzled by the opulence.

The room ran the entire width of the hotel and was two stories tall. The night air had been hot and humid but inside the lobby was cool and airy. Gooseflesh broke out on my arms, and I was instantly sorry I had not worn gloves, both for modesty and for warmth. As we crossed the marble floor, our heels clicking elegantly, I craned my neck and looked around. The wall facing the park had five huge arched windows and opposite these were balconies with wrought iron railings. The cavernous space was mostly empty of people at this late hour, but still I chewed my lip and dropped my eyes to my clothing. The dress I'd so loved for its daring earlier tonight seemed inappropriate here in the well-lit luxury of the Statler Hotel lobby. Enzo sensed my discomfort and put an arm around me.

"You're a vision," he whispered in my ear.

"I—I'm…just a little bit chilled," I stuttered. Warily I eyed the five huge chandeliers looming over my head.

He squeezed my arm, and I thought he might offer me his coat, but he didn't.

Maybe there's a rule about men's dress, I thought. In which case there may be one about women's dress as well, and I doubted my bare shoulders would pass muster. Along the east wall was a massive oak counter, from behind which two pairs of eyes watched us

126

intently. I glanced at Enzo, but he didn't appear concerned, not even bothering to look their way. We walked by potted palms and elegant spindly-legged furniture toward the back of the room, where a short corridor led to a bank of four elevators book-ended by two marble-lined staircases.

As we waited for a car, I kept my legs pressed tightly together and tried to keep my knees from knocking. Precisely what had me so nervous was hard to say. Was I afraid that I wouldn't be able to fend him off if he tried something? Was I scared that my willpower wouldn't be enough to resist his physical overtures? Or was there, beneath it all, an actual fear for my safety? After all, no one knew where I was, and I was allowing a man I knew to be obsessed with power and control to lead me to an undisclosed part of a huge hotel.

"Enzo," I began nervously. "I'm not sure this is a good idea. Maybe if—"

"Hush now, darling." The elevator car arrived and the doors opened before us. He nudged me in front of him, took me by the arms where he'd grabbed me before and whispered in my ear. "You and I have never been a good idea." He steered me into the car and told the operator to take us to the ninth floor.

As the elevator began to ascend, Enzo kept his hands on me. We stood behind the operator, who kept his eyes on the doors in front of him, and a few seconds into the ride, Enzo's right hand slid from my arm across my chest, slowly, possessively. His palm, fingers spread wide, came to rest on my left breast, and he snaked his left arm across my stomach, pulling me back against him.

"I want you." His lips formed the words right at my ear, barely a whisper. He was hard already, his solid erection pressing into the small of my back.

Oh, God.

This might be more difficult than I thought.

Gina. Wedding. Packard. Secrecy. Lies. I reminded myself of the myriad reasons I had to be angry with Enzo, and it worked. When the doors opened, he released me and I stepped out of the car. He followed me into the hall, and when the elevator doors closed, he reached for me again.

"No." I held up one palm toward him. "First, tell me what we're doing here."

"All right. Follow me."

I trailed him down a long carpeted corridor, passing doors on both sides. He finally stopped at a set of double doors straight ahead of us and pulled a key from his pocket. After unlocking the door on the left, he pushed it open and gestured for me to enter first. "After you."

I walked into a dark room, but a moment later Enzo flipped a switch and an overhead light came on. As he shut the door, I moved deeper into an elegantly furnished parlor with a large window opposite the door. I went to it and pushed the filmy white curtains aside, peering down onto Grand Circus Park. Spinning around, I took in the sofa and chair upholstered in gold and brown stripes, the end tables and their lamps dripping with rust-colored fringe, and the low coffee table, upon which sat an amber glass ashtray. The carpet felt thick under my feet.

"Well, what do you think?" Enzo asked.

"Is this your apartment?" A glance to my left revealed another doorway, through which I glimpsed the shadowy outline of a double bed.

"It was." He walked toward me and I backed into the windowsill. When he reached me, pressing his body flush against mine, he leaned back slightly at the waist and dangled the key between us. "Now it's *your* apartment."

"My apartment!"

"Mmhm." He braced his hands behind me and I leaned back. His face hovered above mine, and I looked at his lips. They weren't as full or sensuous as Joey's, but their fine edges and sharp peaks were beautiful, and he was an expert at using them on my body. My insides heated up quickly, and when he lowered his mouth to mine, I let him kiss me. But I didn't put my arms around him, and I kept my lips closed.

"Want to see the bedroom?" He toyed with the straps of my dress.

"No." I elbowed my way out of his reach and put some distance between us.

Sighing, he faced me with an exasperated look on his face.

"Don't give me that look, Enzo. I'm still angry with you. I only came here to hear what you have to say about Joey."

He pressed his lips together. "Why are you always so worried about him?"

"Because he's my friend, and I dragged him into this mess to begin with."

"Really. You instructed him to hijack those trucks and later advised him to steal the opium from the load?"

"No, but…"

"Lupo's a grown man, Tiny. He makes his own decisions, and now he's got another one to make."

An alarm pinged in my head. "About what?"

"Come into the bedroom and I'll tell you."

I scowled at him. "You're impossible."

Enzo smiled and disappeared into the bedroom, and I followed a moment later when he switched on a lamp. The room was even more impressive than the parlor, with two big windows on the left, a large closet with a full mirror on the door, and a private bathroom with a claw-footed tub. The bed, with its scarlet-hued spread and curvy high-backed frame, looked especially inviting. And it wasn't just because I could imagine myself and Enzo naked underneath that coverlet, although that was easy to do—I was exhausted.

"All right. I'm in here. Now tell me."

He took my purse from me and laid it on a chair in the corner. "Do you like the apartment?"

I loved it, but there was no way I would live here at his beck and call. Not when he had a *wife* living with him somewhere else.

I turned away from him. "I'm not doing anything else until you talk."

"You don't have to do anything," he murmured, coming up behind me. He brushed my hair off the back of my neck and rubbed his lips on my nape. His breath sent shivers down my spine, and I willed myself to be strong, even though it felt *so good*. He kissed his way down one side of my neck and slipped one strap from my shoulder. "I simply told him…" He kissed that shoulder. "That I had some information…" He slipped the other strap from my shoulder and pressed his lips there too. "I thought he'd be interested in." He brought his hands to my shoulders and trailed his fingers down the insides of my arms. "Interested enough to trade for the opium."

"What kind of information?" I whispered, my arms tingling.

He bracketed my hips with his hands and pulled me into him. "Well," he said, bending at the knee to grind against me before whispering in my ear, "I know who killed his father."

Chapter Nine

I wrenched myself from Enzo's grasp and stumbled forward. "What did you say?" Pulling the straps of my dress back on my shoulders, I stared at him in disbelief.

"I know who killed his father," he repeated, as if we were discussing the weather. "I know who pulled the trigger outside the station and I know who ordered the hit on Big Leo that killed him."

"But—but how?"

"Nobody keeps a secret for that long in this business. It's been a few years now—eventually you find someone disgruntled with a particular faction and willing to talk, for the right price, of course."

"Of course." My mind was spinning. I knew how badly Joey wanted to find out who'd killed his father—he'd just told me so when we were on the roof. Undoubtedly *he'd* give up the drugs to know who pulled the trigger. But would he stab Angelo in the back? "So...so did you tell him?"

"No. I simply told him I had the information. If he wants the details, he'll have to decide what they're worth." He moved toward me again, but I backed up.

"Just wait." I put my hands out. "I'm a little flustered right now."

"I like you flustered." He kept coming at me and I thought he might back me right into the closet but instead he swept me off my feet and carried me over to the bed.

"Enzo, please."

He set me down and slipped my shoes off. "Please what? I'll do anything you want me to." Running a hand up one leg, he paused at different places—my knee, my thigh, and finally my hip. "I'll kiss you here. And here. And especially here." He slipped his fingers inside the loose edge of my step-in and brushed them against my tingling skin.

Oh, God. He was so handsome and the room was so beautiful and the bed was so inviting and I knew it would feel so good, but—

"No." I pushed his hand away, brought my knees together, and propped myself up on my elbows. "I'm not doing this with you. You're about to marry some other girl, and—"

"Jesus!" he exploded, pounding a fist into the bed. "How many times do I have to tell you? I'm not going to fucking marry her!"

"You lie!" I shouted through gritted teeth. "You're always telling me just what I want to hear and nothing that's actually true. Until you prove to me that you're not stashing me in this apartment just so your *wife* won't see us together, we're not doing this."

He eyed me angrily. "You knew about her last time we did it. And you knew we had to keep our time together a secret. What's changed?"

"I don't know!" I yelled. "But something has."

"Within one week?"

"Yes!"

Enzo breathed deeply through his nose. "What the fuck do you want, Tiny?"

I had no idea. *What's changed?* It was a fair question, in a way—I *had* known he had a fiancée the last two times we'd slept together. True, I hadn't known about the wedding date, but if I was honest with myself, I had to admit there wasn't much of a difference between sleeping with a man who had a fiancée, and sleeping with one who had a fiancée and a wedding date. Both were pretty despicable, separated perhaps by a scant few degrees of despicableness on the scale.

"I don't know, Enzo. I guess…I guess I'll wait until next Saturday and see if you manage to dodge your own wedding. " Slapping a hand over my face, I groaned. "God, that sounds so ridiculous."

"That's a long time away, Tiny." He trailed his fingers along my shin. "I don't think I can wait that long. I don't think you can, either."

"It's one week, Enzo. You can't go seven days without having sex?"

"I just want you so badly." He rubbed my hip, staring at his hand against the ivory material. "Can't we come up with a different plan?"

"No." I got off the bed and located my heels on the floor. "We can't."

"Is this about him?" He watched as I slipped my feet into my shoes.

My cheeks flushed, and I bent over one leg as if I needed to concentrate on the buckle. "No."

"I don't believe you. You have to decide, Tiny. You can't be loyal to two people in this situation."

I straightened so quickly I got dizzy. "Ha! Look who's talking!"

"Gina means nothing to me. In fact, she annoys the hell out of me, and it's pretty clear I am not loyal to her. I never claimed to be."

I bent and buckled the other shoe. When I straightened, Enzo was reaching for the lamp, and a second later the room went black. "I need my purse," I said.

He picked it up from the chair brought it to me. "Are you sure you won't stay?" His voice was lilting and soft again. "I can come back later and stay with you. All night."

I felt a quick tug of arousal, but it disappeared at the thought of him coming straight from Gina's side to my bed. "No. Not until I know for sure that you're not going to marry her."

"How do I know for sure that you're not fooling around with Lupo?" he asked testily. The light coming from the parlor illuminated only one side of his face, leaving the other half dark.

"I'm not."

Silence. "I saw you dancing with him."

My stomach flipped. "So what? It was just dancing. There's nothing between us."

"What if I want you to prove it?"

"How would I do that?"

A smile appeared on his half-shadowed face. "By keeping a secret."

"What secret?"

"This one: The gunman outside the prison was a hitman named Legs Putnam. And the hit was ordered by Sam Scarfone."

I gasped. "Sam Scarfone! But Big Leo was his uncle! Why would he do that?"

"Because Big Leo was the boss. And if you don't like the way things are being run, and you think you deserve more than you're getting or you been screwed one too many times, that's one way to fix it. Take him out."

"Oh my God." I brought a hand to my mouth.

"It was especially smart because Scarfone must have known everyone would blame Provenzano, since that was the big rivalry at the time. But it backfired, because none of the old guard under Big Leo wanted to take orders from pissant Sam and his hot-headed buddies."

That part wasn't new to me—Joey had told me about Sam and his friends leaving the Scarfone faction to start the River Gang. He'd known some of them from school and thought they were decent guys just doing what they could to make a buck.

I swallowed hard. "But…it was *family*."

Enzo shrugged. "Sometimes blood is cheaper than whisky."

#

Out of the apartment. Down the hall. Into the elevator. Through the lobby. Under the awning. One thought held my mind hostage the entire time.

I know who killed Joey's father.

And I couldn't tell him.

Could I?

No. Stay out of this.

As the attendant pulled up in the Packard, Enzo put his hand on my arm. "I need to see someone at the desk a moment. Just wait in the car, OK?"

Another attendant opened the passenger door for me and I got in, my earlier distaste at riding in the wedding gift eclipsed by my anxiety over the information I now had. I knew exactly why Enzo had told me—he wasn't sure he could trust me and this was the test. Enzo wanted to see if I would run to Joey with the knowledge of who killed his father, which would mean I was loyal to Joey over him. Not that I had any guarantee Enzo had given me the truth—when had he ever done that? Giving me false information was just as effective a test as giving me the real names.

I thought of Joey, agonizing over the decision to give in to Enzo's demands in exchange for the information he'd wanted for years. If he did, he'd betray Angelo, who might then be tempted to put Sam wise to the scheme. Sam, whose nickname was *the Barber* because of his skill with a razor, who'd ordered the murder of his own uncle in order to gain a bigger share of the black market spoils.

What would he do to Joey if he found out about the opium?

"God, Joey," I whispered as my eyes filled. "What a fucking mess. Why didn't you just stay in Chicago to begin with?"

My nose began to run a little, and I sniffed, wiping at it with my hand. I needed a handkerchief, but I'd forgotten to put one in my purse. Maybe Enzo had one in here somewhere. I checked the glove compartments in the doors. Nothing. Twisting in my seat, I glanced into the back and thought I saw a bit of white peeking out from under the seat. Enzo was always tossing his coats in the back, so maybe one had slipped out. I opened the door, waving off the attendant who came immediately to assist me. Pulling the rear door open, I leaned into the back and slipped my hand under the seat. My fingers closed around a piece of cloth, and I pulled it up. It wasn't a handkerchief.

It was a pair of women's silk underwear.

I dropped them as if they had scorched me and backed out of the car.

Heart racing, I slammed the rear door and jumped back into the front, tucking my hands between my knees. What the hell was going on? Some girl had been in the back seat of this Packard and left without her knickers? That meant at some point, she'd removed them—or they'd been removed, I thought, scowling—and there was only one reason a girl doffed her underwear in the back seat of an automobile.

Bastard.

Seething, I crossed my arms over my chest. I had no idea what to say to him—part of me wanted to claw his eyes out and tell him he could go fuck himself in his nice apartment because he'd certainly never fuck me there. I recalled the one physical flaw on Enzo's body, a crescent-shaped scar at the top of one sharp cheekbone near his left eye.

Maybe I'd give him a matching one on the right.

Thank God I didn't sleep with him tonight.

The moment he got in the car and turned to me, I slapped him again. "You bastard!" I shouted. "Want to tell me what a pair of women's underwear is doing in the back seat?"

"What?" Enzo grabbed my wrists so I couldn't smack him again, but he struggled to look into the back seat. "What the hell are you talking about?"

"I'm talking about the lacey little knickers on the floor back there."

"I don't see anything."

"You're not denying anything either."

"I have no idea what you're talking about."

"You've never gone parking with Gina in this car, like we did the other night?" My blood boiled as I imagined Enzo in here with me one night and her the next.

"No!"

"Then how do you explain it?"

"I don't know, Tiny! Maybe she had some clothing in here or something. Yes, that must be it. She's been moving some of her things to a new place."

"A new place at the Statler?" I snapped. "How convenient it would be to have your wife and mistress in the same hotel!"

"No." He dropped my arms and rubbed his face with his hands. "Jesus Christ, Tiny. I brought you here tonight because I thought it was what you wanted. You *told* me it was what you wanted. Your own place. Where you can come and go as you please. Where you can do what you want." He looked at me. "Am I wrong? Isn't that what you want?"

I struggled to reply. "Yes. But no. I mean—not like this."

"You don't want the apartment?" He held up a key. "Because that's what I was doing in there. Getting you your own key." When I didn't take it, he dropped it into my lap. "It's yours, Tiny. You want to get out of your father's house? Here's your opportunity."

I stared at the gold key, linked to an oval plate that said Hotel Statler, Detroit, Michigan. "I can't afford it."

"I'll pay the rent."

"I'm not your charity case, Enzo."

"I'll get you a job at the club. I just want you to stay here, so I can see you when I want. When you want. It'll be fun, just like we said."

I sighed, exhausted and overwrought, physically and emotionally. Did I really want to continue fighting him? What did we owe each other, after all? Fidelity? Or just a good time? I played with the key in my lap. "I don't know, Enzo. I need to think about it. Can you take me home now, please? I'm tired."

We went back to the club, where Enzo put me in a different car and instructed one of his men to drive me home. As usual, I had no idea when or where I might see him again, but I was so worn out I didn't much care. I nodded off several times on the way home and fell asleep the moment my head hit the pillow.

#

The next morning I woke up around eight, the sounds and smells of breakfast drifting into my room. The scent of coffee made me whimper a little, and I licked my dry lips. Actually my entire mouth was dry, and my tongue felt swollen. *Dammit, who told me to drink so much?* Every one of my teeth felt as if it was covered in wool. I tried to sit up and promptly fell back when the sunlight stabbed my eyes. Was it always this bright in here in the morning?

I flung an arm over my face. I didn't want to wake up. I didn't want to move. I didn't want to think.

141

But over the clink of plates and cups downstairs, I heard Enzo's voice telling me who killed Joey's father again. *The gunman outside the prison was a hitman named Legs Putnam. And the hit was ordered by Sam Scarfone.*

I couldn't remember all the names of the men brought to trial for the ambush at the police station, but there were several, and Putnam might have been one of them. A few had been held but released for lack of evidence, and the trial had been a joke. I vividly recalled the day the jury reached a verdict—not guilty, of course. No witness had been willing to testify, and every member of that jury was well aware of the danger involved in deciding against a gangster. They reached a verdict in less than an hour.

I swallowed hard. Had the same hitman shot Vince too? What would it do to Bridget, knowing the name of the man who put the bullets in her husband, robbing her children of their father, robbing her of the love of her life? She told me repeatedly she'd never remarry. *It only happens once*, she always claimed, *falling in love that way. I'm grateful I had it at all. Some people never do.*

While I liked the idea of that once-in-a-lifetime love, I wanted her to be wrong too, so she could love someone again. But what did I know? I'd certainly never been in love, and I'd never had anyone say he was in love with me. Given the two offers from men I'd had in the last week, it didn't seem as if love was on the near horizon, either. Joey had invited me to run off to Chicago with him without even so much as a kiss, and Enzo had offered me a luxury apartment, *for free*, with the idea that we could use it for uninterrupted nights of illicit pleasure. But despite telling me how much he wanted me all the time, he wasn't murmuring any words of real affection. Once, he'd even admitted to wanting to kiss me one minute and strangle me the next.

And what about my own feelings?

Last week I'd been willing to overlook the fact that Enzo had a fiancée—it had almost seemed like a fun little twist in the game. I'd sort of convinced myself that it really didn't matter, and a few fiery hot sexual escapades with a gangster seemed like the perfect way to kick off my new life as a flapper.

But was it?

I slapped my hands over my face. What was wrong with me? I was getting everything I'd wanted, wasn't I? Enzo had made good on his promise and come through with the apartment, that beautiful apartment at the Statler with a view of the park, my own bathroom, my own space. Would I take my meals in the dining room there? Order breakfast in my room? At the thought of food, my belly rumbled, and I knew I'd feel better if I ate something.

Swinging my legs over the side of the bed, I counted to three and righted myself. My vision clouded a bit, so I closed my eyes and counted again. When I opened them, the room was still. Getting slowly to my feet, I shuffled toward the dresser and looked at myself in the mirror.

I couldn't help groaning when I saw my reflection. Not only was my red hair tangled and matted, but I'd neglected to remove my eye makeup, which was smudged around my eyes like a raccoon mask, and I'd put my nightgown on backward. As I pulled it over my head, I remembered wearing it the night I'd been with Enzo in the Packard. I tossed it into my hamper. It needed to be cleaned.

#

I spent the day doing household chores with Molly, who was glad to help me out as long as I kept my promise to her about going to the movies without Mary Grace. Daddy had disappeared after breakfast, saying he was emptying the office at the garage of his things and moving them to his new space, and not to hold supper for him. My sisters said goodbye, but I ignored him. We still hadn't exchanged more than two words since he'd forbidden me to move out.

All afternoon Molly and I laundered the linens, scrubbed the bathroom, mopped the kitchen floor, washed the windows with newspaper and vinegar, and took the rugs outside to beat them. With each swish of the mop and pillowcase pinned on the line, I fretted about Joey. What would he do? What would I do in his place?

More important, what should I do in mine?

I had the power to allow Joey to keep a third of the drug money and discover who'd taken his father's life—assuming Enzo had told me the truth. The problem was, Joey didn't just want to know who killed his dad; he wanted to act on it. He wanted revenge. Did I want to be responsible for what he would do with the knowledge? He could go to jail for the rest of his life. Actually, Joey going to jail might be the least painful result—if Sam the Barber heard what he did, there would be consequences. Not to mention what friends of Legs Putnam would do, assuming he had friends. And what price would I pay for betraying Enzo's confidence? I didn't think he'd send me to the bottom of the river, but he'd be plenty mad.

On the other hand, I could just say nothing. Let Joey make his own decision. Let him decide what the information was worth. I hated the idea of keeping something he wanted so badly from him, but it seemed like the safest option.

Between the agonizing and the household drudgery, I was totally miserable.

If I accept Enzo's offer, I'll be free of these chores. In my mind I saw that apartment once more. *I bet the Statler has maid service.*

"Molly." We were hanging sheets on the line in the back yard, and she had to pull a clothespin from between her teeth to answer me.

"Yeah?"

"If I moved out, would you help Daddy with Mary Grace and the house?"

She stuck her neck out so far I almost laughed. "Move out? What are you talking about?" She shrank back, eyes wide. "Are you pregnant?"

I smiled, unable to help it. "No."

"Then why move out? Where are you going?"

145

I continued pinning a sheet and tried to explain without telling the whole truth. "I'd like to move downtown…into an apartment."

"With Evelyn or something?"

"No. By myself."

She burst out laughing. "How are *you* going to afford an apartment downtown by yourself?"

"Well, I'm going to get a job. And the place belongs to a—a friend, so the rent is reasonable." Briefly, I wondered what that suite actually cost.

"Oh." She went back to her sheet. "I guess it would be OK. Yeah. Actually, I know it would." Her tone was more positive with each word, and I imagined she was getting excited about the prospect of one less adult breathing down her neck. "I mean, I'm a better cook than you are, anyway, and Mary Grace is certainly old enough to take over some chores." She stopped and looked at me. "Does Daddy know about this?"

I sighed. "Kind of. I mean, I told him I wanted to move out, but he didn't take the news too well."

"You're an adult. You should be allowed to do as you please."

Grimacing, I reached for another damp pillowcase from the basket. "He doesn't see it that way."

"Well, I support you. If you want to move out, I think you should do it. I know I'd do it if I were you—in fact, I will do it. As soon as I'm out of school, there's no way I'll stay here. A girl's gotta get out and live a little, you know?"

I nodded. It would mean more work for her in the short term, but her support made more sense now that I realized she wanted to do the same thing when she was old enough. And if I did it first, Daddy couldn't stop her. At least, that's the way she saw it. "Well, we'll see. I haven't made my decision yet. Lord, my head is pounding."

"You don't look too good. Your face is a little green. Why don't you go lie down or something? I can finish this." She took the pillowcase from my hands and nudged me toward the house.

"Actually, I prefer the fresh air. Maybe I'll just stretch my legs a bit. Take a walk."

"OK. Just don't be gone too long—I'm leaving right after supper, remember?"

"I remember."

I headed down the driveway and turned right. The sun was hidden behind clouds, so the day had taken on a gray pallor that suited my mood. I sniffed the air and caught a whiff of something strange, almost metallic. Maybe I wouldn't walk that far—it smelled like a storm might be coming.

Chapter Ten

Without really thinking about it, I walked to Bridget's. I stuck my head into the store, waved hello to Martin at the counter and took the back stairs up to her apartment. The scent of roasting potatoes hit me just outside the door, and I breathed deeply. Her place always smelled so good.

"Hello?" I walked into the kitchen without knocking.

"Hello." Bridget stood over an ironing board at one end of the kitchen. It folded down right out of the wall, which was handy, but when the stove was on it made for some hot, sweaty ironing in the summertime. She wiped her forehead with a sleeve. "What are you up to?"

"Just taking a walk. Smells good in here." I wandered over to a chair and dropped into it.

"Thanks. Stay for supper?"

"I can't. I should make something for the girls and Daddy, although God knows when he'll return."

"He's busy with the new shop, huh?"

I pressed my lips together. No good would come of blabbing to Bridget about the gambling if Daddy didn't want her to know. "Yeah."

"And what about you? Now that everything is…settled, are you thinking of returning to school this fall?"

"If I can afford it, perhaps." Clearing my throat, I went on. "I'm actually thinking of moving downtown. Getting a job that pays a little better so I can save up easier."

I figured she'd protest right away, but she just nodded, dropping her eyes to the blouse she was working on. "Oh?"

"Yes. I'm…I just… It's like I told you that day before all that other stuff happened. I'd like some independence."

"I can understand that."

I looked at her, surprise. "You can?"

"Sure I can. I was your age once too, you know. Not that long ago, in fact."

"I know, but you were always so in love with Vince. I never knew you wanted to live on your own."

Bridget tilted her head this way and that. "Well, it wasn't so much that I wanted to live on my own. And I *was* in love with Vince. But we certainly had very few opportunities to be alone without Daddy lurking or you three monkeys hanging all over us, not to mention Vince's overprotective mother who never thought an Irish girl was good enough for her Italian boy."

149

I smiled. "Really?"

"Really. *Oh*, she gave us such a hard time. So did Daddy." She set the iron on its stand and fanned her face. "Jesus, Mary, and Joseph, it's hot in here."

"Why did Daddy give you a hard time?"

"Well, Vince and I wanted to get married and he didn't want us to. Not because Vince was Italian—he was Catholic, at least—but because he didn't want to be without me at home. Same reasons he'd give you if you announced your intention to leave. I was doing the lion's share of the work and had been since Mother died."

"I never knew you asked permission to leave and marry Vince. I thought you got pregnant and had to marry him."

Bridget selected a handkerchief from her laundry basket and laid it flat on the board. "I did."

I scrutinized her closely. Was she blushing? After all this time, she was still ashamed of it? Or was there another reason?

It struck me hard.

"You did it on purpose."

The color in her cheeks deepened to purple.

"You did it on purpose!" I gasped. "Bridget, I don't believe it!" My mouth refused to close, and I slapped the table with my palm. "You asked Daddy if you could leave home to marry Vince and when he said no, you got pregnant on purpose so he'd have to let you go!"

"Shhhhhhhh." Bridget glanced out the window behind her. "Do you want the whole neighborhood to hear you?"

"I just can't believe it." Blinking in surprise, I stared at my older sister, seeing her in a new light. "Was it Vince's idea?"

"No, it was mine." She shook her head as she smoothed out the wrinkled in the white cloth. "And I'm not sorry. I'll never be sorry. The years we had together were worth it. The children are worth it."

I nodded, sadness squeezing my throat.

"And I knew you were able to handle things at home without me." She looked at me then. "And you have. You've been wonderful, Tiny. You kept that house running and those girls in line and made good marks in school too. You deserve a life of your own." Sighing, she dropped her eyes to her ironing again. "I just don't know that Molly is as capable as you were at her age."

We'll see, I thought. My mind was still whirling, and I wanted to know one more thing. "Bridget...can I ask you a personal question?"

"Might as well. But if you're going to sit there, would you mind folding some laundry? There's a basket of the boys' things in the front room."

Nodding, I retrieved the basket and used the kitchen table to fold and sort the little items of clothing. "You once said that you got pregnant with Vince the first time you ever did it. Was that true?"

The color deepened in her cheeks. Slowly, she shook her head.

151

I set a little pair of overalls on one stack. "So you'd been sleeping with Vince before?"

She nodded. "We'd done it a fair amount of times, and we were always careful. We only had to do it a few times without any, you know, precautions, for me to get pregnant."

Dropping my eyes to the basket, I selected a white cotton undershirt.

"Tiny, what's this about? Do you have feelings for someone?" A note of concern crept into her voice.

"I don't know." Chewing my lip, I finished with the shirt and set it down, staring at the stains on its front. I was dying to confide in her. "I might."

"I know you said it wasn't, but...is it Joey?"

I looked at her sharply. "What makes you ask that?"

"I told you last week. It was the way he was talking about you. And the way you two constantly had your heads together. Seemed obvious to me." She grinned. "And you weren't that convincing when you claimed to be just friends."

"I wasn't?"

She shook her head. "No. And neither was he. You know, Vince always used to tease Joey about you. Said he was positive you'd end up together."

"And what did Joey say?"

Bridget's smile deepened, and her eyes glittered wickedly. "A lady should *not* repeat those words."

Rolling my eyes, I flopped back into the chair. "I don't know, Bridget. I'm confused. I feel *something* for Joey, but I don't know what it is. And he's completely frustrated with me right now. Then there's this other guy too, and he's handsome and wealthy and he's... taken quite a shine to me." That was one way of putting it.

"Oh? Quite the popular girl, you are."

I grimaced. "Anyway, this other man has made me sort of—an offer."

Bridget froze and stared at me. "What kind of offer? A marriage proposal?"

Ha! "No. He's not exactly free to do that."

"He's married?"

"Not yet."

"My God, Tiny, that's the last thing you need. Whatever offer he's made you sounds a bit less than honorable."

I threw my arms up. "What's so fun about honor?"

Her eyes went wide and she returned to her ironing. "Well, if all you're looking for is fun, then be my guest. You just be sure you know how to protect yourself."

"I do. I'm not completely foolish." *Although I act like it sometimes.* "One more thing."

"Jesus, Tiny. You want to join the circus or something?"

"Ha, ha. No. I have a question for you." I stood and began folding another little shirt. "If you had some information that you knew a friend had been searching for, that in fact this friend had been obsessed with finding for years, but that might cause that friend to commit violence, would you tell him?"

153

Bridget parked her hands on her hips and stared at me. "What is this about?"

"Just answer me. Would you?"

"I don't know. I'm not much for violence, that's certain."

"Let's say the violence would harm only bad people."

A look of understanding flashed on Bridget's face. "But would there be potential consequences for my friend?"

I nodded glumly.

"Then no, I wouldn't."

"Thanks. That's what I thought."

#

I ate supper with the girls and did the dishes myself, since Molly had done the cooking. As expected, Daddy didn't show. At seven o'clock there was a knock on the door, and Molly flew down the stairs to answer it. She introduced me to a tall boy with wavy blond hair and a friendly smile whose name was Chet, and asked permission to ride in his car to the movies. He looked like a safe enough kid, so I gave it, and she rewarded me with a grateful hug before they left. I wanted to remind her about her curfew, but I bit my tongue, tired of acting like a mother.

Mary Grace and I played tiddlywinks and snacked on a box of Cracker Jack she'd bought earlier in the day, and later she asked to look at my scrapbook. We were upstairs lying on my bed with it when I heard the first roll of thunder in the distance. A moment later, a gust of wind blew in through my open window, ruffling the white curtains.

"We'd better shut the windows." Rolling off the bed and onto my feet, I pulled both my bedroom windows closed and instructed Mary Grace to shut those in the room she shared with Molly, Daddy's room and the bath. I went downstairs and shut them in the kitchen, where rain was already beginning to slant through the screen. Another clap of thunder echoed from the west, and I heard Mary Grace's fast footfalls on the stairs.

"Tiny? Are you down here?" Her voice shook a little.

"Yes, I'm here." Mary Grace got anxious during thunderstorms, and I tried to think of something that would comfort her until this one passed. "Do you want to play another game? Checkers, maybe? Or a card game?"

"Maybe." Rain began to rattle the windowpanes and a few gusts of heavy wind made the house creak. "Do you think the storm will be over soon?"

"Sure it will, these summer storms never last too long." I put my arm around her and walked toward the stairs. "Tell you what. How about we go upstairs and I read a little Ruth Fielding aloud to you and let you sleep in my bed. Does that sound good?"

"Can we put rag curlers in our hair?"

"Absolutely."

Upstairs, we put on our nightgowns and I tied up Mary Grace's hair in rags. Then I sat on my bed while she stood behind me and did her best to tie mine up too. We giggled at our reflections in the mirror, brushed our teeth in the bathroom, and slipped beneath the covers in my bed. The steady, drumming rain on the roof was soothing in a way, but I'd read only a few pages when the lights began to flicker. Mary Grace tensed beside me. I patted her arm and kept reading, and the electricity winked a few more times before it went out altogether.

"Oh no!" She grabbed my arm.

"Don't worry so much, poppet, it's all right. This happens all the time when the wind is rough." I patted her arm again and got off the bed. "I'll go down and find a candle and we'll read by candle-light, like in the old days."

"No, don't go!" She scrambled to her feet and grabbed onto the back of my nightgown. "I'll come with you."

It was hard to move with her tugging on me, but I managed to feel my way down the stairs in the dark, moving along the wall in the front hallway into the kitchen, and from there into the dining room, without stumbling. In the built-in corner cabinet, I located two candles in small silver holders that had probably been a wedding present, and from a kitchen drawer I dug a box of matches. Striking one against the side of the box, I lit both candles and saw the worry in Mary Grace's expression.

"Honey, it's all right," I assured her. "Come on, you want to carry one? I'll carry the other and we'll go back upstairs and finish the chapter, OK?"

"OK." She was trying hard to be brave, but her hand shook so much that I felt better holding on to both candles and letting her hang on to my arm. As we ascended the stairs, guilt over leaving home pounded my heart as hard as the rain against the windowpanes. If I left, who would be left to comfort her? Molly? I swallowed hard. Would she take the job of mothering a ten-year-old girl seriously? Could I ask her to? Granted, both Bridget and I had done it at her age, but Molly was a different sort of person, and I wasn't convinced she would handle the responsibility well. Maybe leaving home was a bad idea.

We made it up to my room, set the candles on my night table, and crawled back under the covers. The thunder and wind let up a little, and though the lights didn't come on, I was able to read by the glow of the candles, and we even laughed a little that this was probably how our mother had read at night as a child. When Mary Grace's eyelids began to droop, I lowered my voice to a hush. When I was certain she'd fallen asleep, I closed the book and checked the clock. It was just after ten. I was exhausted, but I blew out one candle, and took the other one downstairs to wait for Molly to get home. I set the candlestick on the coffee table and curled up on the sofa, chin on my knees, but I kept dozing, so I blew out the flame and waited in the dark. Soon the drizzle on the roof lulled me into a deeper sleep.

The sound of the front door opening and closing woke me with a start, and I picked up my head. The electricity must have been restored, because a lamp in the corner was on. Wiping a bit of drool from my lips, I held my breath until my eyes adjusted and I saw it was Molly, back from her date.

And trying to sneak up the stairs.

"What time is it?" I demanded in a whisper, jumping off the sofa. My muscles and joints felt stiff, as if I had been curled in one position for hours.

"Oh!" She whirled on me and put a hand to her heart. "You scared me! What are you doing down here?"

"Waiting for you. You were supposed to be home by eleven. What time is it?"

"Uh, about midnight?"

"About?"

"Maybe a little after?" She started laughing and clapped a hand over her mouth. "I'm sorry, I know I'm late and you're mad, but you look so funny with those rags going every which way on your head. Did Mary Grace do it?"

"Yes. Now, where were you? And don't tell me you were at the movie theater all this time."

"I—I wasn't."

"So? Where were you?"

"After the movie, we were going to go out for ice cream but the shop had closed early or something. The entire block was dark."

"Electricity went out."

"Right. So we just drove around a bit and then…parked."

"Parked?" Immediately the image of Enzo and I in the front seat of his Packard lodged, unwanted, in my mind.

She sighed. "Yes, OK? Parked. Please don't lecture me. I had such a wonderful night and I didn't do anything to be ashamed of, and for once, I didn't have Mary Grace around to bug me or tease me or tattle. Daddy's car isn't here, so he's not home and he doesn't have to know."

"Unless I tell him."

She gripped the banister with two hands. "Please don't, Tiny! I'm being honest with you, aren't I? I could lie and say we were at someone's house or at a party…but I'm not. I was alone with Chet, in his car, and I was safe."

I held back a sarcastic response, because it wouldn't do any good. I didn't want to argue with her about what was and wasn't safe when you went parking with a boy. And based on our conversation yesterday, she knew more than I thought she did about what boys want from a girl in the dark. *And what girls want too.* I took a deep breath.

"Listen, Molly. I'm glad you had a nice time, and I appreciate knowing the truth about where you were. I'm going to trust that you know right from wrong and that you're aware of what can happen if a girl gets a reputation. I know it's not fair, the boy should have the reputation too," I said when I saw her about to protest, "but that's just the way it is. The more important thing is, you had a curfew and you disobeyed it."

"Not on purpose! We just lost track of time," she whined. "Please don't punish me for it, Tiny. Just let me have this *one night, please*. I'll never do it again, I promise. I'll—"

At the sound of a light knock on the front door, we both gasped. She rushed off the steps and we clutched one another's arms. "Who could that be this late at night?" she whispered.

"I don't know. Maybe Daddy forgot his key?"

Whoever it was knocked lightly again, and then pushed the door open.

"Hello?" The voice was deep and familiar. A face appeared.

"Joey, you scared us half to death!" Molly scolded.

"Sorry. I was out this way, and I saw the light on." He came in and shut the door behind him. His suit and hat were wet, but even so, the sight of him quickened my pulse. He took off his fedora and met my eyes. "I wanted to talk to you."

Frantically, I tried to position my arms so they covered as much of my bare skin as possible. My usual nightgown wasn't dry, so I'd put on an old eyelet-trimmed chemise, which had thin straps, a low neckline, and didn't even reach my knees. I crossed my arms and legs and covered one bare foot with the other, but not before I noticed Joey stealing a glance at my chest.

"What were you doing over here at this hour?" I asked.

"Dropping Rosie off."

"Oh." Jealousy flared in my gut. "Molly, you go on up," I said to my sister. "We can continue our discussion tomorrow."

"Or not." She scurried up the stairs. "We could just forget about it. That's fine, too."

"Sounds like I came at a bad time." Joey tried to make a joke, but I could tell something serious was on his mind. I was pretty sure I knew what it was.

"She was late for curfew."

"Ah. You trying out a new hairdo?" He gestured toward my head with his hat. "Looks like flapper meets Medusa."

Wincing, I brought a hand to my hair and felt the rags there. "Mary Grace did it. I'll take them out so you don't turn to stone when you look at me."

Unbuttoning his coat, he wiped his feet before entering the front room and taking a seat on the sofa while I began tugging the rags from my hair. At first I tried to keep one arm across my chest but gave up on modesty when I realized I'd need two hands to untie the knots Mary Grace had fashioned. *Jesus, what had she done? A sailor couldn't have tied these things tighter.* And she'd gotten half my hair inside the knots too—it was hopelessly tangled. Joey watched me silently for a minute, during which the rain picked up again. "Weather keep you in tonight?"

I angled away from him a little. "I had enough fun last night to last me a while."

"I'll say. You drank too much."

I glared at him over one shoulder. "What do you care how much I drink?"

He put up his hands. "I didn't come here to argue."

"One of us always says that, and we still end up arguing."

That brought a little smile. "Yeah. I guess we do."

"So what *did* you come here to do in the middle the night?" I yanked at a particularly stubborn rag, but only succeeded in pulling the knot tighter. *If I had a mirror, this would be easier.*

"I told you, I came to talk to you." Joey scratched his head. "Do you need some help with those or something?"

"No. Go ahead. Talk."

"I can't talk to you with those things hanging off your head. It's bad enough that you're in your pajamas."

"What did you expect I'd be wearing when you show up at my house at this hour?" Exasperated, I dropped my arms, leaving a few rags dangling in my hair. "Fine, help me."

Joey shrugged out of his coat. "Come sit on the floor here in front of me."

Moving the coffee table out of the way, I dropped onto the floor and backed up against the sofa between Joey's legs. His pants were damp from the rain and felt cool against my bare arms. Gooseflesh prickled across my skin, and a dozen admonishments flickered through my head. *Go up and put a robe on. Joey shouldn't be here. Don't sit so close to him.*

And even though I knew he was going to touch me, I jumped when he put his hands in my hair, unprepared for the buzz that swept from my scalp down my arms and over my legs. It lingered as his fingers carefully worked the knots from the rags.

Neither of us spoke.

It probably only took him a few minutes to remove them, but with each passing second I was more aware of him, of everything around us. Colors and scents and sounds were sharper. The low golden glow of the lamp. The thrumming of the rain on the roof. The tick of the clock on the mantle. The scent of Joey's wet gabardine trousers and leather shoes. My breaths came faster and deeper as I imagined what his hands looked like in my hair, how difficult it must be for masculine fingers to work the thin strips of cloth from my tangled tresses. But his touch was gentle.

Too gentle.

"There. Done." He held the scraps of cotton over my right shoulder, his hand suspended near my collarbone. Beneath my chemise, my nipples peaked against the thin cotton.

Those hands. Those fucking hands.

Even though his knuckles bore the angry red evidence of the fight last night, his hands still had the power to arouse me. Would I never know the feel of them on my skin? Desire and jealousy twined their roots deep inside me. What had he done with Rosie tonight? What affection had he shown her? What

163

physical pleasure had he experienced with her, with any girl, that he never would with me? My heart pumped hard.

I reached up with my right hand, telling myself to simply take the rags, but instead, I wrapped my fingers around his solid wrist. With my other hand, I took the scraps and let them fall. Twisting at the waist, I looked over my shoulder at him, my mouth falling open. Joey's olive skin appeared golden, his eyes almost black. His expression spoke of restraint and frustration, but also undeniable hunger. For so long something had simmered between us, threatening to erupt, and now I had to *know*, or I'd go crazy.

He pressed his lips together and his fingers tightened into a fist, the muscles tensing beneath my grasp. He tried to pull his hand away, but I held on.

Biting my lip, I used my other hand to unbutton the top of my chemise and slip one delicate eyelet strap off my shoulder.

He didn't move.

Oh God, Joey. Please don't say no.

With my heart thumping wildly, I looked down at his fist, unfurled his fingers, and slipped his hand beneath the cotton. Taking a deep breath, I pressed it to my skin and shivered with pleasure when his warm palm covered my breast.

I looked back at him again. For one agonizing eternity of a second, he struggled with his decision.

Well, maybe it was half a second.

He bent forward, grabbed my head with his other hand, and crushed his mouth to mine—oh my

164

God that mouth, those full, luscious lips I'd stared at so many times—how was it possible for them to feel and taste even better than they looked? He kissed me hard, his tongue plunging between our open lips, stroking and sucking. Lust ricocheted throughout my body and centered between my legs. Reaching up to take his face in my hands, I kissed him so deeply and desperately I couldn't breathe, but I cared less about consuming oxygen than I did about consuming Joey.

He lunged off the couch at the same time I struggled to get up on it, and our bodies came together before we tumbled to the floor, frantic to climb inside each other's skin. We ended up on the rug between the sofa and the coffee table, a tangle of twining limbs and searching hands and hungry mouths. Joey's leg slid between my thighs and I squeezed it, lifting my hips. It felt so incredible I nearly exploded right then and there. *My God, it's Joey*, I kept thinking. *It's Joey and me and it's finally real and it feels so fucking good.*

Passion for him surged through me like a lightning storm. My heart pounded against his chest, or was that his pounding against mine? *I have to get closer, there has to be a way to get more of him.* The image of him shirtless in the kitchen popped into my head. I remembered eyeing the muscles in his back, how hot and hard his chest felt under my hands when I checked for bruises. I recalled the way his abdominal muscles rippled down his taut stomach. Oh, God, I wanted to touch him there, touch him everywhere, with my hands, my lips, my tongue. I wanted him naked, next to me, on me, under me, inside me. My head fell back, my jaw dropping in disbelief at the way I wanted Joey.

He moved down my body and took one nipple in his mouth, sucking it through the cotton, and I had to bite down on my own hand to keep from crying out at the pleasure it wrought from deep inside me. Desperate to feel more of his weight on me, I shimmied underneath him, claiming his mouth again with my own and wrapping my legs around him. And then I couldn't help smiling against his lips because I could feel the way he wanted me. Moving my hands around his sides to his round, muscular ass, I pulled him into me, gasping at the huge, hard feel of the bulge in his trousers. *Oh my God, I could come just like this, just feeling his cock rub against me through our clothing, because it's him and this is crazy and my heart is going to burst out of my chest and he feels so good and I never want him to stop and—*

"Christ, Tiny." Joey braced his hands above my shoulders and looked down at me, breathing hard. "What are we doing?"

"I don't know," I whispered, digging my heels into the backs of his thighs. "But don't stop." He groaned, and I lifted my head off the floor and kissed his lips, his chin, his jaw. "Please don't stop." I pressed my lips to his throat and felt his pulse on them. "I want you."

"Since when?"

"Since when?" I panted.

"Yeah, since when do you want me?"

I dropped my head to the floor. That was not the anticipated response. "What do you mean?"

Lifting himself off me, he knelt between my knees. "Last time we talked about this, you said you wanted him, not me."

I propped myself up on my elbows. "I never said that."

"You certainly did. You accused me of judging you for getting what you want. I asked you if you wanted him, and you said yes."

Had I said that? Sighing, I closed my eyes. "I know, but..." God, this was so maddening—my feelings were so twisted up inside me. I *had* wanted Enzo, and everything he'd promised me. But now that he was offering, I wasn't sure I wanted it anymore. Why was that? Was I simply that fickle? Or had I changed my mind because of Joey? I wasn't sure, and I knew the worst thing I could do right now was say something I didn't mean.

I opened my eyes. "I don't know what I want anymore. I'm confused."

"Well, that makes two of us." He got to his feet and snatched his coat off the sofa, shoving his arms through the sleeves.

"And what about you?" I demanded, sitting up. "You're the one who was out on a date tonight, not me!" It was so irritating having to whisper when I wanted to shout. I scrambled to my feet. "Where did you take her?"

"Nowhere, I just gave her a ride home."

"Did you kiss her? Did you?"

167

"No." Joey ran his hands through his hair. "Why the fuck do you even care?" He tried to push past me and go for the front door, but I didn't let him. I caught him by the elbow, spun him around and threw myself at him, grabbing him by the back of his head and pressing my lips to his. He groaned in frustration but slanted his mouth over mine, and I sucked his tongue into my mouth. He tasted so good, like the rain, and *oh my God* I wanted to taste every inch of his body. His arms looped around my lower back, lifting me off my feet, and held me tightly to his chest. But when I tried to twine my legs around his hips again, he set me down and gently pushed me away.

"I can't do this," he said, picking up his hat from the sofa. "I just wanted to say goodbye."

I twisted my hands together. "Where are you going?"

"Chicago."

"Tonight?"

"No. There's something I have to do here first, but I'll have to leave fast after that."

"Something with a gun?"

Joey looked at me carefully. "He told you."

I nodded.

"Then you understand."

I saw the pain of his father's death in his face, and it squeezed my heart. "I do, but...this won't help, Joey. It won't stop here. You kill somebody, his friends retaliate. More death isn't going to solve anything."

"I gotta do it, Tiny. I feel it in my bones."

I tried a different tactic. "So you're giving up the drugs to Enzo? Letting him win?"

"It's already done."

My heart fell to my heels. "What about Angelo? When he finds out, he'll go to Sam, won't he?"

"I'm gonna talk to Angelo, try to make a deal by cutting him in on my first few whisky hauls in Chicago. As for Sam..." Joey fidgeted, and I knew he was struggling with what was safe to tell me. "Look, the less you know, the better," he finally said. "But stay away from Sam, and if he tries to contact you, you should tell Enzo right away."

My mouth fell open in disbelief. "You're telling me to go to Enzo?"

Joey grimaced. "I don't like him, and I don't know what kind of games he's playing with you, but I do believe he'd protect you if you were in harm's way."

I nodded, battling a fierce urge to cry.

He moved for the door.

"Joey, wait."

He turned to me and sighed. "This is useless, Tiny."

"I'm scared. And I don't want you to go."

With one hand on the door, he said, "Give me a reason to stay."

I felt like the wind had been knocked out of me.

Give him a reason. Something, anything. Don't let him walk out that door, because if he's killed trying to avenge his father's death, you'll never have this chance again.

169

"You could be arrested. Or shot."

"I don't care."

"Killing the gunman won't bring your father back," I said, desperate to get through to him. "And your father wouldn't want you to die for him—he'd want you to live for him."

Joey set his hat on his head. "I wasn't asking for a reason from him," he said quietly. "I was asking for a reason from you."

With that he moved quickly for the door and disappeared into the rainy dark.

#

Upstairs, I crawled into bed next to Mary Grace and cried myself to sleep.

Chapter Eleven

The next morning, I woke with puffy eyes, a sore throat, and Mary Grace's stuffed bear tucked underneath my arm. Her small hand was resting on my shoulder.

Love and gratitude washed over me. I tried to move without waking her, but her round blue eyes opened as I sat up.

"Hi," I said. "Thanks for letting me have your bear last night." I held him out to her.

"You're welcome." She took the bear and hugged it close. "You were sad about something. Was it the storm?"

I smiled and shook my head. "No."

"Was it because of Mother? Because I cry about that sometimes too, and I don't even remember her."

"No, it wasn't that either." I tugged on one of the rags in her hair. "You look like her, you know that?"

"Yes. But I like hearing it."

I lay down again, propping my head on my hand. "She had red hair and blue eyes, just like we do."

She squeezed her bear. "It makes me feel close to her, even if I didn't get the chance to love her."

If I'd had tears left, I might have shed them. "Oh, honey, you can still love her."

"Don't you have to know a person to love them?"

I continued stroking her hair, and it reminded me of Joey taking the rags from mine last night. "I guess you do, poppet, but loving your family isn't the same as loving someone else."

She was quiet for a minute. "How do you know if you love someone?"

"Well…" I tried to think of a good way to explain it, but I couldn't. "I'm not really sure. Maybe it's different for everybody."

"I always know if I love someone, because I miss them when they go away," she said. "It makes my heart hurt."

My hand stopped moving. "I think that's a good way to tell, Mary Grace. As good a way as any I've heard."

#

After mass, my sisters and I went to the cemetery, and I couldn't help looking over at the spot where I'd seen Joey last Sunday. But he wasn't there.

172

Disappointment made my feet heavy as we trudged through the wet grass to our mother's grave.

"Where's Daddy?" Mary Grace asked. "How come he didn't come with us?"

"He never comes with us," answered Molly.

"Yes, he does. Sometimes," Mary Grace defended. "And sometimes he comes alone, he told me."

"Does he?" Molly looked at me as we walked.

"I've seen him here once," I admitted. "But he's been busy this week with the new location and moving out of the garage." Why I felt the need to make excuses for the man, I didn't know.

"Daddy says we'll have more money now that he's got the new place," Mary Grace said. "Maybe even enough to hire a housekeeper or a cook."

"What? When did he say that?" I stopped walking and turned Mary Grace to face me.

She shrugged. "I don't know. A few days ago, maybe? He said maybe it will even be Mrs. Schmidt who used to work with mother where she was a maid, at that big house."

Molly and I exchanged a surprised look. "That would be nice," I murmured, starting to walk again. We let Mary Grace run ahead of us and moved to walk shoulder to shoulder.

"Does this mean he's letting you move out?" she wondered.

"I haven't the slightest idea. Daddy never tells me his plans."

We walked silently for a moment, our shoes squishing in the soggy ground. "Are you going to tell him about last night?"

I sighed, lifting my skirt so the hem wouldn't get wet in the tall grass. "I guess not. But if it happens again, I will. You understand?"

She grabbed my arm and tilted her head to my shoulder. "You're the best sister ever. Thank you. I hope Mary Grace is right and Daddy is letting you go."

Of course you do. Then no one will be around to catch you coming in late! It was not a very nice thing to think, but I wasn't in a nice mood. I hadn't slept well, I was worried about Joey, and I still hadn't decided what to do about Enzo. At mass that morning I'd prayed for clarity, but I didn't feel any closer to it than I had last night. My feelings were a jumbled mess.

When we reached our mother's site, we pulled some weeds that had sprung up and stood silently together in prayer. Closing my eyes, I folded my hands together and lowered my chin.

Please, Mother, I begged. *Help me to do things right. I know I don't always act the way I should. I know I've been reckless and self-indulgent and unwise. I know I've had unkind thoughts about my family. I want to be the kind of person you'd be proud of, but I don't know where to go from here.*

Sniffing, I wiped a tear from my cheek with the back of my hand.

For years I've been telling myself that all I want is to get out and live life, because all I've known of it is our house and our family and our neighborhood. Since Bridget left, I've

174

been mother, housekeeper, cook—yes, I know I've been remiss in that area—and I tried not to resent it, but I suppose I did sometimes. And I suppose I went a bit crazy because I've felt trapped, and misbehaving made me feel free and full of life.

I took a deep breath, inhaling the scent of wet earth. Exhaling, I made one last plea.

And Joey…dear God, Mother, please help him. We've made such a mess of things between us, and now he's planning to do something foolish and dangerous, and I didn't know what to say to talk him out of it. Please watch over him—I promise to be a better person and stop tormenting him if you'll protect him the way he protects me. I promise to stop doing things that confuse him, like showing my jealousy over girls he dates, or looking at him with wicked thoughts, and I especially promise to stop kissing him.

Even though I want to. I really want to.

As I crossed myself, a strangled sob escaped my throat, and then another. Saying nothing, Molly and Mary Grace each took a hand and led me away. I saw tears on their cheeks too.

#

I managed to pull myself together for the streetcar ride home, dabbing at my face with a handkerchief and tilting my hat low over my eyes so no one would see how swollen and red they were. From the stop we walked to Bridget's for a visit, and the second I saw her, I burst into tears. My loud keening bounced off the walls in the kitchen as she shooed her wide-eyed boys into the front room with Molly and Mary Grace and dragged me back to her bedroom.

"Stay here," she said. "Let me just get everyone a little lunch and I'll be right back."

Tossing my hat to the floor, I threw myself onto her bed and wailed into the spread. I wasn't even sure what I was crying about exactly. Joey? My mother? My father? The situation with Enzo? My dying dream of independence? Because I knew now I had to say no to Enzo's offer. How could I move into his apartment when I didn't trust him? Gorgeous looks aside, I hardly knew him, and most of what I did know scared me.

And what if I moved in there and felt ashamed of myself? What if he never managed to break things off with Gina and we could never be seen in public together? What would happen if what we felt for each other now died out as quickly as it sparked? Or what if I wanted to leave, and he didn't want me to? I cried harder, knowing that Enzo would not be a man who gave up his possessions without a fight.

Because I saw quite clearly that's what I would be—his possession.

The door flew open and Bridget opened her arms to me. She sat on the bed and I crawled into them, weeping on her shoulder, a little more quietly. After a few minutes, she squeezed me and stood up, going to her dresser. Pulling a clean white handkerchief from the top drawer, she returned to the bed and touched up my face.

"There, there," she soothed. "Nothing can be all that bad. What's happened, love?"

I took the handkerchief from her and swiped at my eyes and nose. "It's a lot of things. I'm scared and exhausted and overwhelmed, and I don't know what to do, and I feel as though I've made such a mess of my life and Mother would be horrified with me."

"Oh, come on now. She wouldn't, either. She'd be so proud of the way you've handled things at home, Tiny. I know she would. And I think she'd want you to have the chance to get out on your own if that's what you want for yourself."

"You don't think she'd tell me to stop being selfish and stay home where I'm needed, like Daddy did?" My words came out between halting breaths.

"No, absolutely not. If anything, she's up there feeling horribly guilty for leaving us girls to take care of things and be a mother before we were ready."

"She didn't leave us by choice."

"No, of course not. But trust me, motherhood has a way of making you feel guilty about many things you have no control over. You'll see, someday when you have your own children."

I sniffed. "If I have children."

"Why wouldn't you? Don't you want a family?"

"I guess so. I've always been so busy with this one, I've not really thought about my own."

"Never? Not even about getting married?"

"Why would I? I've never been in love the way you were with Vince. I don't even know what love feels like." Fresh tears welled in my eyes, and then spilled over.

"Oh, honey." Bridget circled my shoulders with her arm. "You'll know when you find it. It fills you up, so many good feelings, from your toes to the top of your head, until you think you might burst from it. You won't be able to keep it inside of you—you'll want to shout it and share it and give that person everything you have to give. And it still won't feel like enough, but you'll want to keep trying to show him how much he means to you. And the way he'll love you back…" She sighed. "You'll think it's impossible that he loves you the way you love him, but he'll do everything in his power to convince you otherwise. And love makes you do drastic things—look at what Vince and I did!"

I tried to smile. "Love sounds like a lot of work."

She laughed. "It does take work, I won't pretend it doesn't. Both people have to be willing to make themselves vulnerable, to open up. It's not easy to put your heart out there, to offer it up and ask for another's heart in return. Especially for men—they never know exactly what to say, and sometimes it comes out terribly wrong."

I thought of Joey asking me to come with him to Chicago without even telling me how he felt. Was that what she meant? Should I have recognized unspoken affection in his words? How the hell could I be expected to know? I closed my eyes, sighing. It was hopeless.

"What now?" she asked.

"Joey's leaving."

"And you don't want him to?"

I shook my head. "No, but I had no idea what to say to stop him. He *asked* me last night for a reason to stay, and I couldn't give him one."

"He asked you to give him a reason to stay? And you couldn't think of one?" She looked at my tearstained face incredulously.

I could. I could think of one, and I had—maybe I hadn't been willing to admit it yet, even to myself.

But things change.

"I couldn't *then*." I stood and walked to the mirror over Bridget's dresser, taking in my puffy, splotchy face. "But I think I can now." I turned to face her. "Can the girls stay with you tonight? There's something I have to do."

#

After leaving Bridget's, I went home and took a bath, lingering for a long time in warm water I'd scented with a little vanilla extract. I'd thought about something fancier, like rosewater or lavender, but decided Joey would find vanilla harder to resist.

I needed to be irresistible.

I washed my hair with Cocoanut Oil shampoo and combed it out, then I pinned curls to my head and let it dry. Choosing an outfit was a bit of a problem, since I didn't want to wear anything too fancy but my day dresses weren't romantic at all. After agonizing over it for two hours, I chose a simple navy dress with white piping that had been at the back of my tiny closet all summer since it had a tear near the hem and I hadn't felt like mending it. Locating a needle and a spool of navy thread in my sewing kit, I sat on my bed in my black stockings and white chemise and stitched up the tear.

It wasn't as bad as I remembered.

See, broken things can be repaired. Torn cloth can be mended. Apologies offered.

Feelings declared.

As long as I had the guts to do it.

Around three o'clock, I walked to the streetcar stop and took a car heading downtown. As I hurried on foot to the restaurant, I tried to calm my swirling stomach by reminding myself it was just Joey I was going to see. There was no reason to be scared.

But there is, worried a voice inside me. *He could turn me away, he could tell me I'm too late, or worse—he could tell me I was mistaken about what I felt, or what I imagined he felt.*

But I hadn't imagined it last night, I knew I hadn't. When we'd finally come together on the sofa—well, on the floor near the sofa—it was just as Bridget had described. I'd felt so full of passion and relief and want and need and shock and happiness—so many feelings I couldn't even name them all. But it added up to one thing, and I couldn't stop thinking it.

I was in love with him.

I was in love with him.

I was in love with him.

And I wanted to say it to his face.

My stomach tightened. Would he kiss me when I told him? Would he pull me to him like he had last night? Would he let me tear the clothing from his body? *Will he throw me down and ravage me the way I want him to, and let me ravage him in return?*

The thought was enough to make the muscles in my lower body seize up, and I stopped walking. Closing my eyes, I whispered a prayer.

Dear God, please avert your eyes tonight. Because I'm going to do things to Joey Lupo I have never done before, things I've never even imagined doing before.

Licking my lips, I walked two steps before stopping again and glancing up.

And you might want to cover your ears too. Amen.

#

By the time I opened the restaurant door, I was more than ready to confess my love to Joey and beg him not to follow through on his revenge plan. Pulse racing, I walked past the hostess at the entrance to the dining room and took the huge central staircase up two flights, two steps at a time. By the time I reached the third floor I was winded and my hip hurt but I didn't care. The hallway smelled delicious, and I

181

hoped I wouldn't be interrupting dinner. My hands shook as I knocked on the door.

No one answered.

I put my ear to the door and heard conversation. It actually sounded as if a lot of people were in there. Crap, now what was I going to do? What if his mother had company? The scene I imagined between Joey and I could not take place in front of an audience! Disappointed, I nearly turned around and left, but suddenly the door opened.

"Tiny!" Marie shouted. "I knew I heard a knock! Are you alone? Come on in, honey."

Taking me by the arm, she shepherded me into the living room, where, to my horror, the entire Lupo family was gathered. Adults were sitting on the furniture and young children scuttled around underfoot. A quick scan of the room told me Joey wasn't among them.

My heart fell.

"You all remember Tiny? She's Bridget's sister...." Marie switched to Italian and I caught the words *sposata* and *Vincenzo*, so I figured she was introducing me as the sister of the woman who was married to Vince.

Several people crossed themselves; others nodded and smiled. Marie went on with introductions but I knew I'd never recall anyone's name. I only cared about one person, and I didn't see him here. Just as I was about to ask if he was home, Mrs. Lupo rose from her seat on the sofa and kissed my cheeks. "*Cara*, good to see you. You stay for Sunday dinner."

"Oh, I don't want to intrude on your family dinner, I just—"

"Nonsense, Tiny, you're family," insisted Marie. "And if you've never had Joey's *arancine*, you're in for a treat."

"Joey's what?"

"Sorry. They're rice balls," she said. "And they're delicious."

"No one make them better than me but my Giuseppe," Mrs. Lupo said proudly. "He don't even let me come in there today."

"That's right, Ma. You just rest. Joey can handle the cooking today."

A ball of rice didn't sound that appealing to me, but I would've eaten anything they asked me to in order to stay. *He's here!* I glanced at the kitchen door, which was closed. Would it be strange if I asked to go in there? "Can I help with the meal?"

"Absolutely not, you sit down with us." Marie led me to a dining chair, which had been brought out to the front room. Perhaps she'd heard about my cooking somehow. Helplessly, I sank into the seat and looked around. There were three or four older women, one old man and two younger men that I thought might be Joey's brothers-in-law, and probably five or six kids. I didn't see Joey's other two sisters, Joanna and Therese, and I guessed they were in the kitchen with him.

"I'll let Joey know you're here, Tiny. Can I bring you a cup of coffee?" Marie asked.

"Thanks. But no thank you on the coffee. I'm fine."

She smiled at me and went into the kitchen, and my stomach knotted itself worse than the rags in my hair last night. What would Joey do when he heard I was out here?

A moment later, he pushed open the swinging kitchen door and stood in the frame, staring at me through the arched threshold between the dining room and front room. My heart thumped three times in quick succession. My God, he was so beautiful—his face took my breath away. He had a dimple on his chin. Had I not noticed that before? And the lightness in his brown eyes. The lashes so dark and thick I could see them across the room. The mouth. Dear Lord, *that mouth*. My bottom lip fell open as we locked eyes, and my breath was stuck inside me.

He wore an apron over a blue shirt with his sleeves rolled up and dark trousers. He'd removed his collar and tie to work in the kitchen, and the top button of his shirt was undone. He held a dishtowel in his hands.

I felt paralyzed by the sight of him. How had I ever thought he wasn't the one? I wanted him so badly—I felt it in every nerve ending in my body. But now what should I do? I could hardly take off running, hurdle the sofa his mother sat on, and launch myself at him, which is what I wanted to do. And Joey's face was unreadable; I couldn't tell if he was angry at me for coming or glad to see me. I smiled and raised my hand in a pathetic little greeting, and he nodded grimly and backed into the kitchen again, the door swinging shut behind him.

Shit! That reaction was not in the fantasy of how this moment went.

Maybe he didn't want me here. My throat threatened to close up, and I took several deep breaths. Conversation went on around me, but I barely heard it. It was half in Italian, anyway. I'd have to learn some more words if Joey and I were going to be together.

The thought sent chills cascading down my spine.

Joey and I were going to be together.

The more I thought about it, the more certain I was that it was right. I *knew* him, and he *knew* me. He was part of my history, and I was part of his. We had a lot to learn about each other, still, but I knew at the core of his being was devotion to family, a sense of duty, and a huge heart. I had no doubt he had a vast capacity to love someone, and I wanted to be her.

I have to be her.

Staring at the kitchen door, I wondered how insane his family would think it if I just got up, walked through it, and announced to Joey I was in love with him. It wasn't ideal, but if I had to sit here one minute longer, I was going to go mad.

I stood up.

"Tiny? Can I get you something?" Marie asked.

"Uh, would you excuse me for a moment?"

She smiled and pointed toward the hallway off the dining room. "The bathroom is just down the hall there."

185

"Thanks."

With a longing look at the swinging door to the kitchen, I went through the dining room and down the hall to the bathroom. Once inside, I shut the door and stared in the mirror over the sink, arguing with myself.

Coward! Just go in there and tell him! He probably thinks you're here to berate him for his choices again.

I know, but I'm scared! And his family is here…

Figure it out. You're not leaving until he knows how you feel. If he rejects you, so be it, but you're going to tell him. Tonight. Now.

I racked my brain for another minute trying to think up a plan. Then it hit me—a note, I could bring him a note, or ask Marie to take one to him. It wasn't as good as face to face, but it was something. My heart tripped excitedly as I dug through my purse for paper and pencil, but I came up with nothing. Shit! What could I use?

I had a lipstick and a handkerchief. It would have to do.

Kneeling on the floor, I spread out the white square and clicked the red color up the tube. Biting my lip, I printed carefully. There was no room for error—I only had the one handkerchief. The words would not have the same effect on toilet paper.

I love you.

Should I add an apology? Ask for forgiveness?

No, something told me to just go with one simple message. Joey was intuitive where I was concerned. He would know from those words what I was asking for.

Standing, I clicked the lipstick back down, capped it, and tucked it into my purse again. I folded the note, careful not to smudge my letters.

Deep breath. Now to deliver it.

Be brave, be brave, be brave, I told myself as I walked down the hall into the dining room. Instead of returning to my chair in the front room, I squared my shoulders and pushed open the swinging door to the kitchen.

Chapter Twelve

"Tiny!" Joey's oldest sister Joanna greeted me with surprise. She stood at the center table putting together a huge tray of meats, cheeses, vegetables and olives. "What are you doing in here?"

Joey, who was stirring something in a pot on the stove, spun around and stared at me.

I stared back, unable to speak. He was just so *handsome*—my stomach whooshed at the sight of him only five feet away from me. God, I'd rolled around with him on the floor last night and then let him leave?

"Are you staying for dinner?" Joanna asked. "Joey's making arancine one last time before he abandons his family again for Chicago."

She was teasing, but Joey glared at her over his shoulder before turning back to the stove. Either he was really angry or he just didn't know what to say to me.

"I heard," I said, growing bolder. "In fact, Joey promised me a cooking lesson before he left town, and I'm here to see that he makes good on it."

Joey's body stilled and Joanna laughed heartily. "Wonderful," she said. "I keep telling him he should stay on here and run this place. He's got the knack for it, and it needs someone like him to give it some new life."

"I've got other plans." Joey's voice was firm, and he spoke without turning around. "And today's not the best day for a lesson."

"Joey, don't be rude," scolded Joanna.

"I won't get in your way." I walked over to him. With a glance over my shoulder to make sure his sister wasn't watching, I took one of Joey's hands and pressed the tiny white square into it. "And if it's not the right time for a lesson, that's OK."

Joey looked at me with a confused expression. "What's this?"

"Read it." I pleaded with my eyes before backing away.

"So, Tiny, how's your sister Bridget? I haven't seen her in a while," said Joanna.

"She's well," I answered with a shaky voice. From the corner of my eye, I saw Joey unfold the handkerchief and my heart threatened to bounce out of my chest right onto the olives. *Oh God, oh God, oh God. He's reading it.*

And then he looked at me, his lips parted. We stared at each other for a few seconds, and hope rose in me like a hot air balloon.

But he turned away and faced the stove again, and all I could do was blink back tears in disbelief. *He doesn't want me. I'm too late.* My eyes dropped to the floor before closing.

"Bridget was such a good card player," Joanna went on. "I remember how she and Vince used to beat Tony and me at—"

"Tiny." Joey's voice had a new energy to it. I looked up to see him yanking the apron over his head. "I forgot, I need something from the restaurant pantry downstairs. Will you help me bring it up?"

"I can get it," Joanna offered. "What do you need?"

"No, we'll get it. You watch the sauce," Joey said quickly, rushing over and grabbing me by the wrist. "Come on."

He pulled me out the kitchen door and we flew down the back steps, our feet thumping on the wood as quickly as my heart was beating.

When we got to the bottom of the stairs, Joey pushed open the door to the restaurant kitchen and yanked me through it. I had to run to keep up with his strides and we rushed by several cooks and servers who stared after us in confusion, but Joey didn't stop. "Just grabbing something in the pantry," he called out, pushing open a thick wooden door at the back of the kitchen and pulling me into the pitch-black space. He slammed the door shut.

As soon we were alone, what he grabbed was *me.*

First he pulled me into him, his glorious mouth on mine, his tongue driving between our lips. Then he boosted me up with his hands beneath my bottom and pushed my back against the door. "Wrap your legs around me," he demanded, his breath hot against my mouth.

Heat rushed my lower body as I moved my dress out of the way and locked my ankles behind his hips. He put his hands on the door at either side of my head and pushed against me, and I could barely breathe it felt so good. If it was this incredible with our clothes on, I was going to lose my mind once we were naked and pressed skin to skin. How long would I have to wait? Could we get naked in the pantry?

I was honestly considering it.

"Did you mean it?" Joey asked between frantic kisses. "What you wrote?"

"Yes," I breathed, reluctant to take my lips from his even for a moment. "Yes, I meant it. I *mean* it. I love you. And I'm sorry."

"Shhh." He trailed kisses down my neck. "We don't have time for apologies. God, I love your neck. You smell good enough to eat." He licked and sucked a spot below my ear that made my nipples tingle.

I moaned with impatience. "That feels so good. *You* feel so good." *The pantry it is.* With one hand I reached down between us and rubbed my hand on the erection straining at his trousers. "I want you inside me. Now."

He made a strangled sound, the vibrations tickling my throat. "We can't, Tiny."

I ignored him, undoing buttons, slipping my hand inside his underwear and wrapping it around a

191

cock so big and hard my mouth fell open in shock. "Jesus," I whispered. "Maybe you're right. I'm not sure you'll fit inside me."

Groaning, he kissed me again. "You *are* a little bit of a thing." He brought his lips back to mine. "But I've spent too many hours thinking about you for it not to happen."

"Hours, really?"

"Probably more like months, if not years."

"Mmmm, you should have told me sooner." I slid my hand up and down his impressive length. Maybe it was because Joey wasn't very tall, but I had never imagined he'd be so big. "Oh my God, Joey. How do you keep this hidden?"

"Around you, it's an effort," he managed, clearly struggling for control. He dropped his forehead onto my shoulder and gasped. "Fuck, that feels good. God, I shouldn't say fuck in front of you. Sorry."

"We don't have time for apologies, remember? And you can say fuck in front of me. Better yet, you can just fuck me, how's that?" I squeezed him tighter in my fist.

He picked up his head. "Oh, Christ. Listen, I'm gonna be sorry for a whole lot more than that you if you don't stop doing…what you're doing," he said, alarm in his voice. "I'm going to make a mess of our clothes, and then we'll have some explaining to do."

I laughed, withdrawing my hand and dropping my feet to the floor. "Ok, then we'll save that for later. But I don't want to leave yet…" I pushed the braces off his shoulders and shoved his trousers down at the sides.

"Jesus, Tiny, now what are you doing?"

"Shhh. Just let me." Dropping to my knees, I ran both hands all over his cock. It felt firm and thick and hot. I gripped him with one hand and rubbed the silk-smooth tip with the other. Immediately it was slick with a few drops of liquid warmth. *I want to taste him.*

The moment I put my lips on him, Joey braced himself against the door with two hands again. "Oh, fuck. Oh my God."

I rubbed my lips back and forth over the slippery tip before sliding it into my mouth and swirling my tongue along its velvety surface. I wasn't sure, but I thought Joey's knees might have buckled a little. Then I sucked on it as I rubbed my hands up and down his solid length. Joey inhaled sharply.

"You better stop, Tiny." His voice held a warning.

But I didn't want to stop.

Taking him out of my mouth, I held him in two hands and licked him like an ice cream cone, all around. Then I slipped my wet lips over the top again and took him in as far as my throat would allow, but I was *still* able to wrap my hands around the base. My mind raced ahead to the way he could tear me apart, and my own legs trembled. Slowly I lifted and lowered my mouth again and again, while he breathed heavier and harder and said fuck more times than I'd ever heard anyone say it. Placing one hand on his hip, I braved pulling him into me a bit, not too fast, but at a quicker rhythm. I loved feeling him hit the back of my throat.

"Jesus Christ, Tiny. If you don't stop now—"

I pulled him from my lips with a little pop. "I won't stop, so you might as well enjoy yourself. It's my first time, you know. How am I doing?"

"Oh, *fuck*," he said again as I slid his hot, hard cock between my lips once more. Joey must have given up on bringing things to a halt because he began to thrust into my mouth, tiny little stabs that sent bolts of lust straight between my legs. My underwear was damp and I imagined how fucking amazing it was going to feel to have Joey's unbelievable cock pounding into me. The thought of it had me moaning, my mouth and throat vibrating with sound.

Joey stiffened and gasped, his erection throbbing as he swayed forward. Immediately my mouth was filled with pulsing hot liquid, but I'd been expecting it and didn't stop. I waited until his body had shuddered and stilled and only the sound of his labored breathing could be heard over my fast-beating heart, and then I slipped him out of my mouth and swallowed.

"God, that was incredible. I wish I could've seen you," Joey said when he could speak again, "although it probably would have been over even faster."

"Guess I'll have to do it again sometime."

"Oh, Christ." Joey dropped to his knees in front of me and took my head in his hands. "I've thought about you so many nights, but even my fantasies didn't get this good."

"Really?"

"Really. That was…oh, forget it. There are no words to tell you how that was for me. I'm sorry, I wish I could find some."

"We need to stop apologizing to each other."

He kissed me hard on the mouth. "You're right. We do."

"But we might have to apologize to your mother for ruining Sunday dinner if we don't get back upstairs."

"Just wait. One more minute won't hurt." Joey pulled me in close, laying my cheek on his chest and wrapping an arm around my waist. As he spoke, brushed the hair back from my face with his other hand. "Thank you for coming here today. For writing me that note. For taking a chance on me."

I picked up my head but pressed me to his chest again. "Let me finish. The day I saw you after I got back in town, even before all the stuff with your dad, it hit me how I felt about you. Remember when you pushed me into the dirt at the boathouse? I think I fell in love with you that moment."

I laughed. I did remember that—he'd made me so angry that day, but when I'd pushed him and he'd pulled me down with him, something had stirred within me at the feel of our bodies pressed together. At the time it had just made me angrier.

"And I wanted to tell you, but I just couldn't. I thought you'd laugh in my face, maybe even spit in it."

"I probably would have. Just to spite you."

"But every time I was near you, I felt it like a punch in the gut how bad I wanted you."

"You hid it well," I said. "After that kiss in the boat, I thought there might be something happening between us, but you acted so aloof, as if you weren't even affected. It drove me crazy."

"I've got a good poker face," he said seriously. "That kiss fucking terrified me."

I smiled. "Good."

"*You* terrify me."

"I do?"

"Yes. Because in all my life, I have never wanted to be as close to someone as I want to be to you. I've never wanted to make someone happy the way I want to make you happy. I've never wanted to protect someone the way I want to protect you." He dropped his head to speak low in my ear. "And I've never wanted to do to another person the things I want to do to you. Oh my *God*, the things I'm going to do to you…"

My stomach fluttered at the gravelly intensity in his voice. "What's so terrifying about that?"

"It's terrifying because I think I'm a pretty tough person, but I had no idea how… unprotected you would make me feel. That probably doesn't even make sense."

"No, it does." Wrapping my arms around his torso, I thought about what Bridget said, how you make yourself vulnerable when you love someone, and I knew that's what he meant. "But you don't have to worry. I feel the same. I thought I was going to die of fright on the way over here."

"Why?"

"I had no idea what to expect, after last night. All I knew was that I had to see you and tell you how I felt. Then it would be up to you." I paused. "But I did have a few fun things in mind to persuade you if you gave me any trouble."

Joey laughed. "I was too easy, then."

"I got to do one of them anyway."

He groaned with pleasure at the memory. "That's true, you did. And next it's my turn." His tongue flicked at my earlobe before he took it in his mouth, sucking gently. "But I need more light," he said, kissing down my neck as I arched back slightly. He moved a hand to the other side of my throat and held me against his mouth as he whispered hot words against my skin. "I want to see your body while I worship every inch of it with my tongue. I want to look in your eyes when I get inside you. I want to watch you lose control, over and over again..." He circled the flat of his tongue on my neck before closing his mouth over it and sucking hard.

I think I whimpered.

With a low laugh, he released me. "So now, I'm going to button my pants and we'll go back upstairs, suffer through what is sure to be the longest fucking Sunday dinner in the history of men, and then I will spend the rest of the night—and hopefully a hell of a lot more nights in the future—doing and saying things to you I've only fantasized about."

My belly flipped. "Should I be scared?"

He helped me to my feet and leaned in close. "Terrified," he whispered.

Oh. My. God.

How the hell was I supposed to get through dinner?

#

Giggling like schoolchildren, we raced out of the pantry, avoided meeting anyone's eyes in the kitchen and scurried back up to the apartment. Joanna eyed us suspiciously when we entered.

"I thought you said you were just going to the pantry, Joey Lupo. What did you need there again?" She transferred a huge plate of what looked like meatballs coated with breadcrumbs from the table to a counter near the stove, tossing him a knowing look over her shoulder.

"Uh…" At the sink washing his hands, Joey looked over his shoulder and met my eyes. I had to clap a hand over my mouth to keep from laughing. "I forgot," he said.

"What? What on earth has gotten into you two?" Joanna looked back and forth between us, scrutinized my neck for a moment, and shook her head. "Forget it. I don't want to know." She took the apron she was wearing and threw it at Joey. "Finish these up, the oil is hot. I always overcook them. And Tiny, why don't you help me set the table?"

"I'd be glad to." I couldn't stop smiling. Joanna must have thought we were crazy. "Just let me wash my hands."

In the bathroom, I noticed Joey had sucked my neck so hard a bruise had formed. I slapped a hand on it and laughed silently as I looked at my rosy cheeks in the mirror. After trying unsuccessfully to arrange my collar to cover the red and purple spot, I gave up and went back to the kitchen. When Joanna's back was turned, I flashed Joey my neck and he burst out laughing. I slapped his shoulder and Joanna turned to us, rolling her eyes. "Honestly. We have company for dinner. Pull yourselves together!"

But pulling myself together was out of the question. Just watching Joey prepare Sunday dinner for his family was enough to make my legs quiver and my insides clench. Whenever he turned around and I got a glimpse of his gorgeous face, flushed with heat from the stove or maybe from what we'd done—I nearly swooned.

Had I never noticed the way he moved? Joey didn't have Enzo's height or lithe grace, but his muscular body brimmed with caged aggression, more feral than feline. Even doing mundane things like bending for something low in a cupboard or reaching high on a shelf, or moving from the stove to the icebox to the table, his physicality spoke volumes about the way he'd move when unrestrained by clothing or convention.

I lost track of how many times I licked my lips and crossed my legs, tight.

Somehow we made it though dinner, although I was fairly certain we weren't fooling anybody. We sat next to each other, and neither of us did a very good job of paying attention to conversation. When we weren't sneaking glances at each other or sharing secret smiles, we were just staring at our plates, grinning like idiots, and several times I caught both of us eyeing the clock, willing its hands to move faster so this dinner would end and we could be alone. I don't think I ate more than three bites, although the food was delicious.

"Tiny, how old are you now, dear?" Joey's oldest sister Therese smiled at me from across the table, which had been extended to accommodate all the adults.

"Twenty. I'll be twenty-one next month."

"And are you working or going to school, or does your father keep you busy at home?"

"Well, I've been working for Bridget at the store and I attended nursing school at the University of Detroit for a bit over the last year or so. I'd like to go back, if I can save up tuition money."

"Oh." She took another bite from her plate and chewed thoughtfully. "So you'd like to work a while then, before you have a family?"

"I'm sorry?"

Therese exchanged a look with Joanna. "Do you plan on having a family?"

Joey and I locked eyes for a second. "Uh, I... haven't really thought about it. Not too much, I mean. My own sisters have kept me pretty busy."

"Oh, they should be plenty able to care for themselves by now, shouldn't they? You should start thinking about your own."

"Therese. Leave her alone," Joey scolded. "Tiny can make her own decisions." He scooped another helping of roasted zucchini onto his plate and turned to me. "Can I get you some more?"

I shook my head—I still had a full plate of food.

Joey's sisters exchanged another look.

"So, Joey," Therese said. "Going back to Chicago now that Ma is settled at Marie's, I hear?"

Joey sipped his wine. "That's the plan."

I set down my fork and picked up my wine as well.

"I wish you wouldn't go," Joanna piped up. "I've been trying hard to convince him to stay and run this place, Tiny, but he won't listen to me. Maybe you'll have more luck."

"*Basta*, Joanna." Joey's voice held a warning.

She put her hands up. "Don't get mad, I'm only saying it because I think you'd be so good at it. And it's breaking Ma's heart to have to sell." She lowered her voice to a whisper and gestured toward the other end of the table, where Joey's mother sat with the older adults.

"Nice. Pin Ma's broken heart on me now, too." Joey forked a rice ball with vehemence.

"Well, anyone can see she doesn't want to give it up. It was her dream to run this place. And Papa's too."

He glared at her and she dropped the subject. But from that point on, something in Joey was less than it had been. He still smiled at me affectionately, and in his eyes was a promise of what was to come later, but I knew that he'd been bothered by the mention of his father. We hadn't even spoken about what he planned to do with the information Enzo had given him. And what about Chicago? Would he still go? Dread settled in the pit of my stomach. I'd just gotten him. Would I lose him already?

Over cannolis and coffee, I brooded a little. As thrilling as falling in love was, Bridget and Joey were right—it left you vulnerable, unprotected. Had I offered my heart to Joey only to have it broken when he left? Was he still bent on seeking revenge for his father, or would I be enough to convince him to leave the past alone?

Then there was the other kind of danger—the kind that might occur once Enzo realized I'd been less than truthful about Joey and me. And even though I hadn't exactly lied, I knew he wouldn't see it that way. Fear seized me, and my coffee cup clattered against the saucer in my hands.

Joey put his fingers on my wrist, and I looked into his concerned eyes, which made me hot through the center all over again. Lord, when would his family leave? I was desperate to get him alone. At the same time, we both glanced behind us at the clock on the mantel. When we realized it, we shared a genuine grin, and my hands steadied.

And when his relative finally gathered their hats, purses, and children to leave, my pulse began to race.

Chapter Thirteen

Goodbyes in Joey's family were endless. Endless! Just when I thought he'd hugged and kissed the last relative goodbye, there was another one standing with open arms. All of them hugged me and kissed my cheeks as well, and his mother made Joey promise to send me home with a big plate of food for my father and sisters. She and Marie's brood were the last ones out the door, and she looked around longingly at the front room before going.

Her eyes were shiny with tears, and I understood. It must have been hard for her to move out, leaving all the relics of her past here. She pointed a finger at Joey. "You take her right home. I don't want her father to think I don't raise a gentleman."

"Ma, for cripes sake." Joey turned her by the shoulder and steered her out the door into the hallway. He looked back at me. "I'll be right back. I'm just going to see them off."

Nodding, I watched Marie's two young children scurry out after them, which left only Marie and I in the front room.

"I'll be down in a minute," she called, securing her hat to her head. Then she turned to me, a smile on her lips. "He's crazy about you."

I dropped my eyes to my shoes. I'd worn my nicest ones, the black heels, even though they were a bit much for Sunday dinner. "Oh, I don't know."

She laughed. "Yes, you do. I could see it last time you were here, but today it's even more obvious. I think even Uncle Manny could see it, and he's half-blind!"

A smile took over my face. "Well, maybe we won't have to hide it anymore."

"Oh, I hope not. You'd be perfect together. Just don't let him go running off to Chicago, for heaven's sake. What's that boy thinking? He should stay here. Then Ma wouldn't have to sell this place."

"We…we haven't really had a chance to talk about that yet." And I really wasn't terribly interested in doing a lot of *talking* tonight.

Swoosh went my insides.

I crossed my legs at the ankle and stood with my thighs pressed tightly together, as if Marie could read my mind. On a small table to my right, the statue of the Virgin Mary eyed me suspiciously.

"He's just always been so stubborn, you know. He gets an idea in his head and thinks he has to follow through with it, even if it's the dumbest idea ever. And we all know he's had plenty of those!" She shook her head. "*Madonna*, the things he put Ma through… Some days I know she's just glad he's still here." She crossed herself and put her hand on my arm. "If he loves you, and I believe he does, then he'll stop all that gang nonsense and settle down."

"I don't know that I'm—"

She waved a hand in the air to stop me. "Forget I said anything. Honestly, my mouth runs away from me sometimes. And I'm terribly emotional these days." Dropping her hand to her pregnant belly, she laughed. "I fall apart at the drop of a hat. Just you wait and see—oh, for Pete's sake, I'll stop pestering you now—"

"Impossible." Joey appeared at the door. "You'll never stop pestering. But unless you want to walk home, you better go down and get in the car."

"I'm going, I'm going. Good night!" She waved and disappeared down the stairs.

Joey shut the door after her and leaned back against it. "They know."

I smiled. "They know."

He reached into his trousers and pulled out the handkerchief with my lipstick confession on it. "I left this on the counter by mistake. Joanna found it."

My eyes went wide, and I clapped my hands to my face. "What!"

Grinning ruefully, he said, "I was just so excited to get you alone, I thought I put it in my pocket, but I guess I didn't. She gave it to me just now."

"After showing the rest of your sisters, no doubt." My cheeks were searing hot under my palms.

"No doubt."

"Does it bother you?"

"Not at all. I want to tell the entire world I'm in love with you"—and here my breath stopped—"but not tonight."

My insides went from simmer to full boil. *We're alone.*

Inside a heartbeat we lunged for each other, locking together from mouth to hip. Joey lifted me right off my feet, and I twined my legs around him. Walking backward, he tried to move us around the sofa and into the dining room, but since neither of us was willing to break off the kiss and look where we were going, we kept bumping into things. First we pushed the sofa and coffee table out of place. My leg knocked a lamp off an end table and his elbow nudged a painting of Jesus off the wall. We thumped the china cabinet and the contents rattled precariously.

We didn't care.

Finally, we got through the dining room into the hall and Joey was able to walk forward and get us to his bedroom. He kicked the door shut with his heel as I cupped his jaw in my hands and kissed his top lip, then his bottom lip, running my tongue along them, sucking them into my mouth, rubbing my lips back and forth against them. "God, I love your mouth," I murmured. "I can't stop thinking about it. And your hands—I've never told you how much I love your hands."

Heading straight for the bed, he crawled up on it with my arms and legs still wrapped around him. When he finally lowered his weight onto me, kissing me long and deep, I thought I would scream if I couldn't have him naked, fast.

I tugged at his sleeves and he knelt, one knee on either side of my hips, to free his arms from his braces and wrest his shirt from his body. Then he grabbed his white athletic tank from the back and yanked it over his head as I watched, mesmerized by the rough masculine movements, the twitching muscles in his arms and chest, the way the lines on his abdomen undulated as he breathed. My fingers flew to them and I sat up, running my palms over his hot, tight skin. Grabbing his hips, I brought my mouth to his stomach and brushed my lips across it. Planting soft kisses on hard muscles, I placed a hand between his legs, thrilling at the feel of the bulge there. He sucked in his breath, and I looked up at his dark eyes and tousled hair, my heart pounding.

"Should we draw the curtains?" I asked.

"No. I want to see you." He moved backward on his knees and stepped off the end of the bed. "Come here."

I crawled to the edge.

He reached for me. "Stand up."

I did as I was told, feeling the damp heat between my legs as I stood.

Taking me by the shoulders, he turned me around, and I felt his hands at the back of my neck and then working their way down the row of buttons to the sash at my hips. When the dress was loose, I slipped my arms from the sleeves and let it drop to the floor. I turned to face him wearing just my chemise, step-in, and black stockings rolled thigh-high.

The sight of him shirtless and hungry-eyed was too much for me to bear. I reached for his trousers. "Wait," he said, grabbing my wrists. "I want to look at you."

"I want you to do more than look."

"I promise you, baby, I will. Raise your arms." Reaching for the bottom of my chemise, he lifted the simple white garment over my head and set it aside. Then he crouched in front of me and pulled down my step-in. I held his shoulders and lifted one foot from them, then the other. But when I went to remove my stockings, he took my hands again. "Leave them on."

I stood before him, naked except for my stockings and shoes. I'd worn less in front of another man, but somehow this felt like the most naked moment of my life. Every inch of my skin was sizzling as he swept his ravenous eyes over my body. The tension inside me pulled tighter. My nipples grew harder under his stare, and when he licked his lips, I felt a flutter between my legs as if he had licked me there.

"You're so beautiful," he whispered, bringing his hands to my hips and guiding them to the bed. Then he dropped to his knees and slid his hands down my thighs, pushing them apart.

My mouth fell open.

Moving his hands to the small of my back, he pulled me toward him, closing his mouth over one breast. I inhaled deeply when he dragged his tongue around my nipple in lazy circles and flicked it with tiny strokes. When his teeth closed on it, I grabbed his head, filling both hands with his thick, wavy hair. Heat rushed my center, which was cradled against his stomach. "Now, Joey. Please."

He switched his mouth to the other breast and ran a hand up my ribcage to the first, torturing me with his thumb and fingers in a way that made me pant.

Jesus, does he want me to beg?

Because I would.

"You're making me crazy," I whined, looking down at his lips closing over my nipple. Leaving the drapes open made everything he did even more arousing because I could see it.

"I'm just getting started." His breath tickled my wet skin. I shivered at the cool tingle on my breast and the nearly unbearable hum between my legs. He moved a hand to the top of my thigh, his thumb brushing my sensitive outer folds, and then softly circling over my clitoris.

"Yes," I whispered. "Yes, yes."

"Now lie back." He brought his hands to my shoulders and gently laid me back. Standing for a moment, he leaned over me and kissed my neck, a moan rumbling from his throat. "Mmmmm, I can't get enough of the way you smell." He kissed his way down my chest, stopping to take each breast in his mouth again before continuing down my stomach. "Or the way you taste." Planting a kiss on each of my hips, he licked a circle around my belly button before trailing his hot, wet tongue in a line straight south. "I want to taste you everywhere."

He took a moment to slip my heels off my feet. Then he dropped to his knees between my legs again, hooked his arms beneath my thighs and pulled me to him.

When he put my knees over his shoulders, I flung my arms over my head.

At first, I felt only cool air at my center, and then warm air as he exhaled. My body was coiled so tight as I waited for his mouth on me I thought I might explode the moment I actually felt it.

I nearly did.

Slowly he licked his way up the silky wet seam at my center, and my legs trembled. When he reached the top, he lingered there and swirled circles with the flat of his tongue before flicking lightly with the tip. Then he did it again, and I felt the telltale tightening of my muscles in my lower body. I'd never fought an orgasm before, but now I knew the exquisite torture Joey had experienced in the pantry. Soft, tender strokes every which way, barely-there flicks that left me panting, loops and lines and curves...*Jesus, he could write poetry with his tongue.*

"Joey," I whispered. "Please..." But then I couldn't even form a coherent sentence, because he chose that moment to take the tiny bud, tingling with heat, into his mouth and suck, and at the same time he slipped his fingers inside me. My heels dug into his back. My toes pointed like a ballerina's. My hands flew to the bedcovers next to my hips, clawing them in tight fists. He pushed his fingers deep inside me and somehow twisted them to press upward on some magnificent spot I never even knew existed. Working me with both fingers and mouth, he brought me to a peak so high, so hot, so deliciously fraught with tension that I thrashed my head from side to side, my mouth open in a silent scream. When he moaned against my throbbing center, I couldn't hold on any longer. Letting go completely, I was rewarded with an orgasm so powerful, my body went completely stiff with ecstasy as I yelled his name between gasps.

For a moment afterward, I didn't move or speak or even breathe. Joey kissed each of my inner thighs before standing and removing the rest of his clothes. When I propped myself up on shaky elbows and saw him naked before me, I nearly cried with need to feel that body on mine. In the light of the setting sun that crept in through the open drapes, his skin was golden, and every muscle was etched in line and shadow. He had the kind of body immortalized in marble by Italian sculptors four hundred years ago.

Plus an erection that would rival the leaning tower of Pisa.

He picked up one of my legs, set my foot on his chest and removed my stocking. Then he kissed each of my toes, my instep, the inside of my ankle, the back of my knee.

Oh, dear God—how had I never imagined how good his lips would feel at the back of my knee?

He picked up my other leg and repeated the process.

I was shaking. "Joey, inside me. Now."

He grinned crookedly. "You're always so bossy." Leaning down to kiss me, he hooked an arm around my back and dragged us up the bed. "But I'm going to give you what you want." He stretched over me. "Just the way you want it. I promise."

I felt like screaming at how good his skin felt against mine, how blissful his weight was on my body. Our lips and tongues molded, sucked and stroked, and my hands traveled all over him—his back, his arms, his face, his hair. His cock pushed into my thigh and I wanted it pushing into me. I scooted down, knees wide, putting him exactly where I wanted him.

"Tiny." Joey braced himself on his hands above my shoulders and looked down at me with serious eyes. "Are you sure?"

"Yes, yes, yes." I punctuated the words with kisses pressed to his chin, his jaw, his neck.

"I wasn't planning for this, so don't have anything to, you know…stop things from…"

"I don't care. I love you, and I've never wanted anything more than this. We can be careful."

"I'll go slow." Reaching between us, he guided himself to the entrance of my body, and I bit my lip. Would it hurt? I closed my eyes and willed myself to open up to him. *It's Joey*, I kept thinking. The first couple inches slid in, tight and hot with friction. *Oh, God. More. Now.* I put my hands on his ass and pulled, panting with frustration.

Joey let out a strangled groan. "I'm trying really hard to be a gentleman here."

"Fuck being a gentleman." I opened my eyes and dug my nails into his skin. "I want you all the way inside me, and I want it now."

At that his eyes blazed with heat and he rammed into me. I gasped and threw my head to the side, crying out at the sudden shock of being stretched so tight and filled so completely. He pulled out and then slammed into me again, hitting a place so deep inside I was rendered soundless, if not actually mindless. Then he slowed down, and with several long, deep thrusts, he taught my body how to take him in, how to surrender completely to being pushed to the limit.

When I could finally breathe again, I looked up at him. His eyes were open, and in them I saw the battle between how much he loved me, which meant he didn't want to hurt me, and how badly he wanted to pound his cock into me until I screamed for mercy. And even though a sliver of fear still lingered that my body wouldn't be able to handle it, I knew what I wanted. When he hit the deepest spot again, I held him there; then I tilted my hips so I could feel pressure exactly where I needed it.

"Right there, baby?" he whispered, rocking into me with smaller movements.

"Yes," I breathed, closing my eyes as pleasure triumphed over pain. Staying deep within me, he circled his hips in a slow, steady rhythm. Within seconds I grew wetter and hotter and the buzzing tension began building again at my center.

"Fuck, you feel so good," he said. "I had no idea, no fucking idea…"

"Me either," I breathed. "I used to dream about your hands on me, and even that was enough to make me crazy."

"I used to think about exactly what I'd do to you if I had the chance. All the ways I'd touch you. How you'd feel wrapped around me. How you'd smell, how you'd *taste*. There isn't one fucking inch of your body I haven't dreamed about. And now you're here," he said, his voice going hoarse, "and you're so fucking beautiful." He began to move faster, harder, and I wanted it, I wanted everything. My lower body hummed and coiled, and the euphoria began to overtake me again. "Oh my God," I panted, completely lost to him. "Oh my God, you're so good. You're so gorgeous and big and hard and you feel so fucking good."

Over and over he pounded into me, hard and steady and deep. His mouth came close to mine but we were so out of our minds with rapture we couldn't even kiss—our eyes locked and our breath mingled and our bodies moved together in an unceasing, savage rhythm.

"Christ, I'm gonna come," he said through clenched teeth. "So if you don't want me inside you—"

Gripping him tight to my body, I lifted my head and pressed my mouth against his. "Don't leave me."

With powerful, primal sounds coming from deep within his throat, he pumped himself into my body even harder and throbbed inside me, over and over again. Powerless against the torrent any longer, every cell in my body burst open in a glorious fireworks of light and sound and color. I turned my cheek to the bed and cried out, short, repeated screams of pleasure beyond belief that echoed through my head and were probably loud enough to burst Joey's eardrums.

The moment our bodies stilled, Joey propped himself on his elbows and dropped his head to mine, pressing his damp forehead to my temple. "Tell me this is real." His chest rose and fell from exertion.

I finally closed my mouth and licked my lips. "I hope it is."

He put his lips on my cheekbone and held them there, and inexplicably, a lump jumped into my throat.

What the hell? I was perfectly happy and my body was totally sated. What on earth could I possibly have to cry about? But the tears were coming, and there was nothing I could do about it. Completely mortified, I felt one slip from the corner of my eye, and a sob wrenched itself from my chest.

Joey picked up his head. "What's wrong, baby? Oh God, I should have pulled out."

I grimaced through tears. "No, no, it's not that. Nothing is wrong, I swear to you, nothing." Sniffing, I squeezed my eyes shut. "This is so dumb, I don't know why I'm crying because I'm actually really happy right now."

Laughing gently, he wiped a tear from my cheek. "Doesn't look like it."

"I know! That's why it's so dumb!" Incredibly, I continued to sob, and even though Joey must have thought I was crazy, he wrapped his arms around me and flipped us onto our sides, keeping our bodies joined.

"Come here. It's OK."

I circled his torso with my arms and buried my face in his chest, loving the warm feel and smell of his skin and detesting myself for ruining this moment. Weeping like a child, I let him hold me. Joey kissed the top of my head and rested his chin there, rubbing my back with slow, soothing strokes.

Thankfully, my insanity passed and I was able to stem the tears after a minute or two. "Sorry." I sniffled. "I suppose I'm just emotional."

"You? Emotional over me?" He squeezed me tight. "Then go ahead. Cry all you want, doll."

I slapped his chest and picked up my head to look at him—messy hair, smiling mouth, and best of all, eyes full of content and adoration. No one had ever looked at me that way before. "No, I'm done now."

"Oh. Well, in that case..." He deftly slipped underneath me so I was sitting on his hips, my hands propped on his chest. We were still connected, and I felt him stirring inside me again. "God, you're so beautiful. Even with a red nose and puffy eyes."

I slapped my palms over my face. "Don't look at me."

He took my wrists and brought them to his chest again. "Let me." As his eyes took me in, they warmed with unmistakable intention.

I wouldn't have thought we had anything left.

I was wrong.

Chapter Fourteen

"I said sprinkle, not pour!" Joey rolled his eyes when he saw how much sugar I'd dumped over the apples in the pan. "That looks like an avalanche."

"Well, sorry," I said, laughing. "I thought I was sprinkling. And you never said how much to sprinkle so I just guessed." He was teaching me how to make a dessert called Brown Betty Pudding, but I wasn't a very good student. Who could blame me? We'd been in his bedroom for hours working up an appetite, and Joey was still shirtless and barefoot, wearing only a pair of black pants that sat low on his hips. He'd offered me one of his shirts to wear, and I insisted on the one he'd worn today. I couldn't stop sniffing it.

"Jesus. Give me that." Joey took the canister of sugar and spoon from my hands. "Go into the pantry and get cinnamon and bread crumbs."

"You're supposed to be giving me a lesson. How am I going to learn to cook if I miss what you're doing?"

"I'm just adding the butter and salt. Did you at least manage to heat the water?" He looked skeptically at another pan on the stovetop.

"I think so. Even I can't screw that up."

Joey didn't look convinced of that, but I was in too good a mood to bicker so I went to the pantry. I found the cinnamon pretty quickly, but didn't see any bread crumbs. "Joey?"

"Yeah?"

"I need help."

A moment later he appeared in the pantry doorway. "Geez, Tiny, I'm beginning to think even lessons from me aren't going to help you. Maybe you should stick to rum running."

"Ha, ha. I found the cinnamon but I don't see any bread crumbs. Are they in a box?"

"Oh. No, they're probably in a container but it might be labeled in Italian." He glanced up at a shelf and pulled down a canister with something handwritten on the front. Flipping the lid, he peeked in, a curious expression on his face. "Aha."

"Bread crumbs?"

"Nope." He reached in and pulled out…a gun?

I jumped back. "Jesus, Joey! What is that and why is it in your pantry?"

He set it on the shelf and closed up the container. "It's a pistol. My dad's. He used to keep it in there just in case, and my mom probably forgot about it. Don't worry. I won't shoot you, even if you ruin dessert."

I stuck my tongue out at him, and he swept me up in one arm and kissed me. "But if you stick that tongue out at me again, I might have to end this lesson early."

I grinned and kissed him back. When he let me go, I couldn't resist hopping from one foot to the other out of pure joy. Joey laughed at me as he set the empty canister back on the shelf and retrieved the bread crumbs.

"What are you doing, dancing?"

"Why not?" I skipped out of the pantry and twirled around in the kitchen on bare toes. "I just realized on Friday night how much I love dancing. I never knew it before I danced with you."

Joey followed me out, groaning and shaking his head. "You have no idea how hard that night was for me. First of all, seeing you there, in that dress, and thinking you were there for someone else." He set the bread crumbs on the counter. "And then when you asked to dance with me, I couldn't resist saying yes even though I knew it would be a bad idea."

"What are you talking about? It was a great idea!" I bounced around some more and sniffed the inside of his shirt again.

"I didn't think so at the time. I wanted to throttle you for getting me so worked up and thinking it was all a big joke."

"I didn't think that at all." Coming up behind him, I wrapped my arms around his waist and laid my head on his back.

"I didn't know that at the time. Move for just a second, OK, baby?"

I let go of him and watched as he added more butter, sugar and cinnamon atop the bread and poured the hot water around the edges of the pan. He stuck the whole thing in the oven, closed the oven door and took me in his arms again.

"I figured you'd only asked me to make Rosie mad. But even then, I couldn't resist the chance to get that close to you."

I snuggled into his chest. "I'm glad you couldn't. But I didn't ask you only to make Rosie mad—although that was an added benefit, I'll admit. I asked you because suddenly the thought of you leaving the club was unbearable to me."

He kissed the top of my head. "Well, I'm glad you asked, although keeping my hands to myself during that song was the hardest thing I've ever done. No—I take it back. Leaving your house last night was the hardest thing I've ever done."

Squeezing him tighter, I shivered. "I can't believe I let you go. After you walked out the door, I cried myself to sleep."

"You slept?"

I looked up at him and smiled. "Maybe just a little."

He swatted my backside and I yelped in protest. "Hey!" I said, scooting backward with my hands on my butt. "You were the one out with someone else. What went on with Rosie after you left the club? And why were you out with her again last night?"

Joey's eyes lit up. "Jealous?"

I shrugged. "Maybe a little."

"You've got nothing to worry about. I took her straight home both nights, and dancing at the club was the closest I got to her."

"It was close, all right." I sniffed, crossing my arms in front of me. "I thought I'd have to peel her off you."

"Well, you didn't. And *you're* here now, not her. In fact, you're the only girl I've ever had here."

"Really?"

"Really."

"But there were…other girls before me?" It was the kind of question no girl should ask, but I had to torture myself a little.

Joey shrugged. "No one like you."

"What's that mean?"

"It means no, you're not the first girl I've ever been with, but you are definitely the first girl I've ever loved."

I took a deep breath. I'd assumed I wasn't his first—and I hadn't been a virgin before seven o'clock tonight, either—but it was still hard to hear. I didn't want to think about his hands or lips or any other body part on any other girl. And I didn't want to be with anyone else again either. Ever.

Suddenly Bridget's scheme to marry Vince made perfect sense to me. Now that I knew what it was like to love someone this way, I understood the desperation they'd felt to be together. *And Joey is planning to move away.* We hadn't even talked about that yet. But before I could bring it up, he took me in his arms and kissed me, slow and deep and sweet.

221

"I promise you," he said, resting his forehead on mine. "I've never loved anyone the way I love you. I never will."

And then my throat closed up too tightly to talk anyway.

When the pudding was ready, we sat at the table and ate right from the pan with one spoon. The combination of apples and butter and sugar and cinnamon and shirtless Joey was enough to make any girl moan.

As we neared the bottom of the pan, Joey began smearing it on my lips and licking it off. Then he got more creative, unbuttoned my shirt, and dripped some on my neck, down my chest and onto my stomach, all of which he ate off my body with great relish. He was just licking some from my inner thigh when we heard the front door open and slam.

"Which rosary, Ma? There's more than one here. Well, I don't know, so you might as well come up and get it. Cripes, Joey didn't even turn off all the lights before he left. Is he still here?"

Joey and I exchanged a panicked look. His mother and Marie were here, and we were stuck in the kitchen, nearly naked, and I was covered in sticky Brown Betty sauce! If they caught us, there was no possible way to explain ourselves, and we couldn't get to the bedroom without coming out of the kitchen.

"Come here!" he whispered. Grabbing my hand, he pulled me into the pantry and shut the door silently. I saw nothing but blackness and heard nothing but the gunfire of my heart.

"I'm scared," I whispered.

"It's OK." Joey put his arms around me from behind. "She just forgot her rosaries and made Marie bring her back to get them."

"This late at night?"

"She's religious. Something must have been keeping her up. They'll be gone soon."

I hoped he was right. We heard nothing for a few minutes, and I began to relax.

So did Joey. "Your neck is sticky," he said. "Mmmmmm." He began licking the back of my neck, and within seconds, I felt him hard against my lower back. A quickening in my stomach made me close my eyes and squeeze my thighs together.

"Joey, no."

"Yes." He took his arms from me for a moment and I heard him unbutton his pants. Then he lifted the bottom of the shirt I wore. I had nothing on underneath it.

"Spread your legs," he said in my ear. My resolve splintered.

I widened my legs and he pushed up into me from behind, lifting me onto my toes and nearly off the floor. Gasping, I had to bite down on my lip to keep from crying out. My hands braced against a shelf.

I would never look at a pantry the same way again. Ever.

Leaning forward slightly, I whimpered softly as he began to move in and out of me, slow and rhythmic. I moved my hands to a higher shelf and my right fingers brushed something cool and metal—the pistol.

Oh my God, sex and guns in the pantry. This is my life now. Somehow the thought of it spiked my desire even more.

Then he reached around and rubbed me from the front with wet fingers, and I forgot about everything else but his magic hands.

"Does it feel good, baby?" he whispered.

I nodded, unable to speak and terrified I was going to scream with pleasure before we were through. The way Joey moved, it was as if he could read my mind, or at least my body. He knew exactly where I wanted to be touched and how. He knew the perfect way to angle himself inside me and how fast or slow I wanted him to go. He knew just what words to whisper in my ear to rattle my insides and make me clench around him. Grabbing the shelf harder, I sucked in my breath and willed myself not to yell or moan or even squeak.

Suddenly we heard voices in the kitchen.

Joey put his other hand over my mouth.

"What is all this mess? Dear God, Ma, don't even come in here."

Oh my God oh my God oh my God. This it is. This is my punishment, isn't it? This is the consequence of all my awful behavior, my sins, my criminal activities. I'll be caught fucking Joey in the pantry by his mother and she'll faint from the shock and never let us be together again and Joey will hear her call me all sorts of names and oh God he's still hard, how is that possible and why don't they just leave, I'm so hot and tight and tingly and yes, yes, yes—just like that...

224

At the slam of the front door, Joey started moving again. "They're gone," he said. But he kept the hand over my mouth, and I sucked two fingers between my teeth and ran my tongue along them. He groaned, shoving into me deep and hard and driving me to insanity with his other hand. "God, you're so wet," he breathed. "And so tight, and so hot, and I never want to stop fucking you, ever…"

Neither of us lasted another ten seconds.

#

"You have perfect toes," Joey said. We were in the bathtub, leaning back against opposite ends, and Joey held my foot up near his face. We'd locked the heavy wooden bathroom door, of course, but we'd also been smart enough to throw the deadbolt on the apartment's front door as well. No need to invite further calamity.

"Thank you." I bowed my head graciously, and rubbed my hands along the backs of his calves, which were alongside my hips. We'd already soaped and rinsed each other, and now we lingered in the warm water, pruney and damp-haired but happy.

"And your feet are so small," he went on, holding up his hand to compare the size. "Do you have to shop for shoes at a children's store?"

I pulled my foot from his hands and kicked water at him. "*Still* with the jokes about my size? Are you ever going to let me be?"

225

Joey laughed deep and loud, the sound echoing off the black and white tiles. "I'm sorry, I'll be nice." He fished underwater for my foot again. "Let me have it back."

I let him, and he brought it to his lips and kissed it. "I love your toes." He sucked on each one, sending a frisson of delight up my leg. "I love every perfect part of you. Except maybe your temper."

I sat up and pushed a huge wall of water at him, which soaked his face and splashed over the edge of the tub. Sputtering with laughter, he wiped his eyes and grabbed for me. "You got water in my mouth!"

"Serves you right."

Grinning, he got me by the arms and traded places with me, pulling me against him, stomach to stomach. His skin on mine felt so warm, so good, it melted every other feeling but contentment. I kissed his collarbone and rested my head there, tracing the letters of my name on his chest with one finger. His arms wrapped around me, and I closed my eyes. We were back to our comfortable silences.

But in a moment, icy fingers of fear crept beneath the warmth. How could I let him do something I knew might get him arrested or killed?

"Joey, please don't do it." The words slipped out before I had an argument prepared.

He said nothing.

"Don't. Please. I'm scared."

"I have to, Tiny. I have to do it—I promised myself."

"But things are different now."

226

"Between you and me they are. But that situation hasn't changed." His voice had a harder edge to it than I'd heard all night.

"If you kill that man, Joey—"

"When I kill him."

I picked my head up. He looked at me, but his eyes were cool. "You're scaring me."

"This is who I am, Tiny. This is part of me."

"That's not true—what you *are* is not what you do. You're so much more than that."

He was silent a moment, staring into the water. "If you think I can let this go, you don't know me very well."

"But I do! I *do* know you well." Agitated, I got to my knees between his legs. "I know you love your family more than anything in the world, and I know you would do anything for them. I love that about you." Taking his hands in mine, I squeezed them tight. "And I know you were hurt when your father died, but—"

"I was in the car. Did you know that?"

Confused, I just looked at him.

"I was in the car waiting when my father came out of the station."

"Oh, honey." My heart broke for him.

"I heard those bastards come around the corner and start firing. I heard my pop yell for me to get down, and you know what I did? I fucking ducked. I covered my head and ducked down below the window like a frightened kid."

"You were scared! Anyone would've been scared. And you did what your father wanted you to do—you stayed safe!"

He shook his head, his jaw protruding. "His gun was on the seat. I could've grabbed it then. I could've shot back. I could've done something. But I didn't."

"You might have been killed yourself, Joey!" Slamming my eyes shut, I lowered my chin, my lower lip trembling. "Is this how it's always going to be?"

"I promised myself. I promised myself that day that I would never be a coward again. That I would stand up for myself and my family the way he would have. I can't let it go."

"Not even for me?"

He met my eyes, and I saw how hard it would be for him to actually say it. "I love you. You know I do."

"But not enough."

"Don't say it like that."

Sighing, I toppled forward onto him again, fitting myself against his body as tightly as possible. "I love you too. But I don't know if I can live like this…I'll be constantly worried about your safety, wondering if today's the day your luck will run out." I snaked my arms behind his lower back and ran my palms along his solid muscles.

His arms locked around me, and he brought his lips to my head as he squeezed me close. "Don't give up on me. Please."

I didn't want to. Bridget said love was work, and I was willing to work hard at loving him. And I'd never felt as cherished as I did lying there in Joey's arms—I knew he loved me too. But the fear that he could be taken from me at any moment on any average day was enough to give me pause. "Are you still going to work for Sam Scarfone?"

Joey's body stiffened. "I don't want to. But I have to tread carefully. I didn't get a chance to talk to Angelo today, but he's gonna be looking for me. If he goes to Sam—"

My eyes flew open. "I thought you said he wouldn't!"

"I said I didn't see how it would do him any good—but I don't put anything past anyone, and you shouldn't either."

Biting my lip, I kept rubbing Joey's back. Between Sam, Angelo, and Enzo, there were going to be a whole hell of a lot of gangsters unhappy with us. "And after that? Are you still going to Chicago?"

"I was planning on it. But that was before."

"Before what?"

He kissed my head again. "Before I got your note."

I couldn't help smiling at the memory of that. "I'll never forget the look on your face when you turned around."

"I'll bet it was something else."

"It was."

I felt him swallow. "Come with me. To Chicago."

"I thought you said you wouldn't ask me again," I teased, but my heart was pounding.

"This is different. That was a stupid thing to do that night. I should have told you how I felt but I was mad and jealous and I didn't know what to do. But now I do."

"You do?"

"Yes." He took me by the shoulders and held me away from away from him slightly. "Marry me, Tiny."

My jaw fell open. "What?"

"Marry me. I love you, and I want us to live together."

I stared at him with wide eyes. His hair was wet and disheveled, and his jaw was shadowed with whiskers, but his eyes were serious and I saw no sign of a teasing smile on his lips. But still, this was *Joey*. "Is this a joke?"

That brought a smile. "No! I'm serious. I've never been more serious. Will you marry me? Please?"

"Oh my God, Joey." All I could do was stare at him in disbelief. He was *proposing* to me? In the *tub*?

He shimmied my shoulders lightly. "You're starting to make me nervous here. I've asked three times now."

"I'm sorry, I'm just so surprised—I never imagined—I mean, I love you, but—"

"But what? You think that will change?"

"No, but—"

"You want to keep living with your father and sisters?"

"Definitely not."

"You didn't enjoy yourself in the pantry—I'm sorry, pant*ries*?"

My cheeks flushed. "I did, but—"

"Then say yes! You're killing me." The look in his eyes was equal parts love and torture. God, he was so handsome. And strong and sexy and loyal and hard-working and funny and sweet and smart.

He adored me. I adored him.

I chewed my lip. "I want to, Joey. I want to say yes."

"Then say yes. Vince always said we'd end up together."

A rueful smile stretched my lips. "I heard."

Yes was on the tip of my tongue.

He'd be a great father someday.

Our own apartment.

And the cooking. My God, the cooking.

But then I thought about other things. Guns. Bullets. Coffins.

Vince was hardly older than Joey was now when he was killed.

I took a breath. "I have to think about it." At his devastated face, my heart ached. "It's not that I don't want to marry you, Joey." The words *marry you* made my stomach flip.

"But you're not ready? You think you're too young?"

"Not exactly. I mean, yes, we're young, but my parents were young. Bridget and Vince were young."

"Then what? You think I don't love you enough?" he went on, getting more worked up. "Because I do—I love that you've spent your life taking care of your family. I love that you were willing to risk your life to keep them safe. I love how smart you are,

231

how brave you are, how beautiful you are. I love that you want to get out and see the world—I do too. You want to go to school? I'll find a way to pay for it. I love that you want to be a nurse."

"Joey—"

"Let me finish. I love that you can't reach the high shelf in the pantry. I love that you can't cook worth a damn. I love the expression on your face when I catch you staring at me. And I love the way you came here tonight, ready to fight for me. Now I'll fight for you." He kissed my lips. "Say yes."

My throat was so full. "I can't."

His face fell. It hurt me not to give him the answer he wanted, but I didn't want to end up like my sister, widowed at twenty-three with three children.

"Look at Bridget, Joey," I said softly. "She asked Vince to do something else with his life, but he wouldn't. He said nothing would happen to him."

"When you came here tonight, you knew all this about me," he said sadly. "And yet you still came."

"I couldn't stay away." Of that I was positive.

"And we haven't been careful tonight."

I grimaced. "No, we haven't."

"So what happens now?"

"I don't know, Joey. I need to think." Laying my head on his chest again, I shivered. "We should get out. The water's getting cold."

#

232

I spent the entire night in Joey's bed, wrapped in the warm comfort of his arms. We didn't talk any more about Chicago or getting married. I slept a little, my body spooned in the curve of his, his right arm tucked securely around my chest, our right hands clasped. From time to time, I brought my lips to his fingers and kissed them. And more than once I awoke to find him brushing the hair back from my face or rubbing his lips against my shoulder. Countless times, my throat tightened and tears threatened, but there was no point in crying.

Toward dawn, Joey rolled onto his back and I turned over, propping my head on my hand. With his features in repose I could see the little boy he'd been in that First Holy Communion picture. I saw the devil-eyed mischief-maker who'd stolen my underwear. And I saw the full-grown man who wanted to spend the rest of his life making me happy, if only I'd let him.

My gaze wandered down his body, exposed to the waist, and my belly tightened at the sight of his chest, his stomach, the line of dark hair trailing from underneath his belly button. My hands itched to touch him again. My insides felt hollow with need again. If I'd been wearing underwear, it would've been damp again.

I sighed. There was no use pretending I could stay away from him—I knew better.

Joey was who he was. And he was offering himself to me, everything he had. His heart, a home, a family, a life together.

What more could I ask him to give?

By sunrise, I'd made up my mind.

Chapter Fifteen

"Joey," I whispered, gently shaking his shoulder. "Wake up. The answer is yes."

"Hmm?" Joey's brow wrinkled and he sniffed but didn't open his eyes.

"The answer is yes. I'll marry you." Saying it out loud made my entire body radiate with excitement.

His eyes opened and he turned his head to look at me. "Did I hear that right?" He sat up and shook his head in disbelief. "Did you say yes, you'll marry me?"

I nodded. "Yes. I'll marry you. I'll *marry you*, can you believe that?" I slapped his shoulder. "After all the years of your mean old short jokes and my giving you lip?"

Pure elation lit his features, and he tackled me, throwing me down and raining kisses all over my face. "I love your lip. You can give it to me any time you want."

I rolled my eyes. "That's not what I meant."

"God, Tiny, do you really mean it?" He stopped and looked down at me, and I threw my arms around his neck.

"Yes. I really do. I want to marry you. I want to be your wife." I laughed. "That sounds so strange—your wife. You're gonna have a wife!"

"You're damn right I am." He kissed my lips. "I knew you'd come around."

I circled his neck with my hands and pretended to choke him.

He flipped to his back and set me on top of him, straddling his stomach. "Tell me again that you'll marry me."

"I'll marry you. Now enough talking." Reaching behind me, I took his cock in my hand—it was already hard. I raised an eyebrow. "Already? I just woke you up thirty seconds ago!"

He grinned. "Better get used to that. Every morning."

"Every morning? Yes, please."

Grinning, he shimmied down so my knees rested on either side of his head, and without further warning, buried his tongue inside me.

I tipped forward, clutching the headboard with white knuckles, and wondered how I'd ever thought I needed anything or anyone else to feel alive.

#

A couple hours later, we sat in the kitchen—dressed properly, this time—drinking coffee and eating eggs and toast. *This is what it will be like*, I thought, staring at Joey's hands as he brought his coffee cup to his lips. I grinned involuntarily.

"Happy?" he asked.

"Yes. But I still can't believe how much things have changed in just one day."

"Or one month," he said. "A few weeks ago, you couldn't stand me. I lost track of how many times you told me to go to hell."

I lifted my chin. "I make no apologies. You can be very exasperating sometimes."

"Well, I suppose enduring your temper is a fair price to pay to have you for breakfast—I mean, at my breakfast table."

I brought a forkful of eggs to my mouth. "And I'll put up with your teasing if you'll cook for me. I've decided I'm not going to learn how."

"That, my sweet, is a relief to both of us."

I glared at him, but my gaze softened when he glanced at the clock. It was going on nine, and we'd have to part soon. "So what will you do today?" I set down my fork.

"I need to talk to Angelo first thing, convince him I can pay him off in whisky hauls."

"Will you tell him the truth?"

"I don't have a better story, so yeah. I guess so."

I nodded. "I can help you with the whisky."

Joey shook his head. "You're done with the whisky business, doll. You're going back to school, remember?"

"Telling me what to do already?" I arched a brow at him.

"Sorry. But I'll be the bootlegger in the family, OK?" He stood and carried his dishes to the sink to rinse them.

"What about…the other thing?"

Without turning around, he said, "What about it?"

"Are you still going to do it?"

He didn't answer right away. "I don't know."

Hope surged within me. "Really?"

He turned off the faucet and stayed where he was. "I'm reconsidering."

"Oh my God." I jumped out of my chair and rushed to him, circling his torso with my arms and pressing my entire body to his back. I didn't say anything else, didn't want to push further. Just knowing he was having second thoughts was enough.

"I had a dream this morning, after we fell back asleep. After you said yes."

"You did?"

"About my dad." He swallowed hard before continuing.

"Tell me about it."

"We were sitting up on the roof like we used to do, like I did with you that one time."

"Oh?"

238

"And he was smoking a cigarette just like he used to, and he gave one to me and told me not to tell my mom. But I was grown, and I knew he was dead, so I told him, 'You're not supposed to be here.' And he said, 'I have to tell you something.'"

My arms prickled with gooseflesh. "What did he tell you?"

"This is the weird thing. I thought for sure he was going to say something about killing the man who shot him, tell me not to do it or something. But he didn't."

"He didn't? What did he say?"

"He said, 'Teach them about stars.'"

"Teach who about stars?"

"Well, at first it wasn't clear who he meant, and I was confused. The dream ended there, but ever since I woke up, I've been thinking about it, and I think I know what he meant."

"You do?"

"Yeah." His voice caught, and he turned in my arms to face me. Brushing my hair back from my face, he said, "I think he meant my children. Our children."

I couldn't have spoken even if I wanted to.

"And I got to thinking, if anything were to happen to me…" He struggled to finish the thought. "Anyway, I understood better what you meant when you talked about Vince and your sister. I don't want that to be us."

"Me either."

"I haven't made up my mind completely yet, but that promise I made to myself seems less important

239

today than it did yesterday. And I know I gave up all that money just to find out who it was, but you know what? It doesn't matter. What matters is you."

I smiled up at him. "You mean it?"

"Yeah. I do. I can't promise to get out of the business right away, but I'll do everything I can to make things right with Angelo and get out clean. It'll be hard, and I'll miss the money, that's for sure—"

"I don't care about money."

He smiled. "You don't want a nice ring?"

"No." I pursed my lips. "Wait, yes I do."

Laughing, he hugged me close. "Don't worry. I'll find a job that makes decent money. Who knows, maybe my sisters are right and I should stay here take over this place."

My heart thumped happily. "You should! You should!"

"I'll think about it. Right now I should take you home and then settle up with Angelo." I couldn't see his face, but I heard the dread in his voice. "God, I wish I'd never hijacked that stupid shipment and stolen those drugs."

"No sense thinking that way." There were plenty of things I wished I hadn't done either, but regrets never helped anybody. "Let's look ahead, OK? We've got a lot to do."

We finished the breakfast dishes together before Joey drove me home. We were quiet on the way, each of us thinking about the conversations we had to have today and dreading them. But I wasn't one to wait around chewing my fingernails when there was something unpleasant to be done. I wasn't looking forward to turning down Enzo's offer and explaining the sudden existence of a fiancé in my life—especially since I'd made such a big deal about his—but it had to be done. No use putting it off.

And maybe he wouldn't even be that angry. After all, he didn't love me. Ours had not been an affair of the heart, only of the body. We barely knew each other. Certainly, we had enjoyed each other physically, but he could have any woman he wanted—it wasn't as if I was the only one who could please him. And half the time I drove him crazy anyway. By the time Joey kissed me goodbye and promised to call me later, I was certain I could explain things to Enzo in a way that would have him positively glad to be rid of me.

#

The house was empty when I got home, and I skipped up the stairs to my bedroom humming a tune. As soon as I was cleaned up, I walked down to Bridget's. I couldn't remember the last time I'd walked with a spring in my step, but I practically bounced along the sidewalk toward the store. It was sunny and hot, and even though I knew the humidity would do awful things to my hair, I didn't care. I was still wearing my navy blue dress, which was perhaps a bit wrinkled from spending the night on Joey's bedroom floor, but I had clean undergarments on and anyway, each little crease in the skirt reminded me of him. I started humming again.

When I turned the corner into the alley, I noticed Daddy's sign above the garage door was gone, the one that read Jack's Auto Repair. I saw no sign of activity and wondered if the Prohees that had questioned him had given up on the case or still lurked around town trying to investigate. It was an impossible job. Nobody I knew obeyed the dry law, and I was certain there were very few people who wanted to risk the ire of the big mobsters who now bootlegged most of the booze around here. Too many stories in the papers these days about where you might end up if you ratted on them.

Spying a produce truck behind the store, I grinned like an idiot. The day I'd first heard Joey was back in town, he'd helped Bridget unload produce at the store. He often helped her out if Martin wasn't available, and for free too, or maybe just for a sandwich or bowl of soup. Bridget said he wouldn't take money from family. At the time I'd rolled my eyes and declared him a dope, but now I understood him better. Family meant everything to him.

I'd be his family soon.

I may have squealed just a little at the thought.

Letting myself in the back door, I headed through the stock room and into the front, where Molly was teaching Mary Grace to use the cash register, and Bridget's boys were stacking candy behind the counter. "Good morning, everyone," I chirped gaily, stopping to ruffle the dark hair on my nephews' heads.

242

They both blinked as if they didn't recognize me. My grin widened and I patted Molly on the shoulder and tweaked Mary Grace's turned-up nose. "Bridget upstairs?"

"Yeah," said Molly, her brow furrowed. "Where were you?"

"At Joey's," I answered. My body felt lighter than the air around it. I'd nearly forgotten what it was like to tell the truth.

"All night?" Molly's eyes were wide.

"Uh huh."

"Tiny, guess what?" Mary Grace either wasn't surprised at that or it didn't faze her. "Molly's teaching me to work the register and Bridget says she'll pay me if I work some hours at the store each week!"

"That's great, poppet. You'll catch on in no time." I ruffled her hair. "I'll be down in a little bit." Tossing them one last smile, I sailed back into the stock room and up the stairs to Bridget's apartment, leaving Molly in open-mouthed stupor.

The back door was open and music drifted into the stairwell from her radio, a piano waltz that took me back to the night Joey and I sat on the roof.

Teach them about stars.

My belly whooshed, and I grabbed onto a chair back for balance. We would. We would teach our children about stars and planets and history and geography. We'd have a map of the world and show them where their Daddy was born, where their grandparents had immigrated from. Joey would teach

243

them to cook meatballs and tomato sauce and *arancine*, and I'd teach them—

I frowned for a second. Well, I'd think of something to teach them.

And I didn't want children yet, anyway. Quickly I put a hand to my stomach, closed my eyes and mumbled a prayer asking God to forgive Joey and me for throwing caution out the pantry door—and the bedroom door, and the bathroom door, and the kitchen door—and to grant us some time together before starting a family. Not that we deserved much pardon; we'd been completely reckless. And if it happened, it happened. I was stunned to realize I'd be all right either way.

"Bridge?" I called, fighting the maniacal grin that seemed to have taken up permanent residence on my face.

"In here," she hollered from the boys' bedroom. I wandered back and found her stripping the sheets from the beds. "Monday. Laundry," she reminded me. "Although I don't know how I'm going to get these sheets to dry, it's so darn humid outside." She was sweaty from the exertion of housework and wiped the back of her wrist across her forehead. Finally she eyed me curiously. "You look happy."

"I am."

"You're positively glowing," she observed, coming around the bed to examine me closer. "What happened with Joey?"

"I told him I was in love with him."

She gasped. "You didn't!"

244

I smiled even wider at the shock on her face and rocked back on my heels. "I did."

"What did he say?" The grin on her face nearly matched mine.

"He said he loved me too."

Bridget clapped her palms to her cheeks. "I don't believe it."

"And," I went on, twirling around before backing up to the dresser and leaning back against it dramatically. "He proposed."

She gasped again. "I don't *believe* it!"

"Believe it." I had no ring to show her, but I didn't care. "I accepted."

She sank onto the bed, her hands still splayed on her face. "Of course you did." She shook her head. "I don't *believe* it. Vince was right all along."

"He must have seen something we didn't."

Finally she dropped her hands and lowered her chin to shoot me a look. "Everyone saw something you two didn't. Mary Grace saw it, for cryin' out loud."

"She did?"

Bridget nodded. "Yes. You weren't fooling anyone but yourselves." She fanned her face. "Well. Well. I just can't seem to think straight."

"I know the feeling."

She smiled. "Have you told Daddy?"

It was the one thing capable of turning my smile into a grimace. Well, that and the thought of the conversation I had to have with Enzo. But I wouldn't think about that now. "No. I wanted to tell someone who'd be happy about it first."

"I think he'll be happy," Bridget said carefully. "He likes Joey. Always has."

"He likes me at home better, though."

She stood. "Leave Daddy to me. If he's anything less than glad for you, I'll take him to task. The girls are old enough to manage the house and themselves at this point, and you deserve to be happy."

"Thank you." I rushed forward and threw my arms around her so forcefully, she staggered backward. "I'll need all the help I can get."

She laughed and squeezed me back. "Want to wear my wedding dress?"

"Oh, Bridget, really?" I held her at arm's length as my excitement soared. Bridget's wedding dress was beautiful.

"Of course. It'll have to be hemmed of course, but I think it will fit you." Her lips tipped up. "We got married fast so no one would notice an expanding waistline."

I groaned. "Hopefully I won't have that problem."

"Hopefully?" Her face went white. "Does that mean—Frances Kathleen O'Mara, have you gone crazy?"

"Never mind about that." I breezed toward the door. "Let's pull your dress from the trunk so I can try it on."

#

Twenty minutes later I stood before the cheval mirror in Bridget's bedroom wearing her wedding dress. She brought a hand to her mouth, fighting tears. "It's beautiful on you, Tiny. It really is."

I caught her eye in the mirror and smiled. "Thank you. I loved it on you, and I'm so grateful you're letting me wear it. You're sure it's OK to alter it a bit?" The fit wasn't terrible, since Bridget was small-framed too, but the length would need to be taken up and the side seam taken in. It was a simple gown, made by a friend of our mother's. Cream-colored lace, three quarter sleeves, rounded neckline. A wide peach-colored satin sash emphasized my small waist and almost made it look like I had a few curves, and the lovely skirt fell in three fluttery lace panels to the floor. On me the final tier puddled a bit, but Bridget knelt at my side and examined the seam where the bottom panel was attached.

"This won't be too hard to fix, Tiny. If I can't do it, I'm sure Mrs. Hobbs would do the work for a reasonable price. She'll like knowing it's being worn again." She looked up at me. "Want to try on the veil?"

I clapped my hands together. "Yes!"

Bridget got to her feet and dug in the trunk we'd lugged from the back of the cedar closet. The veil was boxed and wrapped in tissue paper, and I gasped when she pulled it out. From a thick crown of beads and lace hung a floor-length swath of lace-trimmed tulle. Bridget stepped behind me and settled the crown on my forehead; it rose to a peak in the center. The tulle fell over my ears and shoulders, flowing down my back to the floor. I wouldn't be able to trim it, but that was all right. When I walked it would drift behind me like gossamer, just like it had on Bridget.

I turned to her with tears in my eyes. "I'll take good care of it all."

Fussing with the veil, she blinked back her own tears. "I hope you and Joey are as happy as Vince and I were the day we married." She met my eyes. "And I beg you to convince Joey to choose a different path than his father."

I put a hand on her arm. "I'm trying. I am."

"Good." She went behind me to begin undoing the column of looped buttons running up my back. "And I hope he's more patient than Vince was trying to remove this dress—he tore off three button loops trying to get it off me!"

I grinned at my reflection in the mirror. "I wouldn't count on it."

Chapter Sixteen

Joey called that afternoon around four. "Hello," I said, my insides warming at the sound of his voice.

"How's my girl?"

"Good. Busy."

"Oh?"

"Monday is laundry day," I explained. "The girls are helping me get it all done."

"Good. Make sure they know how to do it because pretty soon you won't be there to show them."

"You sound awfully confident about that, Mr. Lupo."

"That's because I know something you don't, Mrs. Lupo."

My belly turned completely inside out and the floor seemed to tilt beneath my feet. "I'm not Mrs. Lupo yet, you know," I said with the widest grin imaginable. "You shouldn't count your chickens and all that."

He laughed. "These particular chickens, I'm gonna count."

"Tell me what you know that I don't."

"Uh uh, that's no fun at all. You'll just have to wait."

"Joey!" I stamped my foot on the hallway rug. "Tell me, please!"

"And what will I get in exchange for this information?"

I blushed, peeking out the kitchen window to make sure the girls were still outside hanging things on the line. "I'll do that thing," I whispered into the phone.

"What thing?" He whispered too, although he was probably alone.

"You know..." I wobbled one leg. "The thing I did in the restaurant pantry."

"Oh, *that* thing! In that case, I'll tell you—I went down to the garage and spoke to your father."

I stopped fidgeting. "What? You did?"

"Yes. I know you're not the old-fashioned type, but I know my pop would've wanted me to ask your dad for his blessing."

"And did he give it?"

Joey paused, and I closed my eyes, imagining the difficulties we'd face if my father put up impediments to the marriage. I wouldn't care—I was going to marry Joey whether Daddy said it was OK or not.

"He gave it."

"Oh, thank heavens," I breathed. "One less thing to worry about."

"He was surprised but not entirely shocked. And he grumbled about you leaving home a little, but in the end he shook my hand and wished me luck putting up with your sharp tongue and foul temper."

"He did not say that!"

Joey laughed again. He'd probably never stop teasing me, but I could live with it—in fact, I'd learned I couldn't live without it. "So should I come over now?" he asked.

"Now?"

"Yeah. You know. So you can do that thing."

I clucked my tongue. "Good-bye, Joey Lupo. I'm going now and I don't care if you ever call back."

He was still laughing when I hung up.

#

Within the hour, the doorbell rang. *Joey, you fiend.* I was upstairs putting some clean clothing away and raced down the stairs to answer it, smoothing my hair and my blouse. Just before reaching the door, I slowed down as if I'd walked leisurely and put my fingers on the handle. *Relax. He doesn't need to know you're out of your mind with need for him.*

I pulled it open and blinked in surprise—it wasn't Joey. It was a delivery man from a Gianni's Flowers, and he was carrying a long white box. Over his shoulder I spotted his truck, painted dark green with white lettering on the side.

My heart tripped with excitement. My first flowers from Joey!

"Miss O'Mara?" the man asked. When I nodded, he held the box forth. "These are for you."

"Thank you." The box was thick and heavy, and I didn't bother trying to hide my grin. "Have a good day."

He tipped his cap at me. "You too, miss."

He jogged back to his truck, and I shut the door, squealing inwardly. Rushing into the living room, I set the box on the coffee table. When I pulled off the lid, I gasped.

Joey had send me a dozen gorgeous red roses. My hands rose to my heart and then reached to finger the thick, velvety crimson petals, the emerald stems dotted with thorns, even the crinkly white paper. They were the most beautiful flowers I'd ever seen—so pretty they didn't even look real!

Peering closer, I noticed an envelope nestled among the blooms. When I reached for it, I saw that something else was in there too. Lying at the bottom of the box was a smaller parcel wrapped in white paper. I gasped again—had Joey gotten me a wedding gift already? The box looked too big to be a ring, but with Joey, you never knew...he might be teasing me somehow. Maybe he'd placed the ring in a bigger box just to fool me. But wouldn't he want to offer something like that to me himself?

Immediately I glanced out the front window. Was he lurking in the bushes, ready to pop out and surprise me?

Grinning like mad, I pulled the envelope from the box and tore it open. Inside was a plain white card, upon which words were written in spidery black script. As I read, the smile faded from my face, my lips going slack.

The flowers weren't from Joey.

Dear Miss O'Mara,

I'm delighted to find that you are excellent at keeping a secret.

I hope you have had time to consider my offer, as I am anxiously awaiting your acceptance, and I hope the flowers will help persuade you to give it sooner rather than later. I am also returning something that belongs to you, as you mistakenly left it in my motorcar the other night. Wear it tonight when you visit me at the Statler, just the way you wore it in your bedroom. Telephone the number below to reach me so we can arrange a time…although I believe you still have the key.

Until then,

E.D.

Enzo DiFiore. I didn't even have to open the smaller box inside the flowers—I knew it contained the diamond choker. The one he'd bought for Gina as an engagement gift. The one Raymond had stolen from his brother's room and sent to me as a misguided attempt at affection. The one I'd worn in my bedroom, naked everywhere else, when Enzo had snuck in and surprised me. My face burned.

253

You can't think that way. What's past is past, and the escapades with Enzo are part of your history. It was just a bit of fun, just a girl reacting to being responsible her whole life, and finally getting a taste of freedom.

A taste? OK, more like a meal.

A really attractive five-course meal, served searing hot.

But I wasn't the type to wallow about my mistakes, even if Enzo was the biggest one I'd ever made. No sense in it. What made sense was that I needed to tell him right away that I wouldn't be accepting his offer, that what was between us was done, and he should focus on Gina or switch his attentions to some other girl he could control easier than me. But not tonight. Not when we were alone in that apartment with darkness pressing at the windows. I was in love in Joey and trusted myself not to give in to Enzo, but I didn't trust that Enzo would be a gentleman. I'd barely managed to put him off last time we were there together, and he was not a man who liked being told no.

I needed to phone him right away. But I felt that I'd have more success in person than on the telephone convincing him not to be angry, and I had to return the key and choker. A daytime meeting would be best, or one in a crowded location. Would he agree to see me on my terms?

Chewing my lip, I went to the telephone and dialed the number. I wondered if it was the number to the apartment at the Statler and got my answer when the hotel switchboard operator came on the line.

"Mr. Enzo DiFiore, please," I requested.

"One moment, thank you."

While she made the connection, I wondered briefly what a switchboard operator made. If I didn't return to school right away, I'd have to get some sort of job. I didn't much relish the thought of sitting in a small room plugging wires all day long, but maybe as something temporary, it would do.

"Hello, darling." Enzo's deep, smooth voice sent a chill down my arms. This wouldn't be easy.

"Hello. Thank you for the flowers."

"You got them."

"Yes, they're beautiful."

"They'd better be. And the necklace was inside?"

I glanced nervously at the box on the coffee table. "Yes. It's there."

"Good. Otherwise I'd have to have a word with the florist."

I laughed uneasily.

"Will you come tonight?"

"Actually, I can't tonight. I have to...stay with my sisters."

Enzo clucked his tongue. "You see, darling, this is why you need to accept my offer. No girl as tempting as you should be alone in her bed at night."

"I—I can't tonight. I'll be with my family."

He sighed. "Tomorrow, then?"

"All right. Tomorrow."

"I'll be at the club."

"I'll come there." The club—perfect.

"Wear the necklace, Tiny. And plan on staying."

The connection went dead.

#

That night we ate together as a family for the first time since the day Bridget and the girls returned from vacation. She came over a bit early to give me a hand in the kitchen, while Molly and Mary Grace took the boys outside to play in the yard.

Actually, Bridget did most of the work in the kitchen. I sat at the table doodling my name and Joey's on a piece of scrap paper when I was supposed to be writing down Bridget's method for frying pork chops.

Tiny Lupo.

Frances Kathleen Lupo.

Mr. and Mrs. Joseph Lupo.

Huh, what was his middle name?

"Are you writing this down?" she barked at me for the tenth time when she caught me staring into space.

"What? Oh, yes. Egg. Bread crumbs." I scribbled it down. *Bread crumbs…* Of course, my mind wandered to the pantry and nothing Bridget said got through after that. Eventually, she gave up.

"You're not listening to a word I say," she complained over the hiss of frying meat.

"I'm sorry, I'm too distracted. And besides, I think Joey will be doing the cooking for us."

"I hope so, otherwise you're going to starve." She shook her head. "Just set the table, will you?"

Happy to oblige, I set eight places around the table and even hummed a tune while I worked. Bridget laughed.

"My, my. Such a difference in you, Tiny O'Mara! Just look what love does!"

I stuck my tongue out at her, but even my tongue reminded me of Joey and I got lost in dreamy thoughts again. Would he come over tonight? I'd gone almost twenty-one years without seeing him every night, but now the prospect of a single night without him seemed unthinkable.

When Daddy came in I held my breath, wondering what he'd say to me. But he said nothing unusual, just poured his customary evening whisky and poked his head out the back door to wave at the boys. Bridget and I exchanged a glance. I'd told her what Joey told me, and she was thrilled that Daddy wasn't giving me trouble like he'd given her. But he wasn't exactly jumping for joy either. I couldn't help being a little disappointed—it wasn't that Daddy was the type of father to be effusive with praise or affection. But when he felt strongly about something, he got worked up, and it seemed to me this was something he should feel strongly about, one way or another. I'd almost rather have an argument than silence.

Bridget called everybody inside and they took turns washing up at the sink. We sat down and Daddy started to say grace. With my eyes closed and head lowered, my mind began to drift again, but it snapped to attention when Daddy said, "And now, Lord, a word about my Frances Kathleen."

From the corner of my eye, I saw Bridget peeking at me from the corner of hers.

"She's borne the load around here for a while since her dear mother departed, and today I gave my blessing for her marriage, even though it will be a struggle without her. Please be with her and Joseph in their marriage and help us get along without her here. And, Lord, let her know that I'm proud of her and if her mother were here, she'd want nothing more for Tiny than the good man she's chosen. Amen."

"Amen," everyone echoed. Everyone but me—I couldn't speak quite yet.

"Tiny," breathed Molly, staring at me from across the table. "Are you and Joey getting married?"

I looked at Daddy but he was already reaching for a pork chop. Evidently that was all the fanfare my news was going to get, but it was enough for me. I'd take quiet approval and a reluctant admission of pride over his blustering any day. Flashing Molly a smile, I nodded.

"But—but..." she stammered. "It's so soon."

"Sometimes, Molly," I said, reaching for the potatoes, "you don't realize a thing is staring you in the face until you're hit over the head with it."

"Joey hit you?" Mary Grace asked, her eyes wide. "That doesn't seem like him."

The three older sisters at the table burst out laughing. "Not really, poppet. It's just a way to say

Joey had been there all along but I didn't realize how we felt about each other until now."

"Oh." She gave me a smug face. "Well, *I* could have told you how you felt about each other. It was positively obvious to *me* all along."

I grinned and reached for a pork chop. It was the nicest supper we'd had as a family in a long time. We talked a little about the wedding, although I didn't have any details the girls cared about yet but for the dress I'd wear. Daddy said business was going well at his new location, and I tried to read his face, wondering if the gambling arrangement was working out, but he kept his eyes on his plate. When he was finished, he retired to the front room with his whisky to read the paper, and I left him alone. If he was satisfied with his life working for a man like Angel DiFiore, so be it. I wanted nothing to do with it. My only hope was that he'd bring home enough money to take care of the girls, and when they were ready, pay for their schooling. I might have to enlist Bridget's help to convince him to do it, but I'd worry about that later.

Molly and I did the dishes after supper, and I was still drying when there was a knock on the front door. Mary Grace pulled it open, and a moment later I heard Joey's voice.

"Hi." I rushed into the front hall. He looked even more handsome than I remembered, if that were possible, even though he only wore work clothes and the old floppy cap.

"Hi." He removed the cap and came forward to kiss my cheek. Mary Grace elbowed Molly and the two of them stood there beaming like idiots.

"Scat, girls," I told them. "Go finish the dishes."

"Oh, just a minute," Molly scoffed, stepping toward Joey and offering a hug. "We heard the news, Joey, and we're really happy. Congratulations."

Joey hugged her, giving me a surprised look over her shoulder. Mary Grace, not to be outdone, threw her arms around Joey and Molly's waists.

"Well, thank you." Joey laughed as he embraced both girls. "Just what I always wanted—more sisters."

"OK, you said your congratulations, now away with you. Finish the dishes." I pointed a finger toward the kitchen.

"Sure will be nice not to hear that anymore, won't it?" Molly said to Mary Grace as they headed down the hall.

Rolling my eyes, I turned back to Joey. The way he looked at me—like he was barely able to keep his hands to himself—sent my heart pounding. Before supper I'd changed into a peasant blouse and an old blue skirt, but he looked at me as if I wore diamonds and silk. *Or maybe nothing at all.* Simultaneously, we glanced to our left, where my father sat reading the paper only ten feet away.

Then we grinned at each other. "Can you come for a ride?" he whispered.

"Maybe." I raised my voice and called to Daddy. "Is it OK if I go for a ride with Joey?" Daddy nodded without lifting his eyes from the paper, and my excitement ratcheted up ten notches. "Thanks."

I grabbed my purse off the hall table and followed Joey to his car. It wasn't quite full dark yet, and the warm air was filled with all the sounds of a summer night. Soft breeze, noisy cicadas, tinny music from a phonograph drifting through an open window. Joey opened and closed the door for me before getting in on the driver's side. The moment his door was shut he grabbed my face and pressed his lips to mine, his tongue sliding into my mouth in a way that told me exactly what he was thinking. Blood rushed to my center.

"God, I've been thinking about you all day," he whispered, putting our foreheads together. "And I can't go another hour without your body next to mine."

I put my hands to the back of his head and pulled him to me, my pulse racing faster and faster as the kiss grew more frenzied. I lavished the attention on his lips and tongue I wanted to lavish on other parts of his body.

After a moment, he groaned. "We can't do this here."

"Let's go to your house," I said breathlessly.

He grimaced. "Can't go there either. My Ma and Marie are there packing up come things she forgot in the attic. She keeps coming back," he whined.

I thought fast. Where could we be alone? "The boat house. You still have a key?"

Without a word, he started the motor and tore down the street. My head was thrown back against the seat and the wind rushed to meet me, and I laughed, the air around me crackling with energy.

On the short drive to the boathouse, I didn't bother to keep my hands off him. Unbuttoning his pants, I freed his hot, hard erection and tantalized him with my fingers and palms, the backs of my hands and the inside of my wrists.

"Jesus, Tiny. I can barely drive." Joey gripped the steering wheel hard.

With a wicked grin, I lowered my head and licked him like a lollipop.

"Oh, fuck, now I really can't drive. Oh my God. Oh Christ. Where the fuck is that boathouse, I can't even remember the way right now."

I laughed with him inside my mouth, the hum from my lips making him even harder. Tasting the salty sweetness of his imminent release, I took him deeper, relishing the feel of him at the back of my throat.

He must have remembered where the driveway was, because my head thumped the steering wheel as the Ford traversed the pocked dirt road that led down to the dock. Giggling again, I sat up. "Ouch. Guess I better stop for a minute."

He parked under the willow tree and grabbed my hand, hauling me out of the driver's side and racing for the boathouse without even shutting the car door. At the boathouse entrance, he fumbled with the key.

"Hurry," I whispered, wrapping my arms around his torso and kissing his back.

Finally the lock gave. The moment we were inside we tore frantically at each other's clothing, our lips and tongues and teeth colliding hungrily. The short amount of time that had elapsed since we'd last had our hands and mouths on each other was completely out of proportion with the appetites we'd built up. With impatient fingers I pushed the braces from Joey's shoulders and shoved the buttons of his shirt through their holes. He managed to get my skirt off before shrugging off his shirt and pulling his undershirt over his head. Giving up on the tiny buttons on my blouse, he bent and yanked my underwear to my ankles. I kicked it off and jumped up, twining my stocking-clad legs around his waist.

When he licked his fingers and reached low, I opened my mouth to tell him he needn't bother, I was already wet, but then his fingers were rubbing me, inside and out, and all I could do was sigh with pleasure.

Satisfied he wouldn't hurt me, he moved toward the door. I cried out as he shoved his cock inside me, slamming my body against the wood. My eyes rolled back in my head and I dug my nails into his skin. But he didn't stop. Again and again, he drove me into the wall with powerful, deep thrusts, shocking me with his violent need to fill me so completely.

When I regained the capacity to respond, I covered his face with feverish kisses. Between gasps, I breathed his name, pulled his hair, licked and sucked his neck, his mouth, his tongue. And when he put his hands on my ass and altered his angle just enough so that I rode him tighter to his body, the rock hard base of his cock rubbed me just the right way. I clutched him hard with arms and legs. "Right there," I whispered against his lips. "Fuck me right there. Yes, yes, yes." Something deep inside me was tightening and coiling in a way I'd never experienced. It wasn't only just the delicious friction between our bodies; it was some hidden place in my body he was able to reach this way, and I had no words, no thoughts, no voice for what he was doing to me.

Higher and higher I climbed as he moved with utter abandon, until my muscles clenched and pulsed around him. Starbursts of color exploded in front of my eyes and I moaned his name over and over through the shimmering waves of bliss.

"Fuck, I can feel you," he whispered. "Oh my God, I'm gonna come so hard."

"Do it," I panted. "Now, Joey. I want to feel it, *now*."

Slamming me back into the door again, he groaned long and hard as he poured into me. I felt his shuddering release as deeply as I'd felt my own and exploded once more, the delicious rippling at my center lingering even longer than before.

Joey dropped his forehead to my shoulder. I hadn't even realized my eyes were closed until I opened them and the colors disappeared. One by one, my senses returned. Beyond Joey's dark hair, I saw the glow of the moon through the high windows. I felt the damp heat of his shoulders under my hands. I heard our heavy breathing as our lungs recovered and smelled the musty wood of the boathouse walls. Lowering my lips to his neck, I slipped my tongue through them and tasted the salty warmth of his skin.

"You keep doing that, I'm gonna have to pound you into the wall again." Joey's voice was muffled in my shoulder.

"Promise?"

He turned his face into my neck and inhaled deeply. "Mmmmm. Yes."

"Good, because I liked it."

Joey chuckled before picking up his head. "I used to wonder what you'd be like. I had a feeling you'd be a firecracker."

"And? Am I a firecracker?"

"Doll, TNT's got nothing on you."

I laughed. "I'll take that as a compliment."

"You should."

"I used to wonder what you'd be like too."

"Yeah?"

"Yeah. And I used to touch myself all over, imagining my hands were yours," I whispered.

I thought his eyes would pop from their sockets. "Really?"

"Really."

"Maybe you'll show me sometime."

"I'll show you right now."

Joey staggered backward as if he'd been shot. "Oh my God, Tiny. You're killing me." Keeping me hoisted around his waist, he dropped to his knees on the cement floor, and then onto his bottom. My knees came to rest beside his hips and he leaned back on his elbows. "Show me," he said.

I bit my lip. Was he serious? Down on the floor, the shadows were thick, and I could barely make out his expression.

But then I felt him stir inside me. "Show me," he said again.

Oh, what the hell.

Slowly I unbuttoned my blouse while he watched. When it was undone completely, I did the same with the tiny row of buttons down the front of my chemise. With each new inch of my skin exposed, he grew harder. I let the blouse slip from my shoulders, but kept the chemise on, open at the chest. My thighs were pale above the tops of my black stockings. When I looked down, I saw the place where our bodies were joined, and a rush of arousal swept over me. My skin tingled. Involuntarily, I clenched around him.

He grew harder.

I brought my hands to my breasts, kneading them as I began to rock my hips a little. "First I'd do this," I whispered, keeping my eyes on his. "And I'd pretend it was your hands on me."

Joey's mouth fell open and he made no effort to close it.

My breasts were small but responsive, and as I played with my nipples they tightened and peaked. I brushed my fingers over the taut pink skin, pinching and pulling them. His cock continued to swell, and I closed my eyes as I circled my hips.

"Oh my God," Joey moaned.

"And then," I said, sliding one hand down my body, "I'd do this." When my fingers reached the warm, slick spot just above where our bodies were connected, I rubbed myself slowly.

By now Joey was fully hard and I could feel him moving his hips, trying to push up inside me. "Christ, you are so beautiful," he said. "I'm dying to touch you but I don't want you to stop."

I laughed, luxuriating in not only the compliment, but the intimacy of the moment and the erotic pleasure of the act. "Remember the night you slept on the couch at my house?" I asked. "I could barely sleep that night, knowing you were downstairs." Taking my other hand from my chest, I leaned back slightly, placing it on his leg behind me. The new angle increased the pressure to that place inside me that made me gasp and arch.

Joey groaned as if in agony. "Me either. God, I wanted you so badly that night."

"And then the next morning, you stayed to cook breakfast and I went upstairs to take a bath."

"Yeah?"

"Yes, and this is what I did while I thought about you. Your hands on me, your mouth on me, your cock inside me."

"Oh my God." Joey sat up fast and took a nipple between his teeth. Crying out at his bite and the uncontrollable urge raging through my body, I held on to his thick, muscular shoulders and rocked against him. Nothing had ever felt so good in my entire life, and as the frenzy inside me hit the tipping point, I flung myself forward, knocking Joey onto his back and pinning my hands on his chest. Bucking wildly on top of him, I thrilled at the sound of his rasps and strangled grunts and the sight of his gorgeous jaw dropping open as another climax hit him. He gripped my hips hard as we came together, our bodies pulsing in perfect sync.

When I could move again, I brushed the hair from his forehead. "You know, that was actually even better than it was in my fantasy."

"Mine too," he whispered, eyes closed.

"Now you'll have to show me how you touched yourself when you thought about me. It's only fair."

He opened one eye and looked at me. "You're killing me."

"Not *right* now, silly. Maybe next time."

"Deal." He shut his eyes again and sighed. "God, I love you. And I don't want to go, but I promised to meet Angelo at ten. I should get you home."

I couldn't bring myself to release him yet. "How much will you owe him?"

He grimaced. "Probably about ten grand. I'll have to run booze from Chicago to keep Sam's nose out of it. Or maybe New York. But don't worry about it."

"Ha."

He squeezed my hips once more. "Come on, let's go. Better pull yourself together, though. I don't need your dad after me at this point."

Reluctantly I got to my feet, my knees aching a bit from the cement. "At this point, what would it matter?" I checked for holes in my stockings. "We're getting married, aren't we?"

Still on his back, he lifted his hips and pulled his pants up, a masculine maneuver that somehow made my belly tighten even after I'd already come three times in the last half hour. "Yeah, the sooner the better. Because I want to do this all the time now."

Smiling, I buttoned my blouse and pulled on my skirt. "Me too. Any idea where my underwear went?"

Joey squinted into the shadows. "I think I see something white over there." He walked over and picked them up. "These belong to you?" he asked, swinging them around on one finger.

When I grabbed for them, he held them out of my reach. "Now, hold on just a second. I once made some pretty good dough charging the boys to peek at your knickers. I might be able to afford a ring if you let me keep these."

"Joey Lupo! You give me back my underwear this instant!" I jumped for them.

"Last time you threatened to tell my mother." He held them way over my head.

"Don't think I won't, mister. Or better yet, I'll punish you myself."

He stopped moving and considered that before handing them to me.

"That's what I thought."

On the way back to my house, I asked Joey if he'd told his family about us planning to marry.

"Not yet. I thought we could do it together." He took my hand and squeezed it. "Maybe dinner one night this week over at my apartment?"

His apartment? "So you're going to keep it?"

"For now." He glanced at me. "We can live there after we're married. But I'd like a house eventually. Once I save up the money."

"I'd love that. All of it."

"Good." He kissed my hand. "When do you want to get married?"

"As soon as possible."

"Me too. Let's go see the priest tomorrow, OK?"

"OK." God, there was so much to do—I hadn't even told Evelyn yet! "Where will we do it?"

"Well, if you don't mind, I'd like to get married where my sisters did, at Holy Family."

"That sounds nice." Bridget had been married there too.

"And then maybe luncheon at the restaurant? We could close it for the day. Would you like that?"

"That's perfect!" Inside my chest, my heart thumped a happy rhythm. "Hey, you know what? Drop me off at Evelyn's—I want to tell her the good news if she's home."

"Sure." He turned onto her street and chuckled a bit. "Hope Rosie doesn't throw something at you. She was coming on pretty strong."

270

"Yeah, I saw that. Looked like it was really tough on you."

He grinned. "I liked that it made you jealous."

"Of course you did. Well, not to worry, I'm sure she's on to the next sap by now."

"Swell. She can bring him to our wedding."

"As long as she keeps her hands off the groom, it's fine by me."

"Could be tough. Especially if I wear my nice suit."

I sighed in disgust as he pulled up in front of Evelyn's house. "You know, just when I think you're a nice guy..." I opened the door and started to get out, but he grabbed my arm.

"You know how much I love you, right? How happy we're gonna be?"

"Beat it, Joey Lupo. You're a troublemaker, that's what you are." I leaned closer and lowered my voice. "And if you didn't have such perfect lips and hands, or such a nice big"—I glanced down at his crotch—"apartment, I wouldn't even talk to you."

He laughed out loud, and I pulled my arm away. "No kiss goodnight?" he asked.

"You've had enough kissing. Now go." I slammed the door.

Grinning, he threw me a kiss and took off down the street.

Chapter Seventeen

Later that night, I walked home, my cheeks sore from smiling and laughing so much with Evelyn. Other parts of me were sore too, but even that made me happy.

At the news of my engagement, Evelyn had been stunned, then ecstatic, then envious, and then thrilled when I asked her to be a bridesmaid. After a lot of squealing and hugging and misty eyes, she got practical, going over all the details I'd have to attend to before the wedding took place.

"You'll need bridesmaids dresses—you'll have your sisters, of course—and flowers. You'll have to plan the menu for the party and have Bridget's dress altered and get a license and oh! You will let me throw you a bridal shower, won't you?"

I'd winced and shook my head, telling her I wasn't really the bridal shower type, and anyway, we were moving into Joey's apartment, which already had everything we'd need, assuming his mother let us keep it all. Did I really need my own china or silver tea service to sit unused on a shelf like Bridget's?

Eventually, Evelyn got smug and told me she'd seen it between Joey and me all along, and how even Rosie had admitted that he hadn't laid a finger on her and in fact he had talked about nothing but me the two nights he'd driven her home. When we imagined her sitting next to him in the car, getting huffier and huffier at his inattention, we laughed out loud.

As I rounded the corner onto my block, I thought about Joey's meeting with Angelo. Twisting my hands together, I prayed that everything had gone smoothly. Why hadn't I made him promise to call?

Daddy's car was still in the driveway. I was surprised that he was taking a night off, although it was a Monday. Perhaps the club was closed. I let myself into the house, which was dark and silent. *Everyone must have gone to bed already.* I knew I should too, but I was antsy. I wouldn't be able to sleep worrying about Joey. So when my eye caught Daddy's keys on the front hall table, I swiped them into my hand and went out again.

I wanted everything settled. No point waiting until tomorrow.

I'd talk to Enzo tonight.

#

"Floor, miss?"

"Nine, please." My voice was shaky, and I cleared my throat. "Thank you."

The operator at the Statler pushed nine and the doors closed. As we ascended, my stomach churned incessantly. What would his reaction be? Had I made the wrong decision to come here tonight? I hadn't told anyone where I was going. By the time the elevator pinged and the doors open, I was close to nausea.

But I stepped out, nodding at the operator behind me and taking a few deep breaths. *Come on. You faced Angel down when you were hundreds short on the ransom. You tricked Raymond into all sorts of things, even when you were at gunpoint. You can end things with Enzo without falling apart.*

I put one foot in front of the other and began the walk down the hall to the front apartment. But my knees wobbled. What if Enzo didn't see it my way? What if he tried to change my mind?

No, impossible. I straightened my shoulders and lengthened my strides, confident I wouldn't be seduced by him ever again. *Maybe I won't even find him attractive.*

Somewhere deep in my brain I heard a peal of laughter.

OK fine. But even if I find him attractive, there is nothing he can do or say to make me change my mind about Joey.

Positive of that, I approached the door to his apartment, lifted my fist, and knocked.

No answer.

Maybe he wasn't here? He'd said he would be. I put my ear to the door, and sure enough I heard his voice. It was too muffled to tell what he was saying, but it was definitely his.

I knocked again, louder.

Nothing.

Shifting my weight from one leg to the other, I debated using the key he'd given me. I'd brought it to give back to him, along with the necklace. I raised my hand to knock one more time when suddenly a rhythmic thumping began. I cocked my head—it sounded like it was coming from inside the apartment.

Then laughter. Female.

That's it—I was using the key.

I rummaged in my purse, pulled it out, and slipped it into the lock with trembling fingers. Bursting into the apartment, I took in the low light, the women's heels on the floor near the window, and an evening bag on the coffee table.

Half furious and half elated, I slammed the door loud enough to interrupt.

Sure enough, a minute later, Enzo appeared in the bedroom doorway wrapped in a sheet, and holding a pistol.

"Tiny? What the fuck are you doing here? You said you couldn't come tonight."

"Clearly I was the only one. Who's in there?"

"Enzo? What's going on?" The squeaky voice from the bedroom was unmistakable.

I raised my eyebrows. "Your fiancée. How refreshing."

275

"Just wait a minute." Enzo disappeared into the bedroom for a moment and returned without the gun but wearing pants. Only pants. He ran a hand through his disheveled hair and pulled the door shut behind him.

I was delighted to find that in fact I did not find him as attractive as I feared. Yes, he still had the face and the body, but underneath lurked deception and a darkness I'd never again find beautiful. I threw the apartment key at his head, and he caught it before it struck his cheekbone.

"Tiny, what the hell? Why are you doing this?"

"What a laugh. Why are *you* doing this?"

"Doing what?"

My eyes popped. "Doing what? Fucking another girl in the apartment you just offered to me!"

"It's *my* apartment!"

I folded my arms. "And it's going to stay your apartment."

"Don't be like that," he said quietly, moving deeper into the front room. "This doesn't have anything to do with you."

He probably believed that. "You're right, it doesn't. Because I no longer care what you do."

"I don't understand you. I thought we agreed about exactly what we could be and what we couldn't." He moved closer to me, too close. I could smell Gina's perfume on his skin.

I took a step back. "Maybe we did. But I'm no longer interested in it."

"Oh no?" A seductive smile crept onto his lips and he came toward me again. "Bet I can change your mind."

"No." I tried to take another step back but bumped into the sofa. "You're insane. Your fiancée is in the other room. Probably naked."

"And she's going to stay there if she knows what's good for her."

From my purse I took out the necklace box and slammed it into his waist. "Go back to her, Enzo. You don't care about me or anyone else. You just want what you want when you want it."

"Until now you felt the same way. That's why it worked between us."

"Not anymore."

"Tiny, I want *you*," he breathed, tossing the box on the coffee table and reaching for me. "I've wanted you since the moment I saw you. You know that."

I put my hands out to stop him from touching me. "And I wanted you. And we had each other, and it was fun for a lark, but now it's done. You've got everything you want—the drugs, the whisky, the club, the car, all of it. I just want you to let me go now."

"What if I don't want to let you go?"

"You have no choice."

His eyes flashed with anger. "It's Lupo, isn't it?"

"I didn't tell him what you told me," I said quickly. "I kept the secret."

"Bravo, darling. You passed the test."

"Damn right I did. I never lied to you."

"You told me there was nothing between the two of you. That was a lie."

"There was nothing between us then."

"And now?" His breaths were controlled.

"And now..." I swallowed. "Now there is something."

To my surprise, he laughed. "You want that fucking *boy*?"

Rage exploded inside me, and I shoved his chest. "Go to hell! It's none of your business who or what I choose! It never was."

"You'll change your mind. You'll want what I can give you—I know you, Miss O'Mara. Don't forget that."

"No, you don't. You knew a girl who chased danger for a while, that's all." I backed toward the door.

"You chased more than that, darling."

My face burned. "Maybe I did. But that's done."

He moved toward me, slow and sleek, unfairly handsome. Before I knew it, he had me up against the wall, a hand on either side of my head. "And I say, it isn't done. I still want you."

"You'll find another girl."

He moved a lock of hair off my face. "I don't want another girl. I want this face, and these lips, and this body."

I turned my cheek to prevent him from kissing me. "You can't have me. Leave us alone."

He slammed a hand into the wall and backed away from me, rage radiating from his body. "Go,

278

then. But if you thought I'd let him go unpunished, you were mistaken. He stole from me."

Panic screamed through my veins. "Enzo, please don't do anything to hurt him."

His lips tipped up. "You're too late, darling. It's already done."

It was the smile that frightened me most.

#

I drove straight to Joey's. The restaurant was closed, of course, and the block was dark and deserted. As I parked along the street, I glanced up to the apartment. No lights were on. I had no idea if there were any guests staying in other rooms or renting other apartments, but I wasn't going to be able to get into the building if no one was inside. Chewing my thumbnail, I looked up and down the block. This area was not well lit at night, and I had no weapon of any kind.

Or did I?

Frantically, I looked around inside Daddy's car. Nothing on the floor, nothing under the seat. Standing on the seat, I leaned into the back and checked the secret compartment in the floor, used for hauling whisky.

Nothing.

Dammit, Daddy, you were a bootlegger. Couldn't you at least be the kind that carried a gun? But he wasn't. Bootlegging hadn't been violent until recently, and

Daddy's favorite weapons were his fists, anyway. Slumping back down in the front, I looked at my own fists. Pathetically small. I had nothing to fight back with.

But I had to find Joey.

Exiting the car, I gritted my teeth and took the steps up to the double doors at the recessed entrance. I was completely in shadow. My teeth chattered as I rang the buzzer.

No one came.

Cupping my hands over my eyes, I peered inside and saw the silent lobby, the dark wood staircase. I pounded on the glass pane with the heel of my hand.

No one came.

Tears welled. Where was he? Had Enzo done something to him? Why did one man have to be so greedy? I knew it was futile but I tried opening the door before I pushed the buzzer again, three times. *Now don't get hysterical. He's probably just still out.* But I wasn't going to feel better until I saw him, held him, safe and sound. Weeping openly, I rushed down the steps and around the side of the building. Maybe I could climb the fire escape.

In the alley, dark and silent and smelling of rotting food, I held my breath and said a prayer I'd be tall enough to pull down the ladder.

But it was already down.

Something about that seemed off, but I climbed it and then raced up the steps to the third floor—*oh, shit.*

The back door was open.

"Joey?" I peered into the kitchen, my heart knocking painfully against my ribs. It was dark, but my eyes adjusted fairly quickly—no one was there. I entered and crossed to the swinging door to the dining room.

But before I pushed it open, I heard Joey's voice. "No! Just let her go, Sam, she has nothing to do with this." His words sounded muffled and strange, as if he had a mouth full of cotton.

"Shut the fuck up, Lupo. I should cut you right now for hiding that dope from me."

I pulled my hand off the door as if it had burned me, backing up until my butt hit the kitchen cabinet, which rattled noisily.

Shit!

In a panic, I grabbed a butcher knife from a block on the counter, darted into the pantry and shut the door almost all the way. In a moment someone swung into the kitchen.

"Nobody in here!" I heard a voice say over the galloping of my heart.

But it would only be a matter of seconds before whoever it was checked the pantry, and I begged God for the strength I'd need to plunge the knife into human flesh. I didn't want to kill anyone, but I'd need to injure him badly enough so he couldn't hurt me. *Aim for his right side, maybe a shoulder.* My hand shook horribly, and I tightened my grip lest the knife clatter to the floor.

And then I remembered the pistol. I swept my left hand along the shelf.

It was still there.

I dropped the knife, swiped the gun into both hands, and screamed as the pantry door opened, revealing the stocky, thick-necked outline of a guy. More than either of the weapons, I think it was the scream that stunned him. He faltered a little at the noise, and I took advantage of his surprise to draw back one foot and kick him in the balls as hard as I possibly could.

Grunting, he went down hard, his own gun clattering to the floor. I couldn't bring myself to shoot him, even though he might have been willing to shoot me, but I did kick his gun away and clock him over the head with my own.

A few times.

When I was positive I'd knocked him out, I burst into tears and shoved open the door to the dining room.

"Tiny, get out of here!" shouted Joey. But his words still sounded muffled.

Disoriented, I looked through the archway into the front room, where one lamped burned.

My knees nearly buckled.

Joey sat on a chair, the same chair I'd sat in before Sunday dinner, while Sam Scarfone stood to his side, holding a straight edge razor to his throat. His face, his beautiful face, was bruised and bloody, and his wrists and ankles were tied with rope. *Just like Daddy.*

Instinctively, I tucked the pistol I held behind me.

"You heard him. Get the fuck out of here," said Sam. "Where the fuck is Freddy?"

"I…" My voice stuck in my throat. Fear had totally paralyzed me. Somewhere in my mind, a voice said *shoot him*, but I wasn't sure I could do it. I locked eyes with Joey, who silently begged me to go. I could see the desperation in his face, but I wasn't about to leave him. My fingers tightened on the pistol.

Sam glared at me. "Get the fuck out of here, I said, before I show you the way myself."

"You lay one finger on her, and I'll rip you to fucking shreds," Joey said, the clearest words from him yet.

"You got a lot of nerve talking to me like that, Lupo, after what you pulled. I ever hear you held back again, I'm gonna lay more than my finger on her and make you watch."

I saw the rage erupt in Joey and he vaulted out of the chair and hurled himself at Sam, butting his head into Sam's chin.

"Joey, no!" I cried.

Sam was easily able to shove Joey down to the floor, and he grimaced, touching his tongue to one bloody corner of his mouth. "You're gonna pay for that," he said. "I thought you were smarter than Angelo, but I guess I was wrong." He brought the blade to Joey's cheek, and I snapped.

Rushing forward with the pistol out in front of me, I took aim at Sam's chest.

And I pulled the trigger.

Chapter Eighteen

Turns out, I did have it in me to shoot someone.

It also turns out that I'm a horrible shot.

I missed his chest by a mile, putting a bullet in his leg instead. But it was enough to knock him backward, and as he staggered I pulled the trigger again. This time I caught him in the shoulder, and he dropped his blade, groaning in pain. I raced into the room and scooped it up.

To my utter shock, he actually stumbled for the kitchen door and disappeared through it.

"Oh no!" I cried. "Should I go after him?"

"No!" Joey struggled to sit up. "Let him go. Just let him go, he won't get far."

I rushed over to him. "Oh my God," I said, breaking down again. "Are you OK?"

"I'm fine, baby. Where's the other guy—Freddy?"

"He's in the kitchen. I kicked him in the balls and knocked him out with your dad's gun."

Joey actually tried to smile. "He'd be proud of you."

I untied Joey's wrists and ankles. He threw his arms around me and I wept into his chest, relieved and grateful. "Shhhh, it's OK now. It's OK, *cara*." Then he murmured something in Italian, I had no idea what, but his voice was soothing and the lilting, rhythmic words were so beautiful, I grew calmer immediately.

Joey took one of the guns and went into the kitchen, where he discovered Freddy had disappeared as well. However, he must have been too cloudy-headed to handle the fire escape because the police found him in a heap of broken bones beneath the iron staircase as if he'd fallen. Either that or Sam had pushed him.

Turns out there had been someone else in the building, and though she'd been too scared to answer my knock after hearing the shouts from Joey's apartment, she'd called the police. Freddy lived through the fall and was promptly arrested after being released from the hospital.

Sam Scarfone was not so lucky—but it wasn't my bullets that killed him.

Joey once told me that friendships and rivalries change with the wind in organized crime. You can never be sure exactly who your allies or enemies are at any given moment. Someone might shake your hand one day and sign his name with your blood the next. That summer, there were a lot of shifting alliances as the top figures in Detroit's underworld sought to position themselves to make the most money and gain the lion's share of the criminal rackets.

Enzo, unable to handle his jealousy of Joey and seeking to punish him for the hijacking, had extended an offer to Sam Scarfone, unbeknownst to me. If Sam would run booze for Enzo's clubs, Enzo would tell him about River Gang members who'd screwed him out of thousands of dollars on a drug heist. Sam responded by confronting Joey the evening I showed up, and might not have killed him, since they had been friendly before, but I don't know for sure. In their business, there was no greater crime than not paying up.

However, earlier that day Joey had reached out to the old guard of the Scarfone faction, the men who'd split with Sam over control of the Scarfone territory after Big Leo's death. To get even with Sam for ordering the hit that had killed his father, Joey spilled what he knew about Sam's role in his uncle's death, and the old guard agreed—Sam had to pay.

His bullet-riddled body was found in the river a few weeks after the incident at Joey's.

No one was convicted.

Angelo, who had agreed to Joey's offer of a cut of his bootlegging spoils, had been roughed up pretty good by Sam and wore a necklace of scars the rest of his life, but he survived. The River Gang disbanded once Sam was gone, and the leaders of the various powerful outfits in Detroit and the rest of the Midwest got together and agreed on a distribution of territory to cut down on violence. Eventually, even the outfits on the East Coast reached out to make a deal that would set up mutually beneficial smuggling operations.

Joey and Angelo decided to partner up and bought a boat together, and they ran whisky from Canada across the river on a regular basis for ten more years under the protection of the Scarfone outfit—until Prohibition ended. Eventually, they had enough money to buy an airplane, and they partnered with a few Canadian farmers who agreed to let their fields be used as landing sites in exchange for some booze and a fee. I wasn't crazy about Joey staying involved in organized crime, but he promised me it would only be bootlegging, and he'd stay out of trouble. After all, he wanted to dedicate most of his time to running the restaurant and raising a family with me.

As soon as his injuries healed, we were married at Holy Family and feted by friends and family at a reception at the restaurant. The morning of the wedding, a beautiful September Saturday, my sisters and Evelyn helped me dress in my old bedroom.

Bridget, dressed in soft blue, fastened the row of buttons at my back and we exchanged a look in the mirror remembering what she'd said about Joey getting them undone later. Molly and Evelyn, also in blue, settled the veil's crown on my head and adjusted the tulle to fall around my shoulders. Mary Grace, in a sweet white dress, brought me my satin shoes and helped me into them. Bridget and Evelyn were teary-eyed, but I felt nothing but pure joy.

At the back of the church, I stood with Daddy, waiting for the processional to begin. He'd been mostly silent throughout the wedding preparations, grumbling at the price of things here and there, but never denying me something I really wanted. Now, we stood aside in the vestibule with our arms linked, my fingers tight around the stems of white roses.

"Tiny," he said, his voice gruff, but soft. "I need to say something."

"Now?" I whispered, glancing nervously toward the aisle.

"Yes, now." His jaw was set.

"All right, Daddy."

He swallowed. "I'm not good with words or affection like your mother was."

"It's OK."

"Let me finish," he said as the organ bleated the first notes of my processional music. The church coordinator began sending my sisters up the aisle as Daddy tugged me back. "When your mother died I did the best I could, but I know most of the raising fell on Bridget and then you. I could've done better to help."

His voice caught, and I squeezed his arm. When he looked at me, I was stunned to see tears in his eyes. My throat immediately tightened.

"Of all the girls, you're the most like me, Tiny. You're the spittin' image of your mother, but you've always been the most like me and I suppose that's why I've let you get away with more, the whisky and everything, and why I've been harder on you."

"I understand." I shot a nervous glance up front. Was Joey there yet?

"I'm sorry for the things I've done that have hurt you or put you in danger, and I'll always remember how you—did what you did for me. I might not've come through without you."

"I'd do it all again. And you'd do it for me."

"I would." And he put a hand over his heart.

I knew he meant *I love you*, and I leaned over to kiss his cheek. "I love you too, Daddy. We are who we are, and the people who love us have to take us as we are. But now you gotta get me to the front of the church, or Joey's gonna think I changed my mind."

He sniffed. "Let's go, then. I need a jar of whisky, and there ain't any in this church."

I smiled, the lump in my throat dissolving, and we stepped into the center aisle. Mary Grace was just reaching the altar, and we paused a moment, allowing the guests to rise. I was briefly stunned at how many people were there, perhaps more than a hundred, but then I remembered how large Joey's family was. His mother and sisters were so thrilled with our plans to marry, they'd insisted on inviting every last person on the family tree with breath in their body.

For a second, nerves knotted in my stomach, but then Joey walked to the altar, and they unraveled into a thousand butterflies taking flight. Daddy and I began walking toward him at a quick clip, so quick that some guests hid smiles behind gloved hands and handkerchiefs. But I didn't care—Joey was waiting for me. It wasn't just his gorgeous face or the beautiful dark blue suit, or the strong body beneath it. It was that I *knew* that body now, every inch of it. I knew his mind. I knew his heart. I knew his history and his hopes for the future. I knew that he loved me and wanted me and understood me. He wanted to see the world with me. Some people might see marriage as a thing that trapped a girl in her home, but I knew life with Joey would never be dull, even if we never left the house.

In fact, as my eyes traveled from his slicked back hair to his lips and down his torso, I thought never leaving the house sounded like a pretty good idea.

I forced myself to keep my mind as pure as possible—we were in church, after all—and looked Joey in the eye. His were wet, and as I got closer, he blinked and then brought a hand up, thumb rubbing at one eye, fingers at the other. I smiled at him, full to bursting.

Daddy gave me away, Joey took my arm, and the rest of the ceremony was a blur but for the moment Joey slipped the ring on my finger. He'd wanted to surprise me, and he did—my mouth fell open and I didn't stop staring at my hand for a full ten seconds, so long the guests began to chuckle. It was unbelievably beautiful—a large rectangular diamond surrounded by delicate filigree work in a silver band. Later he would tell me the diamond was emerald cut and the metal was platinum. The ring reminded him of me, he said—lovely and strong all at once. I had no idea how he afforded such a ring, and I never asked. Some things I just learned not to question.

We shared a chaste kiss when the priest pronounced us married, and Joey squeezed my hands.

"Mrs. Lupo," he whispered in my ear as our guests cheered.

I loved every moment of our reception—especially one particular moment when I caught Joey watching me from across the restaurant. Rather than smile, he simply locked eyes with me and jerked his head toward the kitchen. I had a feeling I knew what he meant, and my belly tightened with desire. He excused himself from whomever he was talking to with barely a glance, and he came over and grabbed my hand. Moving quickly, he pulled me through the kitchen door and we flew by the surprised staff. I laughed out loud, glad I'd already removed the veil from my head. I'd have tripped for sure.

The moment the pantry door slammed shut, he kissed me for real, wrapping his arms around me and lifting me right off the ground. "Mmmmm." He teased my tongue with his. "I can't wait any longer."

"Me either," I said. "But we can't leave yet."

"Who said we had to leave?" He set me down and ran his hands up my sides.

I laughed. "Joey, this dress!"

"It's beautiful." He kissed his way down my neck, setting my skin on fire. "You're beyond beautiful."

I shivered, cradling his head at my chest. "I still can't believe it. We're married. We're actually *married*."

"I know." His words were muffled as he kissed my breasts through my dress. "So even if they miss us, they can't say anything. And I can't wait to taste you one more minute."

291

He dropped to his knees, lifting the long tiers of my dress up to my waist. Holding them aloft, he pressed his lips to my thighs above the white stockings clipped by garter to my corselette. Moaning again, he brought his mouth to my center, covered by the thinnest layer of loose silk that snapped between my legs. "Back up," he said.

I did, bracing myself against the pantry door.

"Good. Now put your leg on my shoulder." I rested the back of one thigh on top of his shoulder, gasping as he nibbled and sucked at me through the silk. "Now the other." His breath was hot on my skin.

Since his hands were holding up the front of my dress, only his shoulders would hold my weight. But I was so needy for him, I plastered my hands on the door next to my hips and swung my other leg up.

Sometimes being small was a blessing.

Joey easily held me suspended on his shoulders, burying his face between my legs. Unsnapping the step-in *with his teeth*, his magnificent mouth worked the damp silk aside and he slipped his tongue inside me, eliciting a long sigh of pleasure from deep in my throat.

Eventually he let my dress fall over his head and reached under my backside to hold me to him. I had no idea how he managed not to suffocate, but I was so deliriously aroused I didn't give it more than a passing thought. He absolutely devoured me, licking and sucking and fucking me with his tongue until I was panting and digging my heels into his back and pounding my hands on the door behind me. When I finally came, I yelled his name so loud I was positive the entire reception heard. He moaned into my pulsing wetness, making me throw my head back, and it banged the door, hard.

I'd have a lump.

I didn't care.

As I began to breathe again, he kissed each of my inner thighs before helping me stand. "God, I love that." He hugged my legs from his kneeling position. "I want to do that every day. Twice a day."

I laughed. "We'll never leave the house."

"Fine with me, Mrs. Lupo."

The name sent a ripple of joy through me. I looked down at him and wished I could see his face in the dark. Smoothing my hand over his hair, I marveled at how we'd ended up here. "I love you."

He stood and pressed his lips to my forehead before pulling me into his chest. "I love you too."

I breathed in the scent of him, knowing how lucky I was to be in that moment. So many things could have prevented it—from outside threats to our own stubbornness. "Isn't it amazing," I said, "how much has changed this summer?"

"Definitely. Just think about how much you disliked me before now."

I squeezed him tighter. "I didn't dislike you. You just drove me crazy with all your teasing."

"That's how I showed I cared."

"Well, you have better ways now."

He kissed my temple. "Yes, I do. But I'll probably still tease you."

"How would I know I married the real Joey Lupo if you didn't?"

He released me slightly and tipped up my chin. "I'd do anything for you." He kissed me. "Anything. You want me to leave bootlegging behind, I'll do it. You want to move away from Detroit, I'll do it. You want ten kids, I'll do it."

I laughed. "Uh, let's start with one—eventually. And you don't have to leave bootlegging behind, not completely. Just promise me you'll be careful and smart, and if it gets dangerous, you'll quit."

"Promise."

"And there is something you can do for me."

"Name it."

"I want to go to New York and stay in a big hotel like the Astor or the Plaza."

He kissed me again. "Done."

I hugged him close. "So how much longer do we have to stay at this reception? I'm dying to get these clothes off you."

"Say the word and I'll carry you out of here."

"Now."

"That *is* a word you like, I've noticed." After one last kiss, Joey pulled the pantry door open, and led me back through the kitchen. We ignored the knowing looks among the waiters, who elbowed each other and guffawed, keeping our heads up as we re-entered the restaurant. As always, Joey's family said the longest goodbyes in all Creation, each person hugging and kissing us and wishing us well. I endured more than a few jokes about having children soon, and rolled my eyes at Bridget, who was laughing at me from across the room. I knew she understood.

We said goodbye to my family too, Daddy actually kissing my cheek and then Joey's wordlessly. My sisters hugged and kissed us both, and Bridget clung to me for a long moment. "I know you'll be happy together," she whispered. "Vince would be so glad." I squeezed her back and turned to Evelyn, who embraced me while Ted shook Joey's hand.

"I can't believe it, Tiny. You're married. To *Joey*!" She released me but kept my hands in hers.

"I know. I can't believe it either," I admitted. I'm glad you and Ted aren't as stubborn or blind as Joey and I were."

"Me too." She leaned in again to whisper in my ear. "Cross your fingers for me. I think we might be next."

"Crossed," I whispered back in hers.

She giggled. "Now go. Any fool can see how impatient you two are to be alone." Glancing at the ceiling, she added, "And if the chandeliers start shaking, I'll know why."

I gave her one last hug and took Joey's hand, and we walked out the main doors into the lobby. It was there Joey swept me into his arms and carried me up two flights of stairs. I laughed when he started skipping steps on the second flight. "Take it easy. I don't want you worn out before we even get inside."

He grinned. "Never."

Without setting me down, he turned the knob and opened the door to his apartment.

Our apartment.

Inside, he went straight for the bedroom, setting me down at the side of the bed. I grabbed him by the tie and pulled his mouth to mine, tipping backward onto the mattress. He laughed as he fell on top of me, then propped himself up slightly on his hands, pressing his lower body into mine. My breath hitched at feeling him hard on my leg, and I wiggled impatiently beneath him. "Too many clothes between us," I whined. "Get them off, now."

He laughed, and my insides filled with longing again as I looked up at him. I'd never get enough. "Relax, Mrs. Lupo. We're just getting started."

It's only the beginning, I thought as I brought my hands to his face. When he lowered his lips to mine, I remembered thinking the exact same thing the day he'd kissed me in the front hall, only that day the words had filled me with trepidation.

Today, I just felt alive, bursting with life and love and hope, and it was everything I wanted.

Epilogue

Joey and I spent a week in New York after we wed, and a more romantic honeymoon I could not have imagined. Soon after we returned I discovered I was in a family way—of *course* I was, we were terribly careless about precautions from the start—and we began planning for our family. I thought I might feel some regret at expecting so soon, but I never did. Joey still said he'd support my going to school if I wanted to, and I did, in fact, take a few classes before the baby arrived. It was a good thing I was interested in science, because I was only permitted to take classes where the long white lab coats would hide my condition.

But once the baby was born, a girl we named Vincenza Kathleen, I realized school would have to wait. I didn't mind—taking care of Vinnie and keeping accounts for the boarding house kept me busy, although Joey, true to his word, did all the cooking for us. How he managed that plus the restaurant and his bootlegging operation was a mystery to me, but he was smart, hard-working and ambitious, although never so much that ambition overshadowed his devotion to his family.

Unlike Enzo DiFiore.

We didn't cross paths with him for a while, but I heard he married Gina and took over her father's distilleries after Vito Meloni's mysterious death—shot one day while exiting a diner, the victim of a sniper across the street whom no one seemed to notice. The sniper even entered a woman's nearby apartment and called a cab, explaining that his car had broken down, and waited in her front room for twenty minutes before the cab showed up.

Yet she was unable to identify him.

Evelyn told me Rosie was Enzo's mistress of choice for a few months the next year, even staying at his apartment at the Statler. But he grew tired of her and eventually took up with someone else, leaving Rosie to move back home until she married a divorced executive at Ford, moved into his house in Grosse Pointe, and never set foot in J.L. Hudson's dress department again.

As for Evelyn, she married Ted that winter and had twin girls almost as quickly as I had Vinnie. We often met for walks with our girls, pushing the buggies and laughing about how much our lives had changed in just one year. For the most part, it felt like my life began when Joey and I fell in love, and I never even thought about those insane weeks during July of 1923.

Until one day when Enzo showed up at the restaurant with a blond on his arm that was not his wife. Sometimes I helped Joey down there if he was short-staffed, and I happened to see them at a corner table. Immediately, my stomach filled with dread and I sought out Joey in the kitchen.

"It's OK," he assured me. "He came in about a week ago demanding payment. Apparently, territory has been renegotiated once more and this is his block now."

"And?" My heart was pounding with fear. *Not again.*

"And I paid him. And I'll keep paying him as long as he stays out of our lives and doesn't interrupt my bootlegging. We settled on a number and agreed to put the past behind us."

I relaxed a little. "And you trust him?"

"I wouldn't go that far. But I don't think he'll bother us," he continued, his eyes going dark. "Because I told him if he comes near you or our family, I'll fucking kill him."

"What did he say?"

"He said, 'Congratulations,' and he handed me a hundred dollar bill."

It didn't surprise me at all. Doling out favors on the street was part of Enzo's vision of himself as an all-powerful, benevolent mafia don, just like the men he'd seen growing up in Brooklyn. "God, what an asshole," I said.

"Yeah. I told him to keep it. We don't need his money."

"No, we don't." I wrapped my arms around Joey's waist.

When I went back into the restaurant, I looked at Enzo, and he raised his glass to me in a silent toast.

I nodded. *That's right, asshole. Here's to me. I have everything I want, and you'll never be happy. Life isn't about owning things or people or money, but you'll never understand that.*

The next time I saw Enzo's name, it was in the newspaper—he'd been arrested for shooting his brother in an argument over who was stealing money from Club 23.

It didn't even faze me.

As for the rest of my family, Bridget surprised us all by marrying Martin after he graduated from dental school, and they sold the store, bought a home on the east side near Daddy, and raised the boys there, as well as their own two girls that followed. Eventually, Joey and I bought a house in that neighborhood as well, and our eight children grew up playing with their cousins, just as it should be.

Yes, eight. Four of each, within ten years.

We never did get very good about precautions, and we couldn't keep our hands off each other.

Molly and Mary Grace both went away to college—paid for by Daddy, who finally put some money away—but both of them returned to the Detroit area to raise families. In fact, we rented our apartment to Molly and her pharmacist husband Jeff, and they lived there happily for many years.

I did become a nurse, eventually. It took me a while, what with eight children and all, but by the time the second world war broke out, I was working for the

Red Cross. Two of my daughters followed me into medicine—one became a nurse; another, a doctor.

Prohibition ended, of course, and with it went a large portion of our income. But Joey had saved a good deal of cash, and at that point he and Jeff invested in a chain of drug stores that took off, and while we were never overly rich, we were certainly wealthier than either of us had been growing up.

And as the years went by, the summer of 1923 took on an unreal quality—as if it had been the plot of a movie or a book, the events so dramatic it didn't seem as if they could've happened to us in real life. But then Joey would dig out that handkerchief, the one with the words still written on it in red lipstick, faded but still legible. And we'd know it was all real.

The beginning of us.

THE END

A note from the author...

Thank you so much for reading Speak Low. I'm truly grateful for your purchase, as I know there are many amazing books and authors out there.

If you enjoyed the book, please consider leaving a review on a retail site, such as Amazon, or Goodreads. Reviews are a fantastic (and free!) way to support indie authors, and they are much appreciated.

Cheers,
Melanie

ACKNOWLEDGMENTS

I dedicated this book to you, my readers, because without your words of love and support for a scrappy, sexy historical series, this story would not have been written. Your reviews and emails thrill and humble me. THANK YOU.

A huge shout-out to the members of Team Harlow: Lisa, Cristina, Melannie, Brittany, Delilah, Dawn, Jennifer, Jodie, Georgie, Zandalee, and Mia—your enthusiasm for Tiny (and her men) inspired me daily as I wrote this book, and I want to take you all out for cocktails!

Thank you to Tom Barnes for another gorgeous cover, and to Cait Greer for formatting and technical assistance. I'm so grateful to you both.

To the sexy awesome ladies of the Wrahm Society—you're amazing. I'm so lucky to be one of you. Wrahmpage, here we come!

"Tamara Mataya, you're the greatest editor ever," she said, because she can't lay off the dialog tags. "I'd be lost without you in so many ways."

To Bethany Hagen, Gennifer Albin, Kayti McGee, Laura Barnes, and Tamara Mataya—you're the best friends I've never hugged or spilled gin on, and I'm going to remedy that soon. Thank you for the countless times you've made me laugh, cry, drink, swear, flail, squee, and fan myself. Your words, your minds, your beauty, and your friendship are golden.

To my daughters, thank you for giving me the time and space to write, even when you really really really just want me to get up and get the purple paint.

To my husband, whose love and sense of humor I could not live without, thank you for your endless encouragement, patience, and understanding. You've always been the one.

About the Author

Melanie Harlow likes her martinis dry, her lipstick red, and her history with the naughty bits left in. The SPEAK EASY series was inspired by her affection for good gin, her fascination with local history, and her obsession for the Prohibition era. When she's not writing or dancing the Charleston, you might find her sipping a Queen Anne's Revenge at The Sugar House in Detroit or a Double Plus Good at The Oakland in Ferndale. Belly up to the bar and say hello or connect with her online...

Facebook: www.facebook.com/AuthorMelanieHarlow

Twitter: @MelanieHarlow2

Blog: www.melanieharlowwrites.blogspot.com

Email: melanieharlowwrites@gmail.com